EPITAPH

for a

DREAM

TERRY MORT

McBooks
Press

Guilford, Connecticut

McBooks
Press

An imprint of Globe Pequot, the trade division of
The Rowman & Littlefield Publishing Group, Inc.
4501 Forbes Blvd., Ste. 200
Lanham, MD 20706
www.rowman.com

Distributed by NATIONAL BOOK NETWORK

British Library Cataloguing in Publication Information available

Library of Congress Cataloging-in-Publication Data available

ISBN 978-1-4930-6195-2 (paperback) | ISBN 978-1-4930-6500-4 (ebook)

∞™ The paper used in this publication meets the minimum requirements of American
National Standard for Information Sciences—Permanence of Paper for Printed Library
Materials, ANSI/NISO Z39.48-1992.

To Sondra, the best and the bravest

Chapter One

After the funeral, we went to a bar. I was surprised when Marvin asked me to join him. I didn't really know him all that well. He was a movie producer, and I was a private dick who worked on the fringes of the business, now and then. But I wasn't what you'd call well connected. Not with the business side of Hollywood, anyway.

After we ordered drinks I said, "I'm sorry about ...Elaine."

"Thanks," he said. "She didn't deserve that."

Elaine was his wife and the centerpiece of the funeral. The accident happened at 3 a.m. on Santa Monica Boulevard. She'd been crossing the street in the rain. The guy didn't see her, and when he hit her he didn't even slow down. They hadn't caught him yet, and chances were, they wouldn't. They weren't even sure it was a guy.

The only witness said he didn't see the driver, but he thought the car was a Hudson. That didn't narrow it down much. Hudsons were popular cars. This same witness had been with her just before it happened. He was nervous about saying why, but there was no mystery about it. They'd been in the corner booth of a quiet bar most of the night. He asked the cops and the newspaper boys not to put his name and picture in the paper. They just laughed.

The accident had happened one week before and the driver could be anywhere, most likely in some place where no one would notice a Hudson with a dent in the front fender. She wasn't a big woman, so it probably wasn't much of a dent. Chances are he'd had it fixed, anyway.

"Truth is," Marvin said, "she shouldn't have been there that time of night."

I kept a straight face.

"What about the guy she was with?" Was this tactful of me? Maybe not. But I was interested.

"Him? Nobody. A pretty boy wannabe actor waiting tables during the day. He'll never work in this town. Not now."

He said this with what I thought was a curious absence of malice, as if snuffing out the guy's career, such as it was, was just routine. No more than brushing off a flake of dandruff.

Marvin took a long pull on his drink and looked thoughtful. Well, I suppose that was natural, under the circumstances.

"You know, the hell of it is," he said after a while, "now she'll never know how I really felt about her."

I nodded sympathetically. People usually say things like this after a funeral. They regret not having told the departed how much they loved them, that sort of thing. That kind of guilt is understandable. Temporary, but understandable. But that's not quite what he meant.

"She'll never know how little I cared. She was ... a deeply, deeply unpleasant woman. Fact is, a lot of the time, I hated her."

"Oh."

"She'll never know how big a favor I was doing her, staying with her."

Not now. But it occurred to me -- wasn't hatred a kind of caring? I don't know. Probably that's a question for a shrink or philosopher. But it seemed likely that she must have had *some* idea of how he felt. Having drinks with a pretty boy at 3 a.m. sounded like either a symptom or a cause of an unhappy marriage. Maybe both. But I didn't say anything. This conversation was apparently leading somewhere. I was in no hurry.

"And I gave up a lot – that's another thing she'll never know. I stayed with her, even though most of the time I didn't care whether she lived or died," he said. "And do you know why I stayed with her?"

"No."

"Neither do I."

I wondered – could it have been the prospect of alimony?

"Too conventional, I guess," he said, ruefully.

In this town? I must have smirked.

"I get it – it's hard for you to believe," he said. "It's hard for *me* to believe. But it doesn't matter anymore." He took a long drink and rattled the ice cubes for a refill. "Can you guess how I feel at this very moment?"

"Not really." But it obviously had nothing to do with grief. I could tell, because he was smiling.

"Free. I feel free for the first time in a long time. Does that shock you?"

"No. But not much does."

He laughed.

"So you fit right in – in this town."

3

"That's the rumor."

"Good. So ... you're wondering why I asked you to join me."

"A little. I figured you'd get around to it."

"You're a private detective, right?"

"Yes."

"Ethel Welkin says you know your stuff."

Good old Ethel, my affectionate admirer. She was the pint-sized wife of a big time producer and an all-around nice lady with a taste for gymnastics and experimentation, usually on Wednesday afternoons. She'd steered business to me before, and apparently she'd done it again.

"I do. Know my business, I mean." Modesty doesn't work in this town. People don't know what it is, and it confuses them.

"Good. I have a job for you. I want you to find someone."

Chapter Two

About an hour later, I drove back to my place, which was a bungalow at the Garden of Allah Hotel.

The hotel used to be the home of an old-time silent movie star named Alla Nazinova. That wasn't her real name, but she was a real Russian and had had a few hits back in the day when film acting meant elaborate gestures and lots of eye shadow. But when talkies came in, her career went south. She turned her house into a hotel and built twenty-five bungalows behind and around the pool that was shaped like the Crimea – a nostalgic nod to her homeland. The bungalows were arranged around winding brick walkways and garden beds with flowering oleanders and bougainvillea and other pleasant, scented plants. If you wanted a place that said "Southern California," this was it. It was a magnet for actors and writers who shared a taste for gin and late nights and who were mostly transient. But there were a few of us semi-permanent residents. When Alla went bankrupt, she sold the hotel, and the new owners added an *H* to the name, but didn't change much else. It was Hollywood's fraternity house. I liked living there.

EPITAPH FOR A DREAM

One of the other semi-permanent residents was my friend Hobey Baker. When I got back from my meeting he was at his usual place on a chaise longue beside the pool. Beside him on the table was a martini shaker. Underneath his chair was a gin bottle – his reserve. It wasn't quite cocktail hour, but that didn't matter to him or anyone else who lived there.

"Greetings, Old Sport," he said when he saw me. "Join me. Have a drink."

"Thanks, I will."

"Hobey" wasn't his real name, but it was the one he preferred. He'd been a famous writer ten years before, and he and his outrageous wife had done outrageous things like jumping into fountains outside the Plaza Hotel in New York and riding bareback on the coach horses in Central Park. They'd been by no means alone in their antics. It was a good time to be young and a writer, if your stories sold. Hobey's did. He and his wife always got a pass from everyone, including the newspapers, because they were good looking and young and successful. But the Jazz Age faded and was replaced by Prohibition and then the Depression, and money got tight and youthful good looks and high spirits faded along with the money, and the golden couple more or less separated, though they stayed married. Hobey came west to repair his ravaged bank account by writing for the movies. His wife stayed in New York and wrote letters to him complaining when the checks didn't arrive on time. The arrangement worked, more or less. He rode the Hollywood roller coaster with its high points of lucrative writing assignments and its low points of unemployment. He was regularly hired and then fired by producers who didn't care two bits about Hobey's reputation or his very real literary talent. The money men knew what sold, and a lot of the time Hobey didn't. He was constantly trying to turn the movies into high art. He'd take a Three Stooges script and rewrite it as *The Brothers Karamazov, Part Two*. That annoyed the producers, who understood that the Stooges were more popular than Dostoyevsky and always would be. Probably with good reason. He called himself Hobey Baker after his college hero at Princeton, a handsome football star who was killed in the war and who fit Hobey's ideal of a Romantic Hero. It was his way of trying to forget his past. It didn't work completely, but it worked a little. Gin helped, too, as did a succession of girlfriends. And, underneath it all, Hobey knew perfectly well that his pen name was also a joke he played on himself. He looked more like a prep school Classics teacher than a romantic hero. One of his favorite sayings was "I appreciate irony and multiple levels of meaning." He usually said that ironically, but he meant it, too. That didn't play in the movie business, either – not in terms of reliable, steady employment, anyway. The moguls only wanted one level of meaning, which boiled down to a simple precept – the hero ends up with the girl. But Hobey was amazingly resilient and always managed to get by. A new job buoyed his spirits beyond all reason, just as the inevitable firing plunged him into temporary gloom. But he had a strange sort of luck. Something always came up just at the point when he was about to go under for the final time. He almost never had to borrow money from his friends, and when he did he generally paid it back.

I sat down next to him and helped myself from his martini shaker.

"I just came from Elaine Ginsberg's funeral," I said.

"Yes, I heard about that. I met her once at a party. Seemed nice enough. How is Marvin holding up?"

"They've been married ten years. He hated her."

"Really? That's interesting. Makes you wonder why he stayed with her. Maybe she was sick, wasting away like *La Dame aux Camélias*, and he faced a moral imperative – no choice but to do his duty by her."

"I doubt it. Just before she got run over she was bar hopping with a waiter."

"Oh. Probably rules out a tragic, lingering disease. Did you know that the original story by Dumas *fils* was based on a real courtesan, which is a fancy French word for prostitute?"

"No, I didn't." Hobey had a habit of veering off subject into literary references and cul de sacs. I didn't mind. I was still working on my education.

"She wore a white camellia when she was available to her lovers and a red one when she was indisposed. The color significance is obvious. I read the novel in college. It was interesting, but as Doctor Johnson said about *Paradise Lost*, 'None wished it longer.' Anyway, why did you go to the funeral? Did you know Elaine well?"

"Not really. Marvin asked me to, and then wanted to talk after the ceremony. He has a job for me."

"Tracking down the killer?"

"No, as far as Marvin's concerned, the guy did him a favor. He wants me to find a girl. Seems he met her a while back on a transatlantic voyage."

"Shipboard romance? Bit of a cliché, don't you think? I'm surprised he didn't turn it into a script."

"He told me he was thinking about it."

"Typical. But maybe I should call him."

"Wouldn't hurt. Besides, it's not a cliché to Marvin."
Hobey was a well-known pest to producers, great and small.
Whenever there was a sniff of a project, he turned up with a
fistful of ideas and a hopeful smile.

"It never is when you're living it."

"He says he saw her first in the dining room of The
France, and he was 'transformed' – his word."

"Really! You wouldn't think a movie producer would
have it in him. I think of them as soulless robots, like the
Baltic Knights in *Alexander Nevsky*."

"We're all the same, sad fools, Hobey."

"Men, you mean? Yes, I suppose so, although some of us
are sadder and more foolish than the average. I bow to no
man in that regard. So he wants you to find her? That
suggests she's gone missing."

"Nothing gets by you, does it?"

"Not much."

"It seems they fell in love somewhere in the middle of the
Atlantic and had a few blissful days on route to Le Havre.
From there they went to Paris for more blissfulness –"

"But then she disappeared? A wasting disease? Mental
breakdown? Sent to a sanitarium in Switzerland?"

"No. She went back to her fiancé, who was waiting for
her somewhere in France. On the Riviera somewhere."

"He wasn't a dashing French aviator, by any chance?"

"No. He's in wholesale vegetables. Does well, apparently.
Why?"

"Just wondering. Please continue."

"So, after days of blissfulness with Marvin, she had
developed doubts about going through with the marriage,

but she did anyway. That's his interpretation – about her doubts, I mean."

"Strange. I've met Marvin. Hardly a maiden's dream. But you know, there's absolutely no explanation for what some women find attractive. The most beautiful women will now and then be drawn to the human equivalent of a hairless Chihuahua. And it has nothing whatever to do with money or equipment, the two usual explanations. They're inscrutable creatures, women."

"You speak from experience."

"Alas."

"Anyway, since they said *au revoir*, Marvin has been writing her passionate letters three times a week. He sends them to her mother's address and hears nothing back. But he's sure her silence is significant. He's convinced she's unhappy and wants to resume their days and nights of blissfulness."

"He finds meaning in silence. Very oriental."

"Not only that, the girl apparently has a bohemian streak. She's an artist. A painter. Before they parted, she gave Marvin a portrait of herself done by one of her friends."

"Well, at least you'll know what she looks like."

"Not exactly. The picture is of a man and woman locked in a naked embrace. Her expression suggests that she's enjoying things, and it's not exactly in a realistic style. According to Marvin."

"Not much is these days."

"But he seems to think it may be very valuable."

"To him, certainly. To anyone else... who knows? But do you think it's possible that this great romance is all in Marvin's head and that the girl in question just had a three-

or four-day fling before going back to real life with her vegetable merchant?"

"Possible? No. I think it's highly likely. But I'm not going to rain on his fantasy."

"No. Especially not when it leads to business."

"The problem is, Marvin doesn't know her married name. She's somewhere in France, and he doesn't know where. Now that he's free, to use his word, he's desperate to find her."

"But why hire you? Why not go himself?"

"I wondered about that, too. But he said he's got too many projects right now."

"Ah! There speaks the heart and soul of a producer. And so enter Riley Fitzhugh, ace private investigator, who goes by the *nom de guerre* of Bruno Feldspar."

"Yes."

"A plum assignment."

"Yes, again. I told him that my fee is twenty-five a day plus expenses and that finding her could take a while. Just getting there will be expensive. He shrugged and said, 'Do you know how much we grossed on our last musical?'"

"Translation: carte blanche for Bruno."

"Yes."

"How nice. You do know, however, that people say there's going to be a war. The Germans are just itching to march into Gay Paree and be snubbed by the waiters."

"I mentioned that. I think the war's another reason he's sending me and not going himself."

"Probably. In fairness, though, Europe these days is not all that welcoming to Ginsbergs. Not many are trying to get *into* Europe."

"True. But I'm not too worried about war. No one thinks the Germans can get through the Maginot Line. France should be safe enough, for the time being."

While that was the conventional wisdom and I did more or less believe it, I also intended to look into the matter a little more thoroughly before booking my ticket.

Hobey sighed and stared into the middle distance. "You know, I spent some happy times in Paris. Back in the Twenties. It was quite the scene then."

"I've heard."

"So, what's your plan? You don't know her married name, so how can you find her?"

"I know her mother's name. I'll start there."

"Out of curiosity, what is the girl's name?"

"Nicole."

"Nicole," he said wistfully. "Yes, it would be, I suppose. I once knew someone with that name. After a fashion. Where is she from?"

"Lyon. I have her mother's address. That's where Marvin sent his letters. To be forwarded."

"Just for the sake of argument, what are you going to do if you do find her and she gives you *le rire du cheval,* which is French for the horselaugh?"

"Is that really a French expression?"

"It could be."

"Well, if that happens, I turn around and come back, give Marvin the sad news and present him with a bill for services rendered. What he does next is up to him."

"Lyon! I spent a couple of days there. With another writer I used to know. We drove from there back to Paris in my car. Good times, though we got rained on. My wife disapproved of autos with tops. Still does, I imagine." He sighed. "Lyon is famous for its chicken. And potatoes lyonnaise, of course. I wish I could go with you."

I had been expecting this. I knew this excursion would appeal to his romantic streak, which was not hard. A lot of things did.

"Why don't you?"

"Are you serious?"

"Why not? What are you doing at the moment?"

He thought about it. "Nothing, really. Just writing the narration for a ten-minute travelogue about Paraguay. Ever heard of it?"

"Vaguely."

"It's only two pages and I could whip that out before Evensong, once I find out where it is."

"I could tell Marvin I need an assistant. Expenses only. I'd be surprised if he balked. Besides, you speak French, don't you?"

"Pretty well."

"That's perfect, then. It would be a great help. I could tell Marvin in all honesty that having you along would make things go faster. Faster means cheaper. Besides, I'd probably have to hire an interpreter at some point, anyway."

"Really? That's *very* tempting."

"But what about Hedda?"

Hedda was Hobey's current girlfriend. She wrote the "Miss Lonelyhearts" advice column for one of the evening papers using the byline "Hedda Gabler." Her real name was Betty something.

"Ah, yes. Hedda. You know how you said Marvin was transformed when he first saw his dream girl?"

"Yes."

"Well, the first time I saw Hedda, I, too, had a vision ... a vision of a woman who used to sell ladies' hats."

"You were not transformed?"

"No. Not even a little bit. Dream girls don't chew gum. Although I will say I felt the stirrings of unholy urges. You've seen her figure."

"Yes, I have. Impressive."

Hedda liked bathing suits that did not conceal much, and she liked to do her work around the pool every afternoon. She would read out loud the pathetic letters coming from her sad correspondents. They made her laugh. Her advice was worthless, but that wasn't the point of the column. It was only there to attract readers by arousing a satisfying mixture of schadenfreude and ersatz pity. It sent the unsubtle message that although your life may be miserable, you were better off than the poor mutts who wrote to Miss Lonelyhearts and expected help.

"Now that I think about it, there's nothing urgent keeping me here at the moment," said Hobey. "And besides, we'll be coming back. Hedda will wait. I'll tell her it's some sort of diplomatic mission. She'll think we're spies, or something glamorous."

"What if she doesn't? Wait, that is."

He shrugged.

"*C'est la vie*. When do we leave?"

Chapter Three

Characteristically, Hobey was enthusiastic about the trip and ready to leave immediately, but I had some things to do before we could get going. I wanted to talk to my friend "Bunny" Finch-Hayton, a professor of art at UCLA and an Englishman who seemed to know a lot more than just the techniques of impressionism. He was well connected in social and even political circles, and well connected with other men's wives, who found him charming and even good-looking, despite – or maybe because of – his aristocratic beakiness. He was tall and thin with flaxen hair, carefully brushed, and he usually wore blue pinstriped suits from Savile Row and the blue-and-white-striped tie of an Old Etonian. I sometimes thought he was an agent of British Intelligence. If he was, he was a good one, because I never could discover any hard evidence. Just hints here and there. He thought much of modern art was a fraud and that the upwardly mobile people who bought it were a bunch of "muffins." Though he moved in fashionable art circles, he thought the art critics and dealers who facilitated the fraud were no more than high-class con men, although he did admit that some of them actually believed what they wrote and said. "It's not hard to fool oneself," he said. "Have you noticed that?" He found the whole business funny – or, rather, "amusing," which, he had been quick to point out to me, was something very different. He would say "A child can find things funny, but it takes years to master the art of being amused."

Bunny's sidelines were appraisals and authentications. Buyers asked his opinion about a painting signed with a famous name, and if he wasn't sure the thing was authentic, he would label it "Possibly genuine, but certainly in the style of so and so." He would then pocket his fee with a clear conscience, thereby allowing the ambitious collectors to believe whatever they wanted to believe. They could tell their friends they had a Monet because it said "Monet" in a bottom corner and because Bunny said it very well might be real. More often than not the hopeful collector was a wealthy and attractive woman of a certain age whom Bunny seduced with art gossip, champagne and harmless, transparent lies. He was a connoisseur of these meaningless love affairs – charming, but detached. Most of the women he went with appreciated that about him, because they no more wanted an entanglement than he did. He managed to remain smoothly aloof and amused, and he never made enemies. You had to admire his balance. I helped him out once on a case of art forgery, although we never did discover who the real forger was. Now and then I suspected it was Bunny himself, but I knew I would never find out for sure. And, frankly, I didn't really want to. I thought we were pretty good friends, but with Bunny you could never be sure – about almost anything.

I called his office at UCLA to see if he was free, and he invited me to come right over.

"Ah, Riley! Good to see you. Have a seat. You're just in time for coffee. Care for some?"

"Yes. Please."

Bunny's office looked more like the smoking room or library of a London club than a professor's lair. That was not the work of some interior designer, but rather Bunny's natural expression of how things looked and were done in a well ordered universe – antique furniture, leather club chairs, floor-to-ceiling bookshelves, photographs from university days, the rich scent of pipe tobacco and his black Labrador retriever, Tom, who napped in the sun beneath the window. Bunny usually had a photograph of his latest amour displayed discreetly on his desk – just in case she dropped by unannounced. The pictures changed regularly, but each one appeared in the same silver frame. "If they offer to give me a photo, I always ask for an 'eight by ten,'" he said.

His secretary emerged from somewhere, as usual anticipating Bunny's every wish. Well, it was four o'clock and Bunny didn't like tea, so the coffee was probably ready to be served whether I was there or not.

"What brings you to Westwood?"

"Advice."

"Buy all the Picassos you can. They have not found him out yet, and it looks like it'll be a while before they do. And just between us, I'm beginning to think that he might be the real thing, here and there."

"Not that kind of advice. I'm going to France, on a job."

"Oh. I see. Interesting?"

"Could be." I explained about Marvin Ginsberg's dream girl.

"I see. The old *amour fou*."

"It happened on a ship heading for Europe."

"Yes. It often does. Do you know Yeats's poem 'The Song of Wandering Aengus'?"

"No."

"It's one of his early ones, which means you can actually make out what he's saying. Rather good, the whole poem, I think. The Dream Vision suddenly appears and bedazzles the poet but then disappears again, leaving the poor fellow bereft. He resolves to spend his life finding her again. Much like your producer friend."

"'The Song of the Wandering Marvin?'"

"So it would appear, yes."

"You are familiar with the phenomenon?"

"Not personally, no. Unfortunately. I'm still waiting for *Her* to appear. I know what she looks like, though I've never seen her."

"So is Hobey – still looking, I mean. He's going with me to France."

"Maybe he'll find his *Her* there. Well, Marvin's suffering is good news for you. I sometimes think that human happiness is a zero sum game."

I wasn't sure what he meant by that, but let it pass.

"How can I help?" he said.

"I'm wondering about the political situation. People say there's going to be a war in Europe."

"There will be. No doubt about that. The only question is when. And, of course, how bad."

"Is France secure?"

"We're depending on it. And when I say 'we,' I mean us Brits. Our navy, their army. Between us we should be able to hold off the Huns. That's the theory and the hope."

"Is the Maginot Line strong enough?"

"Yes, I think so. But, you know, the whole idea of the Line is not to entice the Germans to batter themselves silly trying to break through – they're not that stupid – but to encourage them to go around to the north through Belgium, where we and the French can concentrate and meet them in tight spaces. We'll have the interior lines, and they'll be stretched out on the roads through Belgium. What the Belgians think of this you can probably imagine. But that's the real strategy behind Maginot: funnel the Huns into a space where we can give them a bloody nose and send them back to the brawny arms of their Brunhildes. Either that or entice them into a long drawn out stalemate which we will eventually win, because of the greater resources of the British and French economies and empires."

"Will it work?"

"We'll find out soon enough. But if you're wondering about your assignment, I think you'll be able to move around pretty freely for the foreseeable future. It's just possible I might see you over there – if you stop in London for a bit. I have a little business to take care of."

"Really? Care to tell me what?"

"Oh, nothing much. Something about a Tintoretto that's for sale. Some people have doubts about it. Rather a big price tag. Lots of art is going this way and that these days. People are nervous. Markets are nervous. Quite a few people, especially on the continent, are trying to turn their collections into cash. Others are taking advantage of a buyer's market.   Means big opportunities for the shady characters. Thieves and forgers."

"And for authenticators."

"Them, too, yes."

"Tintoretto?"

"Italian fellow. Sixteenth century."

Well, I more or less knew that, though *Li'l Abner* was more to my taste. My question really had to do with whether a phony Tintoretto was the real reason for his trip.   Did I believe that? Some of it, anyway. As I said, you never really knew about Bunny.

"When are you leaving?"

"Next week. Our chaps at the consulate have arranged for passage on the Pan Am Clipper from New York."

"Nice of them."

"Yes.   I did one of them a favor.   You know how that goes."

"Yes." A favor. Of course.

He looked at his watch.

"Have an appointment?" I said, innocently.

"*Cinq à sept*," he said. It was French for "five to seven," that time of day when a man met his mistress at some neutral location for two hours of champagne and lovemaking, after which both could leave, well pleased – she to her husband and dinner plans, Bunny to whatever social responsibilities he had. Bunny thought the *cinq à sept* idea was the highest expression of French culture. "Matisse is all very well," he said "but the five to seven is an art form all to itself."

"I'll be going, then," I said. "But there is one last thing – have your heard any word from or about ... Amanda?"

"Nothing in any detail. She's a cultural attaché in Berlin, you know."

"Which means she's a spy."

"*C'est possible.*"

Amanda was an aristocrat who had accidentally shot and killed her equally aristocratic husband while working at the British consulate here in L.A. I had helped her out, and we had become friendly. If that's the right word.

"She may not be there long, however," he said. "There's no way to know how long the embassy will be open. If things get too dicey, she may be posted back to London." He looked at me with a sly smile. "Miss her?"

"A bit."

"Me, too. Not in the way you do, of course."

"Yes, well ...."

We finished the coffee and I thanked him and left, wondering if it might just be possible that Amanda and I would meet again. Perhaps in London. It was a long shot, but I figured the odds were at least as good as my finding Marvin's *amour fou*, to use Bunny's expression.

Chapter Four

In the morning I went to my office. I needed to make some calls.

My secretary, Della, was at her desk in the reception room banging away on her typewriter.

I never knew what she was writing, because my business didn't generate a lot of correspondence. She ran an escort service on the side, so I imagined it all had something to do with that. She only came in a couple of days a week, but when she was there she gave the place the proper tone. I think she really thought of it as her office and that I was just a visitor to be tolerated. But she answered my phone and typed up the occasional invoice or report and in general gave the impression that we were a serious outfit. She was middle aged, with henna-colored hair and a Pall Mall perpetually dangling from her mouth. It made her eyes water from the smoke, but she put up with that, because she really liked Pall Malls. She also liked Braunschweiger and onion on rye and a couple of martinis for lunch. She was married to an ex-bosun's mate who ran a water taxi out to the gambling ships.

She didn't have a softer side, she didn't have a heart of gold, and her basic response to the Universe was more or less, "Oh, yeah?" She and her husband, Perry, were well known to or well connected with L.A.'s marginal characters. They knew a lot of what went on below the surface of things. They had helped me out of one or two tricky situations. I was very fond of both of them.

"Good morning, loyal employee," I said.

"You think so?"

"How's the novel coming?" She always said she was working on a novel about a smart aleck LA private eye. I didn't believe it, but it made a decent running joke.

"I have writer's block."

"You can take something for that. Check at Schwab's."

Schwab's was a well-known drug store and lunch counter across Sunset from the Garden. It was where the stars and the hopefuls went for corned beef sandwiches and prescriptions.

"Any calls?" I asked.

"Ethel Welkin. She wants a lube, oil and filter. Followed by lunch at the usual place. Wednesday. I said you were free."

"Oh. Well, I guess that'll work."

After all, I did owe Ethel something for this new assignment. She didn't demand much in return for these favors, but she did have a clear idea of what she wanted. Besides, for a pint-sized forty-ish woman, she was a surprisingly good bed partner. Inventive and acrobatic.

"Shall I put it in your calendar?" said Della. Not that I had one.

"No. I'll remember. But do me a favor and call Blinky."

"Blinky Malone?"

"How many Blinkys do you know?"

"You'd be surprised. What do you want from him?"

"Tell him to come to the office this afternoon." Blinky's place of business was known only to himself and a very few trusted characters. He came to you, you didn't go to him. Like most subterranean creatures, he figured it was safer that way. Even Della only had his phone number.

"OK, Chief." Della enjoyed calling me "Chief."

I had a call to make, too, and went into the inner office. I didn't bother closing the door. There was no sense trying to keep personal business private. I dialed Catherine Moore's home number in Malibu. She answered after five rings. She sounded sleepy.

"Hello, Beautiful," I said.

"Hello, Sparky," she cooed. "To which Sparky am I talking?"

"Sparky, the detective."

She laughed. "I know. I was just pulling your chain."

"Sounds good to me." It was a routine we went through pretty much whenever I called.

"Guess what I'm wearing."

"Well, since it's still morning, I would say ... nothing."

"Wrong. Pearls. Manny just gave them to me before he went to the office. They're very elegant. Opera length, he said. I don't like opera, but I do like pearls."

Manny was her husband and a movie mogul who was besotted with her. She was not besotted with him but liked having a beach house in Malibu and a mansion in Bel Air.

"You're a lucky girl."

"Says you. These things don't come for nothing, you know. But I don't mind. A little schtupping in the morning and then it's over for the day."

"Feel like doing me a favor?"

"Sure. But I haven't had my bath yet. Do you care?"

"Not that kind of favor. At least not now. I want to get hold of Tony, but I don't have his ship to shore number. Would you mind calling him for me and asking what's a good time for me to come out there? I need to talk to him."

"Anything for you, Sparky. Assuming you're the Sparky I think you are."

Tony Scungilli, also known as Tony the Snail, was Catherine's boyfriend. If her husband Manny knew anything about it, he didn't let on, and it had no effect on his besotted-ness, if there is such a word. Tony was a big time gangster and the manager of the *Lucky Lady*, the gambling ship anchored just outside the three-mile limit, which protected it from California's laws, gambling and otherwise.

Catherine had been involved with Tony before she married Manny, and she saw no particular reason to change things just because she went through a five-minute legal ceremony that she didn't really pay attention to. "Is that wrong?" she would say, her blue eyes all wide innocence. She could really do innocence. Tony didn't mind the arrangement either, because he didn't want a full time commitment, and, besides, he already had a wife and family back in New Jersey. He was star-struck by the movie industry and delighted that his girlfriend was part of it. In his heart of hearts, he also thought that he might one day get discovered and become a second George Raft, even though he was short and stocky and spoke the King's English like he grew up in the mean streets of Newark, which, as a matter of fact, he had. He'd been sent west by the mob and had done well and risen in the ranks, to become manager of the largest of the gambling ships off LA. He was a good earner and would continue to rise as long as he didn't put a foot wrong. Or, as he put it, "Just so long's I don't fuck up."

I had done him a favor in the past, and he liked me. This was contingent on a gentlemen's agreement that I wouldn't go to bed with Catherine more than just occasionally and not make a habit of it. That was all right with me, and with Catherine, for that matter. She told me when we first got to know each other, "Don't go falling in love with me. I got enough on my plate." I didn't, not more than half, so we were all friends together. Even so, I didn't have Tony's private number.

Catherine said she'd deliver the message, hung up, made the call and called me right back.

"He says come for lunch today. He's having *frutti di mare*. You want company? I suggest you say 'yes,' because Tony says he wants to see me."

"The answer would be 'yes' in any case."

"Smooth talker. I'll wear my new pearls to make Tony jealous, so he'll think twice about trying to get by on the cheap next time."

"Good. I'll meet you at the pier at 11:30."

About an hour later I drove to the Santa Monica pier in my two-tone cream and tan Packard convertible. A great and beautiful car. When I parked, I wondered if I should put the top up, but it wasn't going to rain and the seagulls were occupied by the various concession stands on the pier. Della's husband, Perry, was standing next to his water taxi.

The boat was as shiny and well maintained as you would expect from an ex-navy bosun's mate.

"Hey, Chief," he said. "Going out to see your buddy, the goombah?"

"Yeah, but I'm waiting for someone. You know Catherine Moore."

"Not as much as I'd like to. I'd make a move, but I restrain myself on account of Della. She ain't the jealous type, but she can be vindicative."

"You mean vindictive?"

"That, too. She tells me she's writing a book about you. A detective story."

"I heard that, too. I don't believe it. Do you?"

"I ain't in the believing business. But if I ain't mistaken, here comes your lady's Rolls."

A spectacularly shiny Rolls Royce pulled up to the entrance of the pier, and Catherine emerged looking exactly like a movie mogul's wife-cum-gangster's girlfriend should look – a vanilla parfait in the flesh.

"Hi, Sparky. How do I look?"

"Like you smell good all over."

"Mmmm. And you know what? I do. Hiya, Perry! How's tricks?"

"Good. Ain't you gonna be a little warm in that mink?"

"Silly. How do you like my pearls?" She leaned over slightly so that her mink would fall open and her pearls reveal themselves.

"Nice ones" said Perry.

"I agree," I said.

EPITAPH FOR A DREAM

"Smooth talkers. Well, let's go, boys. I have to be back pretty early. Manny is throwing a party tonight for some big shots. I'm the decorations."

She waved at her chauffeur, Jesus, who dutifully pulled over to a parking spot to wait. Waiting for Catherine was his chief pleasure in life. His métier.

Twenty minutes later Catherine and I were being ushered into Tony's office at the aft end of the *Lucky Lady*. We had to walk through the smoky main salon, which was one huge room the size of a football field. There was the usual cacophony of slot machines ringing and croupiers calling and people shouting or groaning, and in the background there was a full dance band complete with bandleader smiling and waving his baton and a sultry girl singer standing at a mike and warbling "Heart and Soul." One of the gloomy novelists currently in fashion might say it was an appropriate song, because the *Lucky Lady* was a place where people lost their souls and broke their hearts. But in fact almost everyone was having a good time, and there were very few tears and even fewer personal crises. Plundered and lacerated souls were in short supply. It was a normal scene on the *Lucky Lady*, where it was always 11 p.m., 24 hours a day.

Tony's office was nothing like you would expect from a mobster. No dark imitations of Renaissance Venice, no paintings of fruit bowls or matadors on velvet. A sober-sided banker would have felt at home there. There was one large portrait of a serious-looking old gent with sparse hair, a menacing stare and a decidedly Mediterranean look. The first time I was in Tony's office I asked him who it was.

"If you don't know, you ain't supposed to know" was all he'd say.

A long conference table ran lengthwise and could seat twelve. It was already set for lunch. For three. Tony's massive mahogany desk was in the rear. There were couches and comfortable chairs arranged here and there. When we came in Tony was behind his desk going over the figures from the most recent accounting.

He looked up and smiled when we entered.

"Hi, Doll," he said. "Hiya, kid."

I wasn't really a kid anymore, but I realized this was just Tony being friendly. In this town, it was good when Tony was friendly, and it was good to be his friend. In his vernacular, there were only two kinds of people – "our friends" and everybody else.

Tony pressed a button on his intercom, notifying the kitchen, I suppose, and then came over and hugged Catherine, who cooed appreciatively and professionally. Then he shook my hand. I never looked forward to that. His grip was painful. But he didn't mean anything by it; it was just how he did things.

No more than a minute went by before the office door opened and a nervous-looking waiter came in pushing a massive cart, bearing a huge bowl of seafood pasta, a loaf of campagna bread and two bottles of Valpolicella.

"Let's eat," said Tony. "It's been a long time since breakfast. I gotta restore my energy for later." He grinned at Catherine, who rolled her eyes at him, but smiled.

"Don't be in such a hurry like usual," she said. "You wanna see my new pearls?"

Tony groaned.   Manny's constant flow of jewelry and other expensive gifts cost Tony money, too, just trying to keep up.

"Maybe later."

We started in on the pasta.   Tony tucked a big white napkin in his collar and I did the same.   Frutti di mare sauce is thin and has a tendency to spatter.   Catherine didn't bother with the napkin, though, because it would interfere with our view of her new pearls and her breasts.   She wanted Tony to have a good look at them.

"So, to what do I owe the pleasure of your company?" he said to me.   "Not that I ain't always glad to see you.   If I wanted to adopt a nice Presbyterian kid from Ohio, you'd be on the list, near the top."

"Good to know.   Fact is, I'm hoping you can put me in touch with some of your friends in France."

"France? Why?"

I explained the job and Marvin Ginsberg's obsession.

"What a dipshit," said Tony, when I finished.

"His dipshittedness is my opportunity."

He nodded.

"That's how business happens."

"But it would help if I knew there were some friends in France I could call on, if I needed to."

"What makes you think we got friends in France?"

"Just a guess.   I know that there's a fair amount of business going on – in and out of Marseilles and Paris – the kind of business people here might have some interest in. And I think there's a war coming, and that will mean all sorts of disruptions in normal markets."

"And all sorts of opportunities for our friends? Is that it?"

"Pretty much. There'll be shortages in everything once the shooting starts. I'd be very surprised if people over there weren't already planning for it, and very surprised if they hadn't contacted people over here to see what sort of cooperation might work for everyone's best interest."

"Like what, for instance?"

"Like regular shipments of American cigarettes, for one. That would be like printing money – even if the cigarettes cost a little something over here."

"Even better if they didn't," he said.

I had a mental picture of a semi-truck loaded with Lucky Strikes being hijacked on the way up from North Carolina and then driven to the Port of Elizabeth and loaded onto a steamer bound for Marseilles. American cigarettes would be like gold on the black market – and there *would be* a black market, because of shortages and rationing. How many crates of Luckies could a steamer hold? A lot. I knew that Marseilles was the smuggling capital of France, if not the whole of Europe. And I knew that the mob there had distribution networks all through France and beyond, mostly for narcotics. And if I was sure of anything, I was sure the mobsters on both sides of the Atlantic had already thought this through.

Tony looked at me for a second, smiling slightly and considering what he wanted to say.

"First of all, for the record – I don't know about any this, not first hand, you understand."

"Of course."

"But what you say makes sense. And I wouldn't be surprised if some of our friends in New York weren't having the same kind of thoughts. You're right – as soon as those folks over there start shooting each other, there's going to be shortages on their home front, because the armies will suck up all the cigarettes and toilet paper and razor blades and what have you, and the people back home will be left smoking corn silk and shaving with clam shells. Won't matter which side is winning. Even a stalemate will cause the same sort of thing. Actually, that would be better. Make things last longer. And you're also right that our friends *over there* have probably thought about this, and planned for it. And they've called our friends *over here* to discuss things. Like supplies. But – what's all this mean to you?" said Tony. "Don't tell me you're trying to weasel in on the action. You ain't that stupid."

"No. I don't want anything to do with it. I don't even want to know anything about it. All I'd like is a few names over there, if I get into some kind of trouble. Just a back-up. A number to call. If I had to get out of the country quickly and without being noticed, that sort of thing. I thought you might have some good friends over there who'd like to meet a nice private dick from LA and do a favor for your nice American friend. Chances are I wouldn't ever call on them. But it'd be nice to have the contact in my back pocket."

"That's the wrong place for it. It ain't ever smart to write things down."

"I was speaking, ah, metaphorically."

"I get it. But why bring this to me? Why not check with your FBI buddy?"

"Do you think the FBI has a clue about business in France? Or your kinds of contacts?"

"No. Not a chance."

"Well, then."

The truth is, I was planning to call my friend at the FBI, Bill Patterson, later today or tomorrow. But there was no need to complicate discussions with Tony. Besides, it was perfectly obvious that Tony could be vastly more helpful with contacts than the FBI, who, in all fairness, were pretty much restricted to domestic US business. They might have relationships with the French national police force, but those guys might be some of the ones I was running from.

"I understand what you need. Lemme think about it," he said. In other words, end of discussion. "How's your pasta?"

"Perfect."

"How about you, sugar?"

"I splashed some on my pearls."

"It'll wash off. I'll have someone clean them after lunch, while you ain't wearing them."

"It'll take longer than five minutes," she said, wrinkling her nose at him.

"No, it won't"

After lunch, I left Catherine there with Tony and took the water taxi back to my car. I got to my office a few minutes later. Blinky Malone was waiting for me there.

Chapter Five

"Blinky's inside," said Della. "He's already checked behind the doors and in the closets. When you're finished with your business ask him to show you his latest peeper shots. You'd be surprised at the things people do!"

"Really?"

"Well, maybe not. But people are a whole lot more creative than you'd think. You remember the story about the one-legged jockey and the gerbil?"

"Yeah, I do."

"Well, there you go."

Peeper shots were the kind that photographers took outside motel windows or in bath houses. Guys like Blinky got hired by angry spouses, or their lawyers. Or by blackmailers, not that there's much difference. But Blinky's stock in trade was not just photography. He was also one of the better forgers in LA. He just did peepers when the demand for documents got soft. He always carried a camera, though, because, as he put it, "You never know." He was not a Cartier-Bresson looking for that "decisive moment" that revealed life in an interesting and artistic way. No, Blinky was looking for that decisive moment that someone would be desperate to cover up. And willing to pay to do it. Besides, most official documents of the kind he specialized in required pictures, so he always had his Leica in his pocket.

He was sitting in one of the two oak client chairs with his feet on my desk. He was reading a smutty magazine and chewing the sloppy end of a cheap cigar. He was dressed in his usual checked suit and derby, and he had that pallid complexion common to prison inmates and society ladies who avoid the sun.

"What's up, Blinky," I said as he shot to his feet.

"I found this magazine in a wastebasket on the street," he said, as if I cared that he read porn.

"Don't let your mother see it."

"Won't be hard. She ain't with us anymore."

"Oh. Sorry to hear it."

"She moved to Detroit. They say the weather's better there, but I couldn't say for sure. I ain't ever been west of LA. That's funny ain't it? A guy in my business who ain't never traveled."

"Another of life's mysteries."

He nodded as if to say, "That's how I see it, too."

I sat down and he sat down, and negotiations began. There was no sense spending more time with Blinky than was strictly necessary.

"I need some documents pretty fast. Passports and visas and whatever else I might need for Europe. England and France, mostly. I assume you know what's required."

"Yep. You're dealing with a professional, you know."

"Good. The more visa coverage I can get, the better. Spain, Holland, Belgium. And I want the passports to look like they're well used. Lots of stamps."

Blinky wrote it down in a small notebook with the stub of a pencil.

"How many?"

"Two sets for me. One under 'Riley Fitzhugh,' the other under 'Bruno Feldspar.'"

"We're having a sale this week on three sets," he said with a smirk.

"Good to know, because I need another set for a friend. He may want more than one, too. That'll qualify us for your sale price."

"Oh. I was just fooling about that."

"Didn't your mother ever tell you no one likes a smart ass?"

"My mother? No. She didn't pay much attention to us kids. She'd rather play poker and go bowling. Who's the other guy?"

I gave him Hobey's name and address at the Garden and told Blinky to meet with him.

"You might wear a different suit when you go there," I said. It was not so much that Blinky's outfit outraged the fashion conscious as that it made him conspicuous. For a decidedly nocturnal animal he had a strange taste for the garish. Was it Emerson who said that consistency is the hobgoblin of the unimaginative? Something like that.

"My other suit's in the cleaners," he said. If he was offended, he didn't show it. "How many sets does the other guy need?"

"I don't know. He may have everything he needs already," I said. "But he may want a spare under another name. So ... how long and how much?"

"As for how long, that depends on things like the traffic flow in front of the consulates. You said you wanted used passports, which means we can't print them ourselves. Oh, we can, but it'd be a lot simpler to lift a few and modify them, so to speak. So I'll have Fingers hang around outside the consulates, and it all depends on how many mugs is going in and out every day. We'll pull till we get the right set."

"Fingers" was Blinky's number one pickpocket. It was said he could steal a guy's boxer shorts without breaking stride and without the guy noticing.

"So there's going to be an epidemic of lost passports outside the consulates."

"It's cheaper and faster and more authentic that way. So, yep. But, you understand, the timing depends on the traffic in and out. Usually, though, we can get these things worked out in a week or two."

"Including alteration of the docs?"

"Yep. Like I said – professionals."

"How much?"

He gave me a figure that was twice what I figured, and I told him so. He cut it in half, and we agreed. I didn't really care, though. Marvin was paying for expenses, and he'd get the bill before Blinky finished the job. Blinky was smiling when he left, so I assumed he ended up with more than he'd expected. That was all right. Always let 'em leave thinking they'd screwed you. It makes for good relations with suppliers.

EPITAPH FOR A DREAM

It occurred to me that it was too bad Amanda had left the British consulate in LA. She might have helped out with the documents. But, then, her leaving was too bad for a lot of reasons. The last time I'd seen her she'd been stretched out languidly on our bed at the Beverly Hills Hotel. She had blonde hair and brown eyes and her coloring reminded me of butterscotch. And those brown eyes had been half closed with sleepy pleasure, and she was half smiling.

Thinking of Amanda, and how she looked that last time, suddenly made me think about Marvin's obsession – and start to wonder if what he was feeling for his dream girl might actually be genuine, not just some middle-aged madness of the moment. It could be, I suppose. He certainly thought so. Of course, it was possible she was just the product of his overactive imagination. If so, I could understand that, too. But in that case, was she any less real – to him? I'd have to ask Hobey about that; he was the expert in such things. Mythology. Psychology. Metaphysics. Poetry. All-around bullshit. Marvin didn't come off as a very sympathetic character, hardly a hero of romance. But even so, he *was* a member of our sad fools club. Most of us weren't heroes of romance, either, but we could all be just as susceptible as any knight at arms, "alone and palely loitering." If you're wondering how I know that line from Keats, I should say I'm still working on my education, so I read a lot. Plus, I hang around Hobey and Bunny, and I pick things up. When I was a kid, I worked in the steel mills of Youngstown, Ohio, and there wasn't much time for studying the classics. I came west to be a star in the movies, decided it wasn't for me, and so became a PI. Now I have plenty of time to study more than just how LA's underworld and overworld work. So I do, and I like doing it. Like Catherine's chauffeur, Jesus, I guess I have found my métier.

On the way home, I stopped at the library and looked up the poem that Bunny had mentioned. One of the last lines was "I will find out where she has gone." *All right, then*, I thought. *I get it. I'll do what I can for you, Marvin.* As for myself, well, who could say?

Chapter Six

The next day I called on my friend Bill Patterson at the local FBI office. Bill was mostly a researcher who specialized in uncovering potential Fifth Columnist terror plots against us. Like most everyone else, he expected that there would be a war and took his assignment very seriously. But then again, Bill was a serious guy. He looked more like a grad student than a G-Man, but as with most things, looks could be deceiving. Bill was a graduate of the Naval Academy, had done five years of active duty and had resigned to join the Bureau. He was an analyst, but he knew which end of a gun was dangerous.

I never needed an appointment with Bill. He was usually at his desk surrounded by piles of paper, and he was always glad when someone dropped in. Not many did.

"Riley! For God's sake, have you got a flask in your pocket?"

"No. Sorry. Besides, Mr. Hoover doesn't want you agents drinking on his time."

"Mr. Hoover can shove it. But don't say I said that."

"Job getting you down?"

"You try studying French politics for a week or so and see where you end up."

"What do French politics have to do with us?"

"I asked the same question. The answer was, 'Who knows? But look into it.' So I'm supposed to become the expert in making sense of it – which cannot be done by any man born of woman. See, there's going to be a war, right? Everyone knows that. The Germans are the bad guys. Everyone knows that. They will attack Poland, and then France will declare war, and the Germans will attack France. Everyone knows that. After that, no one knows anything. But consider the possible scenarios. Suppose the French send the Krauts packing. Hooray for the land of Lafayette! Pass the champagne. Maurice Chevalier smiles and sings *All I Want Is Just One Girl*. But... suppose the Krauts break through the Maginot line or, worse yet, find a way around it."

"Bunny says that's the whole idea. To funnel them around the western end."

"Oh, those wily Frogs! But – suppose the Huns are not as dumb as Hitler looks. Suppose they find another way around. Or through. What then, eh?"

"Well?"

"Then the Germans get behind the French lines and the game is up. Could happen."

"And then?"

"Here's the bad part. There are more than a few Frenchmen who wouldn't mind it if something like that *did* happen. They'll make a deal with the Huns. Decide to work together. Life goes on, only better and more orderly, and the undesirable elements – meaning the Jews and the commies – are sent packing. Or worse. Maurice Chevalier changes his tune to *All I Want Is Just One Fraulein*, and things go on pretty much as before. Same smile, same tap dance, slightly different audience."

"That assumes the Germans will cooperate."

"Yes, it does."

"How about the Brits?"

"I'd like to think that they'll never go along with any of this. But you know there's a faction in English politics that thinks the Fascists in general and the Nazis in particular aren't really such bad fellows. Thinks they have a lot of good ideas about how things should be run."

"I've heard that, too. But it's hard to believe."

"I would have said the same thing a couple of weeks ago. But now I'm not so sure. Especially with the French. French domestic politics are a cage of parrots."

"Colorful?"

"No, quarrelsome. It's depressing, but it's something we have to consider. It's entirely possible that France could change sides after getting a bloody nose. And so the Bureau gave me the job of analyzing how likely all these scenarios are and what to do about it, if one of them does happen. I have to say in all modesty that I'm not the only one charged with thinking about this. So what's your tale of woe?"

"Compared to your problem, it seems pretty trivial."

"That's all right."

So I told him about Marvin's French obsession.

"Since you know what's going on over there, what do you think my chances are for finding her?"

"Finding her? Probably very good. After all, you know her mother's address, and with your boyish charm you can probably sweet talk her into telling you where the girl is. Of course, there's the inconvenient husband, but I have confidence you'll solve that little problem."

"Or not. She may give me the French version of the bird."

"*L'oiseau*? Yes. That's a possibility. In which case you'll have done your best and Marvin will have to find consolation in the arms of starlets. But let's assume she thinks coming back to Marvin is a good idea. In this climate, she might very well be glad to leave France, Marvin or no Marvin. In that case, your problem is going to be figuring out how to get her out."

"Why?"

"Is she Jewish?"

"I don't know. But I can find out from Marvin. What's the problem?"

"It makes things more complicated. French anti-Semitism is alive and well. Of course, that's an age-old story. Not that different from other places in Europe, and not as bad as in Germany, but it's real, and the story we hear is that a lot of French Jews are very nervous. A lot are trying to leave, but the paperwork involved makes it hard. You might find you have to spend some money for what we law enforcement professionals call 'bribes.'"

"Why? If there's so much anti-Jew feeling you'd think everyone would be happy to see the back of them."

"French bureaucracy is notorious for being a tangled web they weave in order to create public jobs, and because they seem to like it. But the paperwork involved in getting Jews out is many times worse. I have a feeling it has something to do with the transfer of property, and it certainly has to do with quotas in the countries they want to go to. Lots of them would like to come here, but we can't take all of them."

"What if she's only part Jewish?"

"Doesn't matter. Remember the old South and slaves? Any portion of black blood was enough. In some ways, less was worse. Pretty much the same with the Jews – as far as the anti-Semites are concerned."

"I'm surprised there are so many anti-Semites in France; I thought that was a German problem."

"I was surprised, too. But everyone needs a scapegoat and the Jews seemed to have been appointed for that role all through Europe. All through history, really. Don't ask me why. These are mysteries I can't solve."

"Suppose I can get her out. Any chance that you or your friends back in Washington could help with immigration? Get her through the quotas?"

"I doubt it. I don't have much pull, you know. I'll see what I can do, of course. But first you have to get her out – assuming she wants to get out. Worry about the immigration paperwork afterwards. A simple temporary visa will be good enough for your purposes. She may get here and not like it. Not like Marvin. Miss the baguettes. Miss her husband. In any case, you will have done your job, no?"

"Yes."

"My best advice is to get busy. When the fighting does start the whole country is going to be in turmoil. Right now everyone is very nervous, especially our friends in the national police. They're seeing fifth columnists, spies and infiltrators everywhere. So I hear, anyway. They're going to be very leery of foreigners."

"I was going to ask if you had any contacts with your counterparts over there."

"No, I don't. I suppose some of our guys back in DC might. But my advice to you is to steer clear of French cops, if you can. Especially the national boys. They are in an ugly mood."

"How much time do I have?"

"Couple of months. That's our best estimate. After that, don't stand next to the fan. Of course, there could be some last-minute miracle."

"Think that's likely?"

"Nope. If the Germans go into Poland, all hell will break loose. And everything points to it."

"Well, thanks for the info."

"You're welcome. Next time bring a flask."

I went back to my office and called Marvin's office number. His secretary put me through. Obviously he had given her my name in case I called. I considered this a good sign.

"What's up? Any news?" he said. "I'm in the middle of a meeting. But go ahead."

"Is Nicole Jewish?"

"What? What difference does that make?"

"Do you read the papers?"

"That bad? In France?"

"Yes. Is she?"

"The truth is, I don't know. We didn't talk about it. She doesn't have what you'd call classic Jewish features, but that doesn't necessarily mean anything."

At first I thought it was odd that the subject hadn't come up between them. But then I realized that passionate affairs generally don't leave much room for religious discussions. My Amanda could be a Confucian for all I know.

"OK," I said. "I've been talking to people in the know. They all think the war's going to start sooner rather than later. So I need to get to France in a hurry, and I want to take the Pan Am Clipper. I also want to take an assistant. A guy who knows France and speaks the language. OK?"

"Do it. Whatever you need."

"There'll probably be some bribes involved, too."

"Like I said, whatever you need. Stop by the Hollywood branch of Wells Fargo tomorrow. There'll be a letter of credit waiting for you. You can draw on it over there. I'll make the call right now. Money is no object. Just find her and bring her to me."

"OK. 'I will find out where she has gone,'" I said.

"I hope so," he said, and hung up.

I hadn't expected him to get the reference, and he didn't. Well, I wouldn't have gotten it either, a day or so ago.

Chapter Seven

The Wells Fargo branch was on Hollywood Boulevard. When I went in, gave my name and asked for the manager, I was greeted like a visiting Sultan and taken straight to the office of the resident vice president. He was a genial kind of guy, happy in his work and eager to help me. It was obvious that Marvin had plenty of grease for all sorts of skids.

"How do you do, sir? I'm happy to know you. Mr. Ginsberg called and told me what he wanted, and we have prepared the paperwork for you – a letter of credit in your name in the amount of five thousand dollars."

A nice round sum.

"How does it work, exactly? I've never dealt with one of these."

"You can present it to any of our correspondent banks in France, or really anywhere in Europe, and draw as much money as you like, up to the maximum five thousand, in the equivalent amount of local currency. Or dollars. That's up to you. All the major banks in Europe are our correspondents, so you will have almost complete flexibility. You see, we have accounts with them and they have accounts with us.

EPITAPH FOR A DREAM

When you show up at their counters, provide identification and draw under this letter, they give you the money, debit our account there, notify us, and we debit Mr. Ginsberg's account here. So it's really a matter of bookkeeping, a very convenient and secure way of having money for travelling. You can draw as many times as you like, in any amount that you like."

"What if I lose the letter?"

"Notify the local bank. They'll notify us by telex and we'll cancel the transaction, then issue a new one with new numbers. But I advise you not to lose it. Putting things right can take a little time."

"Is there an expiration date?"

"Yes. Six months from now. Will that suit you?"

"Should be fine." If I didn't find Marvin's dream girl by then, chances were I never would.

"Of course, if you need to, we can roll it over, with Mr. Ginsberg's permission."

"Can it be revoked?" I could see myself stuck in France with a worthless letter of credit because Marvin had a change of heart.

"No. It's irrevocable. It's a safer version of cash."

"What if I don't use it all?"

"It expires after six months and any unused amount in effect reverts to Mr. Ginsberg. In other words, we don't deduct the unused portion from his account."

"That all sounds perfect. Is that all there is to it?"

"Yes."

"Well then, thank you for the service."

"You're welcome. Have a pleasant trip. And thank you for your business. Perhaps you would mention to Mr. Ginsberg that you were happy with our service."

"Of course."

It's good to be a big time movie producer. But I already knew that.

It was Wednesday, so I drove over to the Beverly Hills Hotel and checked into the usual room. Ethel was only a few minutes behind me.

"Hello, darling. I'm late," she said, as she breezed in and started undressing.

I knew what she meant, but I played along with her and pretended to look shocked.

"Late? You mean ... you're... you mean, I'm ..."

"Not that kind of late, silly. As if you really thought so. I still could, though. You know? But whenever Izzy mentions something about starting a family, I get a headache. I've just got to make it to forty, then I'm home free." She was stripping off her dress and silky underwear. She was a fast undresser. She used to do a slow and seductive strip to demonstrate her bona fides as a Delilah, but those days were over, not because she was past her prime and had lost the urge – she wasn't and she hadn't – but because she was usually too busy and in a hurry. Her daily schedule was always full.

"I want to try number 43 again," she said. "I don't think we got it quite right the last time."

Ethel was a devotee of the Kama Sutra and was determined to work her way through however many positions there were. I didn't mind. It's always interesting to learn something new.

49

EPITAPH FOR A DREAM

"You seemed pretty pleased with how it came out. And I was, too." Not that I really remembered. But Ethel never failed to reach the finish line. I could only take partial credit for that.

"Oh, that. Well, of course. I'm always pleased that way with you, darling, but I was thinking of getting it technically correct. If you're going to do something by the book, you might as well follow the book exactly."

"Fine. Do I hop around on one foot or stand on my hands or something? I don't remember the specifics of number 43."

"No. I 'm the one who has to do a bit of stretching, especially with one leg. But I've been working out. Let me show you."

By this time she was out of her clothes and we began, with me taking instruction and following orders like a good student.

You wouldn't think it to look at Ethel in her Givenchy or Chanel couture, but she was a lively bed partner and very flexible. True, she could afford to lose a couple of pounds, but, all things considered, I really had no complaints, especially because she regularly sent me business, and all she expected in return were these afternoon sessions, followed by lunch – which neither of us paid for. It went on the studio's tab.

Ethel was always very efficient and it was no more than forty-five minutes later that we were sitting at a table in the Polo Lounge. Ethel had ordered her usual corned beef on rye and garlic pickle. I was glad we always had lunch after our romp upstairs, instead of before, because that pickle seemed to have its own visible atmosphere.

"So, how did you make out with Marvin?"

"Very well. He's sending me to France to find a girl he met a couple of years ago. I have you to thank for this."

"You're welcome, darling. But you must promise not to get into trouble over there. Things are going to get nasty. I wouldn't want you to get shot and lose something I'm fond of. And be sure to hurry back when you're finished."

"I know. I'll watch myself."

"What did you think of Marvin?"

"He seemed OK."

"He's not a bad guy. His wife was a pain. If she ever actually laughed, I never noticed. A happy or even bearable marriage is impossible when one partner has no sense of humor. I never liked her. No one did, really."

"I wonder why he married her."

She shrugged. "Why does anyone do anything?"

"He didn't seem too disturbed by her death."

"Are you kidding? I'll bet he was glad."

"Well, yes. He seemed to be. Anything you can tell me that might help?"

"I don't think so. All he ever told me about his girlfriend was that she was an artist of some kind. A painter, I think. She gave him a painting by one of her friends over there. Really quite good, I think. Maybe she even did it herself. I'm not sure. The signature is blurred somehow. Marvin says it might be a Picasso. I guess it could be."

"Really?"

"Could be. She's French and Picasso lives there. And from what I hear he's fond of painting naughty pictures and using young girls as models. Marvin's very proud of it, mostly because it came from her. He has it hanging over the fireplace in his den.   He could gaze at it like a lovesick schoolboy and laugh up his sleeve, because Elaine had no clue it was anything but a pair of nudes making love.   It's really a lovely picture, very sexy in a sense, but it's so beautiful that it's not at all lascivious, if you know what I mean.   It's the opposite of porn, and it's very special to Marvin.   I'm sure he thinks it's meant to be him and her locked in love. Frozen in time."

"'Forever panting, forever young.'   Like the lovers in 'A Grecian Urn'."

"You're very literary today, my dear.   But you will remember those lovers never get together." Ethel had studied literature at Brooklyn College, before getting married and coming to Hollywood.   "In Marvin's painting, they're very happily involved. I've seen it. The expression on her face was enough to make me think of calling you, even though it was Saturday. I didn't dare sit down."

"Always at your service."

"I'm glad, but one day a week is about all I can manage, unfortunately.   Izzy keeps me pretty busy, entertaining." Izzy was her husband, the producer. He gave me my first and only job in the movies. That, too, had been thanks to Ethel's influence.

Just then I saw Alphonso, the maître d', heading to our table with the telephone. His real name was Al Jablonski, and he'd been a pretty good stunt man until he broke his leg getting thrown off a horse. Now he just played an Italian maître d' with a limp. He said he'd been wounded in the retreat from Caporetto. He got that story from a Hemingway book. Producers out here bought Hemingway's books for the movies because they were best sellers, but they didn't actually read them, so everyone pretty much accepted Alphonso's story. Or, if they didn't, it didn't matter. One of the chief virtues of this town is that private myths and fictions are not only tolerated but expected and respected. No one challenges anyone's story, regardless of how flimsy. Everyone comes from somewhere else, and almost everyone *is* someone else before coming here. I'm no different.

I assumed the phone call was for Ethel, but it wasn't. It was my friend Lieutenant Ed Kowalski of the LAPD homicide department.

"How'd you know where to find me?" I asked him.

"It's Wednesday. Even if Della hadn't reminded me, I would have remembered it eventually."

"All right. What's up?"

"I believe you know a guy named Marvin Ginsberg."

Uh-oh.

"Yeah. He's a client."

"Not anymore. Someone put a bullet in his head, right where the spinal cord meets the skull. Bullet came out his left eye. I would suggest a closed casket."

"Oh."

"When you finish lunch or whatever you call it, come on down to the station. We need to talk."

I hung up the phone.

"What is it?" said Ethel.

"Bad news."

Chapter Eight

"Any idea who did it?" I asked.

"Nope," said Kowalski. "Nothing seems to be missing from the house. He still had three hundred bucks in his wallet. So we've ruled out robbery, which is too bad. Life is simpler when only money's involved. His housekeeper found him stretched out on the floor of his den. The forensics boys are still going over the house for prints and the usual stuff. I don't suppose you have any ideas about this."

"Nothing much. I just started working for him the other day. How'd you know about me?"

"Your name was in his diary with a note to himself to make a payment. Care to tell your Uncle Ed all about it?"

"He wanted me to find a girl he met. She's somewhere in France."

"I'm guessing that deal is off."

"I suppose so. But maybe not."

But maybe not. I had thought about this on the way to the station. Did I still have some obligation? If so, to whom? The girl? Was she somewhere in France sitting and wondering, maybe regretting her marriage? Maybe she felt as strongly about Marvin as he felt about her. It seemed unlikely, but as more than one sage has said, there is no accounting for the human heart. And if she really loved him, didn't she deserve to be told he was gone? Wouldn't she wonder why his letters suddenly stopped? True, she never answered them. But there could be a lot of reasons for that. Somehow it didn't seem right to send her a letter. That seemed an awfully cold way to let her know her lover was dead. And I had that letter of credit in my pocket made out in my name, and irrevocable. Five thousand bucks, and all I had to do was draw on it at any Wells Fargo or any of their correspondent banks anywhere in the world. That was more temptation than I needed just then. But if I used the money to find the girl, wouldn't that be morally or ethically legitimate? I knew that Marvin didn't have any children, so I couldn't accuse myself of stealing their legacy.

The alternative was to forget the whole thing and let the letter expire. But the money was there waiting to be used, and I *was* curious. I asked myself whether the obligation I was feeling was legitimate or just a rationalization for taking a trip. Well, that part was easy. Who wants to travel to a country on the brink of war? Not me, I guess. But then I remembered Amanda. Was the thought of somehow seeing her again making me fool myself about my motives? Could be. When you're selling yourself a story, your customer's usually a sucker.

Well, maybe my motives were pure, or maybe they were impure, but I'd pretty much decided to find the girl. Or at any rate give it a good shot. That, at the very least, would be better than cashing the five thousand and taking the next couple of years off. And it would be tragic to let the letter expire and revert to a soulless estate managed by bankers and lawyers, all charging fat fees. With no direct heirs, the bulk of the estate would probably go to a cat rescue operation or some such charity – after the lawyers had their generous helping. You see? Sucker.

So I said to Kowalski:

"I've already been paid for the job, Ed."

"Really? How'd you manage that?"

"Boyish charm."

"Boyish bullshit, more like."

"Whatever. But I'd like to earn at least part of the fee."

"Meaning what?"

"Meaning I'd like to stay in touch with the investigation."

"You show me yours and I show you mine?"

"Something like that. Any chance I could see the crime scene? As long as your boys are there I'll stay out of the way."

"Can't hurt, I suppose. You sure you don't have any bright ideas?"

"Well, you might want to question the guy who was with Elaine Ginsberg the night she was killed. All I know is he's a wannabe actor, and Marvin said he was going to put the word out on the street that the guy was toxic."

"Blacklist him?"

"Yep. Don't look, don't touch, or face the wrath of Marvin. I don't know whether Marvin sent out the memo yet, but if the guy knew about it, he'd definitely have a motive. Marvin may have even called to tell him he's toast."

"Wouldn't surprise me."

"He shouldn't be too hard to find. His name was in the accident report."

"Yeah, and his picture was in the papers. I remember him. Looks like a young Ramon Navarro."

"That's him."

"Sounds like he's gonna need a new line of work. Well, he's definitely worth checking out. So, as a tit for your tat, tell the boys at the crime scene I said it was OK for you to look around. You know most of them anyway."

"Yes. Unfortunately, I do."

"Do I have to tell you not to touch anything?"

"One of these days you're going to hurt my feelings. There's one other thing I just thought about. It doesn't violate client confidentiality for me to tell you that Marvin detested his wife."

"That's interesting. What do you make of it?"

"That maybe the hit and run was no accident? Maybe it was just a hit?"

"Motive? After all, lots of guys hate their wives. They don't go around killing them."

"Agreed. And Marvin was able to put up with an unhappy marriage for ten years or so. But then he met this French girl. She arrived like a thunderbolt. Changed everything. He was suddenly overwhelmed. Had to have her."

"Why not just dump the wife? In this town, divorce doesn't raise any eyebrows."

"No, but maybe the idea of alimony gave him a sour stomach."

"Which gave him two motives. Money and sex."

"Right. One might've been enough, but taken together — a pretty strong brew."

"So he hired some guy to run her down and take off."

"It's possible. And maybe the guy he hired was anxious to tie up loose ends. He certainly would have a motive to cut any connection to Marvin. The more professional the killer, the more likely he'd want to erase all traces of the deal – and be willing to hang around, or come back to do it."

"Bravo, my lad. It may surprise you to know that we law enforcement professionals have already considered that and even now are requesting Ginsberg's bank records to see about any funny looking payments. And who to."

"Do you really think Ginsberg would write the guy a check?"

"No. But we've got to be thorough. If there's a large cash withdrawal in the last couple of weeks, that'll at least tell us something."

"What's the going rate for a hit?"

"Depends. Could be anywhere from five hundred to ten thousand, depending. Of course you could always hire some derelict for five bucks and a bottle, but that sort of thing is not done in high society. Besides, those guys always get caught and always spill the beans. Professionals are another story. In and out and gone, usually forever."

"How about the car? Any sign of it?"

"We're still looking. Not much chance of finding it, but it's possible some repair shop will remember fixing a dent in a Hudson. With any luck, there was blood on the fender."

"A pro would have wiped it off."

"No doubt. That comes under the dog that didn't bark theory. Know that story?"

"I've read it. I should have known you'd be onto that angle. A hit, I mean."

"Your tax dollars at work. I don't suppose your buddy Tony Scungilli would have heard anything about this?"

"I can ask him. But I know what he'll say – one, he doesn't know anything and if he did, he wouldn't say, and two, these things are usually done by out of town contractors who are not here long enough to get their shoes shined, let alone check in with their local cousins. Besides, Tony runs a legitimate gambling operation. He's not into this kind of thing."

"Pull the other one."

"I'll ask him, though, if it'll make you happy."

"I don't get happy. But it can't hurt. Even if he's not involved, guys like that hear things."

"Yeah. But they don't say anything."

"Probably so. Speaking of happy, I read in a magazine the other day that penguins mate for life. Do you believe that?"

"Sure. Why not?"

"It started me wondering – does that mean all penguins are happy, or that the unhappy ones are too dumb to figure a way out?"

"Well, they can't fly, and they don't run very well, so maybe that keeps them close to home. But maybe they just don't have any imagination."

"Well, no one ever said a penguin was smart. But you know they all look alike. That could have something to do with it."

"How so?"

"What's the point of switching around?"

EPITAPH FOR A DREAM

"I see. Well, Marvin's a smart guy. Or was. He wouldn't have any trouble dreaming up a way to get rid of Elaine *and* keep his money."

"Two penguins with one Hudson? Could be. I tell you what, though, I think we're gonna find out."

"I'd bet on you."

"Thanks. Well, stay in touch. And if you do go to France, send me a postcard. One of those smutty ones. But send it in a thick envelope, so Lois won't be shocked."

"How is she these days?"

"Gaining weight. Bon voyage. That's French for sayonara."

I stopped at my apartment for a moment and then went straight over to Marvin Ginsberg's house in Bel Air. It was the usual mansion sitting on a small rise. It looked like a French chateau married to a Spanish hacienda. It used to be the home of a silent star named Velma O'Neil who had it designed according to her specifications. She couldn't decide which style she preferred, so she used both. The architect swallowed his standards and took the check. The house was surrounded by a tall brick wall. You entered the property through iron gates. The gates were open and the driveway was tree-lined and ran past a large pond. There were a couple of dozen Canada geese swimming around or pecking at the grass. They mated for life, too. Or so I'd heard. And come to think of it, they all looked alike.

The driveway in front of the house was crowded with cop cars. It was a big house, and the crime scene boys were still there because it took a while to dust the place for prints. But the lead investigator was just leaving when I got there. I knew him from a previous case.

60

"Look what the cat dragged in," he said. "Just in the neighborhood?"

"I was taking the Home of the Stars tour."

"Kowalski know you're here?"

"He sent me to make sure you guys didn't steal the spoons. Any leads?"

"Lots of prints but no IDs yet. Lupe, the housemaid who found him, is still hysterical. You'd think she never saw a guy with his head blown half off."

"Mexicans lead sheltered lives. Kowalski said it was OK if I looked around. Ginsberg was a client."

"Yeah? Too bad for you. But go ahead. We're pretty much finished for the time being. The body's already gone to the morgue, but if you see an eyeball rolling around somewhere, it's probably Ginsberg's."

"What color?"

"Brown and bloodshot."

The crime scene boys were packing up and getting into their cars when I went inside. They were leaving a cop at the front door and were just putting crime scene tape across the entrance as I ducked down and went in. It was pretty spooky in the house. Very quiet. If Lupe was having hysterics, she must be having them somewhere else. I walked down the main hall looking for Ginsberg's den. It wasn't hard to find. It was at the very end of the west wing of the house, the Spanish wing. It was a large and sumptuous room with leather furniture and an ornate desk that Napoleon would have appreciated, all carved wood and gilded legs. There were fancy leather-bound volumes of the classics in the bookshelf – the kind of books interior decorators buy by the yard. There was a large stone fireplace, and above the mantle was the picture I wanted to see. There was no doubt it was the one. It was done in light colors, blue and pink. It was of a man and a woman, both slim and youthful, locked together full length in the missionary style. They were posed as though the painter was above them and only slightly to the side. You could only see the back of the man's head, but I remembered what Ethel said about the expression on the woman's face. I could see how it might cause Ethel some stirrings. She stirred easily. But that painting might have moved something in an anchorite. There was a signature on the bottom left corner. It seemed to be hurried or smudged, and I couldn't make it out. But it could have said "Picasso." If someone wanted to believe that, they could. And there was a date in the upper right corner. I think it was a date, anyway. It said "Argent, Or 1938." Was that a French word for something? Or was it a name? I didn't know, but I knew someone who might.

There was a set of French doors leading to the rear of the house and the swimming pool. Beside the pool was a small house, for dressing and lounging, I suppose. It looked like a Chinese pagoda – more indecision on Velma's part. Or was it eclecticism?

I listened for a second, but the house was still perfectly silent, so I took out a dry cleaning bag that I had brought from my apartment. I took down the painting, put it carefully in the bag and set it just outside the French doors. I removed the picture hook from the stone and put it in my pocket. You could not tell that a picture had ever been there.

I went back through the house to the front and chatted with the cop stationed there and watched the crime scene investigators packing up their cars. The cop told me his feet hurt and he was suffering from piles, so he couldn't decide whether to stand or sit.

"A metaphor for man's condition," I said.

"Ain't it? Look at them ducks over there," he said, pointing to the geese. "Not a care in the world."

"Maybe. But maybe they have their troubles, too," I said.

"It don't look like it," he said.

When all the crime scene boys were gone, I said I wanted to look around the back of the house. He didn't care. He was just a local beat cop logging some overtime.

"Don't steal nothing," he said, grinning.

"Nothing valuable," I said, grinning.

I walked around and retrieved the package. I came back around the side of the house and watched until the cop had his back turned and walked over to my car. I put the package in the back seat, whistled and waved to the cop. He waved back, and I got in the Packard and drove away.

I had a letter in my pocket. It said "To Whom It May Concern, this painting is the property of Riley Fitzhugh. He loaned it to me as a favor and is welcome to retrieve it at his convenience." It was signed "Marvin Ginsberg." It was a very thin cover story, I know, but I figured it would be enough to satisfy the average cop. As it turned out, I didn't need it, but Blinky didn't charge me much for it, even though it was a rush order. I could have asked Della to type it up, but I felt better having Blinky do it. Whenever possible, I prefer to use specialists. Besides, Blinky told me that the signature was an accurate copy of Ginsberg's. How he knew that, or whether it was even true, was something known only to Blinky, who moved in mysterious ways and pretty much kept his own counsel.

EPITAPH FOR A DREAM

I didn't intend to keep the painting. I wanted Bunny to see it, and I wanted him to study it up close and to take his time with it. I had a feeling the painting could tell us something. On the surface, it was just two people, and especially a girl, having a good time. But I felt there had to be something more to it. When I found out what it was, I'd put the picture back. I did like it, though. I sort of hoped it really was an accurate rendering of a moment between Marvin and his Dream Girl. I wondered how many of those moments he'd had. Not enough of them would be my guess. That's probably why he loved the painting. The moment was timeless. And, unlike the lovers on the Grecian Urn, these two had actually gotten together.

Chapter Nine

The next morning I went to the office. Della was there having her morning coffee with cream, sugar and a shot of rye. She had the eternal Pall Mall going, too.

"Morning, Chief," she said. "Your sweetie called a minute ago." She gave me an evil grin as she waited for the question.

"OK. I'll bite. Which sweetie?"

"The producer's wife, the gangster's moll and the private dick's now-and-then all wrapped up in one gorgeous blonde soufflé."

"Is that a line from your novel?"

"It could be."

"Is there such a thing as a blonde soufflé?"

"There could be."

"Did she say what she wanted?"

"Apparently, she has something for you. I wonder what it could be. She said to call her but not till later in the morning, so she can be sure Manny's gone. She's at the beach house."

"Sounds good."

EPITAPH FOR A DREAM

"There's nothing like a now-and-then in the afternoon. Don't tell Perry I said that. He might think I was lying about my years in a convent."

"I thought you were a Baptist."

"It was a Baptist convent. That's my story."

"And Perry bought it?"

"So he says. Our relationship is based on mutual trust and honesty."

"That's the best kind."

"That's what you think. Whatcha got in the package?

"A painting. Want to see it?" I took it out of the bag and propped it against a chair. "What do you think?"

"Oh, my. I feel a hot flash coming on."

"I need to show it to Bunny. Find out what it is."

"I can tell you what it is. Whether it's worth anything is another question. Goodness. How I envy that girl!"

I called Bunny's office to see if he was available. Classes were on summer break, so his secretary said anytime this morning would be fine.

I always enjoyed the drive over to Westwood. I had the top down and the day was perfect in the way it usually is. The car radio was playing Artie Shaw's *Begin the Beguine*, and the palm trees and bougainvilleas were swaying as though they were listening, too. Sea breezes. The sky above was cloudless and bluer than Ginger Rogers' eyes, and everything smelled good. Southern California was a fine place to be, and I reflected ruefully that I was about to leave here and head for a place that was getting ready to fight a war. Why? Good question.

The students at UCLA had scattered for the summer. I always preferred to visit campus when they were away.

66

Seeing them in all their self-assured youth and perfection, troubled by nothing other than having an eight o'clock class, made me jealous and regretful of my misspent youth – and what there was left of it that was being equally misspent, albeit in slightly different and more interesting ways. I wasn't seriously troubled, not really, but these feelings of mild regret always caused a mild "what if." It was the old Robert Frost thing about the road not taken. Everybody has it, now and then. I can live with it.

Bunny was in his office organizing some materials for his trip to London. He was scheduled to leave the following week.

"Welcome. Excuse the mess," he said. He was wearing a white cricket sweater with three lions embroidered down the front, and baggy flannels. "What have you got there?"

"It's a painting that very possibly has a bearing on a murder case. Maybe two murders. I was hoping you could tell me something about it."

"How did you come by it?"

"I took it from the murder scene."

"Legally?"

"Up to a point."

"I see." It was impossible to shock or even surprise Bunny. "Was it Marvin Ginsberg? I heard that he'd been murdered."

"Yes."

"It was in all the papers, of course. I'd met him and his late wife. Rather a bad week for that couple. Well, let's have a look."

EPITAPH FOR A DREAM

I unwrapped the picture and propped it on one of Bunny's leather club chairs.

"Hmmm," he said. "Beautiful. Very beautiful, don't you think?"

"Yes, I do. But does it suggest anything?"

"Well, it's only a first impression, but it's clearly in the style of Picasso."

"Really? I thought he was more into women with noses on the sides of their heads. This seems pretty ... What's the word?"

"Representational? Yes. Although I would say it's more impressionist. But, you know, the thing about Picasso that often gets lost is that he is a brilliant draftsman. If he wanted to do a Norman Rockwell cover for *The Saturday Evening Post,* he could do it. In other words, he can do anything."

"What about the subject?"

"Well, the old boy has an eye for the ladies, and he's done quite a few naughty things, like this. All quite good. He loves to draw or paint his mistresses. Often he puts himself in the picture, too."

"Nude?"

"As a newborn."

"Could this be one of them?"

"Why not? I'm not saying it's genuine, mind you. That signature in the bottom there might suggest a clumsy attempt at forgery. It's smudged a little as though to imply the artist was in a hurry, or maybe that he dashed it off and gave it to the girl who somehow smeared the name. But a signature on a painting is the least useful clue for judging a work. Easiest to forge. In fact, I'd be more inclined to think it a forgery if the signature were perfect."

"What about that word in the upper corner? Argent Or? Is that French for something?"

"'Argent' is French for 'money.' It also means 'silver,' which in this case is probably what the artist intended, since 'or' means 'gold.' Silver and gold. Maybe the artist's title for the picture."

"Any significance?"

"I can't think of any off hand, unless it's the artist's pet name for the girl. Perhaps a loving nickname. Maybe it refers to the two of them."

"How about the guy in the picture? Do you think it could be the artist?"

"That's as good a guess as any. But there's no way to tell from the picture. You say this came from the crime scene?"

"Yes."

"How did Marvin come by the painting?"

"It was given to him by his girlfriend – quite possibly the girl in the picture. She's somewhere in France. They had a shipboard romance, then she went home to get married."

"Could the man in the picture be Marvin?"

"I don't know. Could be. He was said to be terribly fond of it, as though it was the record of a great romance. He was infatuated with the girl who gave it to him and hired me to find her. He paid me in advance, so I feel I should keep looking into it, even though he's past caring. I was hoping maybe this could be helpful. So what do you think? Is this a copy ... or something else?"

"It's early days, as I said. But there are three possibilities. First – this is a very good forgery, meaning that someone is trying – or has already tried successfully – to pass it off as a genuine Picasso."

"In order to sell it."

"Yes."

"So it's possible that the girl didn't actually give it as a present, but sold it to her lover?   And that he bought it thinking that not only was it a memento of his great affair but a bargain Picasso?"

"Entirely possible.   Do you know anything about the girl?"

"Just her name. And her mother's address in France."

"It shouldn't be too difficult to find her, unless she has a reason not to be found."

"If she was party to a forgery and fraud, you mean."

"Yes.   You say it was a shipboard romance?   Can you imagine anyone more susceptible than a middle-aged man who runs into a beautiful girl in the middle of a transatlantic voyage?   The orchestra is playing Cole Porter, the night is balmy, the stars are out in incredible profusion. He sees her standing by the rail of the fantail, the ocean breeze in her hair. He goes up to her. He catches a subtle whiff of her perfume.   She turns and smiles and says 'Allo' in her charming French accent."

"She could have sold him the painting right then and there."

"Or just about anything else.   He was quite a wealthy producer and very capable of paying for an expensive piece of art."

"That sounds more than plausible.   But you said there were three possibilities."

"Yes. If it's not a forgery, it could be a completely innocent imitation of a Picasso done by one of his talented acolytes, maybe someone known to Picasso, or maybe a stranger. Maybe the girl was his model. Maybe the artist innocently gave it to the girl who either gave it or sold it to Marvin."

"Which leads us to the third possibility."

"That it's a genuine Picasso. Once again – Marvin was wealthy. He could afford the real thing."

"I was afraid of that." It was obviously one thing to lift a worthless copy from a crime scene and quite another to take a valuable work of art. People, meaning the cops, might wonder about your motives and ask questions.

"I can't begin to determine what it is," said Bunny. "In fact, I may not ever be able to. But if I had some time to spend with it and some time to make a few inquiries, I might have a better answer for you. May I keep it? At least until I leave for London? That will give me three or four days."

"Well, I don't suppose it will matter. The owners, the husband and wife, are both dead. The Mexican maid is having hysterics, and I doubt she would notice the thing is missing even on a good day. And even if she did, she couldn't know who took it or when or how."

"Of course, if you feel uncomfortable, I quite understand. If it's real, it's worth serious money."

"What are the odds of that?"

"There's no way to tell, just yet. But we have a very secure facility here. No need to worry about it."

"I'm sure it will be OK." Bunny was thoroughly trustworthy. People sent him paintings to be authenticated all the time, and he had facilities that were more secure than those of most museums. His reputation depended on it. "I'm pretty sure it's important to know one way or the other."

"Well, I'll look into it, if you're comfortable leaving it with me."

"Of course."

Besides, I thought, no one but the two of us – and Della – know that the thing has gone missing from Marvin's house. What's the worst that can happen? Then I remembered the old joke about Napoleon saying something similar to Josephine, as he was leaving for Russia.

I left the picture with Bunny and drove back to my office. I needed to call Catherine. I wasn't all that interested in finding out if Tony knew anything about a contract killing. I knew he wouldn't tell me anyway. But I was interested in what Catherine had for me. She sometimes had the most delightful whims.

It was almost noon, so I figured the coast was clear at Catherine's house. Even better, Della was gone for her usual lunch of a Braunschweiger on rye and martini on the rocks, so I could make a call in some privacy.

Catherine picked up on the second ring.

"Hello, beautiful," I said.

"Hello, Sparky," she cooed. "Is this Sparky the Detective?"

"At your service."

"Yum. And I knew it was you. I was just pretending, to get a rise out of you."

"You don't need to pretend to get that."

"Just being me is enough?"

"More than enough."

"Smooth talker. Then how about coming over to the house? The maid has the day off and Manny's not here, and I have something to tell you from Tony. He said to give it to you in person and not over the phone, so I'm going to. And I also have some cold lobster and champagne on ice, so what do you say, huh, Sparky?"

"I've got a fast V8 Packard."

"That's good. We can have lunch down by the water and take a skinny dip, but then we can come back up to the house. It's too sandy on the beach. It gets in places."

Catherine had a referral for me from Tony. It was a name and a telephone number in Marseilles.

"Tony said to tell you that this guy is one of our friends, even though he's French," said Catherine, as we drank the champagne on the beach. She was wearing a bathing suit that was more of a suggestion than a garment, and she had her string of opera-length pearls reversed so that the long strand went halfway down her back, which was tanned and had no strap lines. "He said you should call him when you get there and introduce yourself, 'cause he could be very useful in case you get in trouble somehow. Or if you want to get into trouble, if you know what I mean. But he said don't write it down, and if you forget it, that's too bad for you. Those were his words, but if I were you I'd write it down somewhere, 'cause it's a funny name and the phone number is pretty funny, too."

"What is it?"

"Mole Yair. But it's spelled 'M-O-L-I-E-R-E,' which is why it's funny."

"You know what Mark Twain said about foreigners."

73

"No, but I bet you do."

"He said they always spell better than they pronounce."

"He could have said it the other way around, too."

"Probably. But I think I can remember that name. I will write down the phone number, though. There's a way of doing it that will keep it safe."

"Tony said, when you call this guy, to say right away that Tony Scungilli was a friend and associate of Paulie Vedozzi of New Jersey, and that you are a friend of Tony's who might need a friend over there sometime. Lots of friends, huh? Like a room full of Quakers."

"How'd you know the Quakers were called 'Friends?'"

"Manny told me. He was thinking about making a movie about them but decided there wasn't enough sex or fighting. They must be pretty dull people. Do you know their preachers don't say anything when they give their sermons?"

"I've heard."

"Funny, huh?"

"Yeah. Anyway, thanks for the name, honey," I said. "I hope I don't have to call on this guy for something, but it's good to know he's there."

"You know what else is good to know? Manny is out of town and won't be back for a week. Want to take a shower?"

Chapter Ten

Two weeks later Hobey and I landed in Marseilles aboard the Pan Am Clipper flying boat. Pan Am had just started the service a couple of months before. Blinky Malone had performed prodigies of forgery and provided passports and visas for both of us in various names. I paid him with money from the letter of credit and booked our air passages across the US and then across the Atlantic. I lost track of how many take-offs and landings we made. I thought of going via London, but the flight to Marseilles made more sense, and we could catch a train from there due north to Lyon. That was the starting point for finding the girl. I figured there'd be time enough to stop in London on the way back, and if Amanda was there, so much the better. Maybe I could talk her into a romantic Atlantic crossing on an ocean liner, assuming the Germans hadn't started torpedoing English and French shipping by then. It was mid-summer when we left and tensions were high. The Germans were threatening Poland and the Brits and the French were pledged to defend the Poles if the Germans went in. It was not a good time to be in Europe, but it was the only time we had, and with luck we'd be able to get in and out before the shooting started.

My buddy Ed Kowalski had given me a "To Whom It May Concern" letter that introduced me to the French police and told them I was a legitimate officer of the law engaged in a case of missing persons that might be tied to a murder. I thought it looked impressive. I had another letter from Bill Patterson saying much the same thing. It was on FBI stationery and was strictly against the rules. But Bill didn't seem to care. "You'd only get one from Blinky, anyway," he said, "so I might as well give you a real one." In addition to Blinky's forgery and photography business, he was an FBI informant and so was well known to Bill. These letters of introduction were little more than pieces of paper, but I thought they might come in handy with French officials who, everyone said, were impressed by paper, and the more of it the better. Neither of these favors was strictly kosher, but favors often aren't. I'd done enough in my time to know that. And they were better than forgeries from Blinky, because it was just possible the French cops might contact either LAPD or the FBI, and both of my buddies said they'd stand by my story. In this business, the truth, or at least something close to it, is usually better, except when it isn't.

Speaking of truth, Bunny called me just before he left for London.

"I've got the picture in my safe at school. I have a few ideas, but I'm waiting to hear back from my colleagues in France, and I'm afraid I won't have a final answer for you until I get back. Is that all right? If not, please come and pick it up. I'll understand perfectly, if you'd rather."

"No. Not at all. It's safer in your custody. And besides, no one has said anything about a missing painting. I'm sure no one has noticed."

"All right, then. See you when I get back – and when you get back. Bon voyage!"

It occurred to me to wonder what would happen if Bunny didn't make it back. Accidents did happen, after all. How could I retrieve the painting? Well, there was no sense worrying about that now. "Sufficient onto the day is the evil thereof." Or, as a Hollywood producer once said to me, "I'll jump off that bridge when I come to it."

The French customs guys were no match for Blinky's artwork. One of them looked surprised that Hobey's two middle names were "Nassau Hall," but Hobey explained that they were old family names and distant relatives of the Dutch royal family. He carried it off with such airy aplomb that the Frenchman stamped his papers and moved on to me. He raised his eyebrows a little at 'Bruno Feldspar,' too. But I shrugged and smiled. I was used to getting odd reactions to my nom de guerre.

"*Juif?*" he said, more as a matter of curiosity than menace, as if to say, why the hell are *you* coming *here* now? It didn't seem like an official question.

"No. Presbyterian. From Ohio, originally," I said, with a disarming, all-American smile. I knew what "*Juif*" meant, from seeing newsreels.

"*Bon. Bienvenus. Je suppose.*"

Marseilles was crowded with people trying to get out of the country. It was the port of departure for French Africa and from there to points west. There were lots of nervous people hanging around the customs offices, and more than a few sinister types offering to sell you anything you wanted, including false passports or a date with their sister who had just come from the doctors and was clean and fresh as the day she was born and had a paper to prove it. The area around the docks was jammed with people pushing and shoving in order to get to their ship, or shouting at a port official about a ship that was late or was not coming at all. All of it made you think that it wouldn't take much to start a panic or a riot.

There was no reason to hang around in Marseilles and a very good reason to get out of there. We wanted to get to Lyon as soon as possible and track down Nicole Bertrand's mother, so we didn't bother with sightseeing and went immediately to the train station. The station was also crowded with people getting off trains arriving from Paris and points north. Most of them had that nervous look of the hunted, and quite a few had big bundles of things, last remnants of a former life, I suppose. Almost no one was getting on the northbound trains. We changed some money at the station kiosk and then had no trouble buying first class tickets, with Hobey doing the transaction. And at first we had a compartment to ourselves.

I liked the way the French trains were set up – compartments for six or eight people, like an old-time stagecoach, with two padded bench seats facing each other. You walked along a narrow hallway outside the compartments and peered into each compartment to find one that was congenial, either because it was empty, or because there was someone interesting already sitting there. Once inside, you could easily imagine locking the door, pulling down the blinds and making love to a mysterious and seductive French girl you'd only just met.

But no such mysterious girl, French or otherwise, came into our compartment. Instead, it was a dapper little man in a dark pin-striped suit and black derby. He had a fussy little moustache with waxed tips and he wore what's known as a pince-nez attached to his buttonhole with a black ribbon. All he needed was a carnation in his lapel. He looked in, opened the door and sat down on the same bench as Hobey, opposite me.

"Do I disturb your privacy?" he asked, politely and in English. "If so, I do not apologize. It is obvious that I do, so why say I am sorry? It would be hypocrisy. You are Americans, I perceive."

"What gives you that idea?" said Hobey, mildly offended. He thought of himself as a cosmopolitan man of the world, especially in France, because he had spent so much time there. But he was wearing an old tweed sport coat, a black and orange Princeton tie and a button-down shirt. He looked like a faintly gone-to-seed Dink Stover.

"It is my business to know these things," said the little man. "No one here wears those collars with the buttons on the tips, only Americans. And you are holding a package of Chesterfield cigarettes, which are difficult to find in France at the moment. I fear that soon they will be available only on the black market. *Et voilà*: Americans."

"Well, Hercule, I congratulate you," said Hobey. "Your little grey cells seem to be active today."

"Hercule! Ha! You make a jest, isn't it? But your witticism contains a soupçon of unintended irony, for I am in fact Inspecteur Jacques Montpelier, of the Sûreté. This is the national police and security organization. Perhaps you have heard of it."

I smiled slightly. He didn't look much like a cop.

"You find that amusing?" he said, pleasantly. "I understand. You say to yourself – here is a little man who looks like an actor in a play. He cannot be *un homme sérieux*. Much less a police official. Isn't it? Yes, I read these thoughts in your expression. Others have made that same mistake."

He reached into his coat pocket and pulled out a tiny revolver. Hobey and I stiffened.

"Say ... What's —"

"Do not be alarmed, *mes amis*. I only make a small demonstration." He opened the barrel and extracted a bullet.

"I wonder," he said "have you ever seen a point two-two bullet? Like this one?"

"Yes," I said. "I'm familiar with that caliber. We call them .22s."

"It is very small, *n'est-ce pas*? And when you shoot, it hardly makes a pop. Not even like a bursting of a small balloon."

"Yes."

"*Bon*. Now suppose some giant of a man, a man who bends iron bars in the circus and lifts three smiling milkmaids with one hand, suppose such a man tried to attack you, and suppose you pulled out this tiny gun and fired it into the giant's forehead. What would you have? I will answer my own question. You would have a very small hole in the forehead of a very large dead body. There is a lesson there. You see?"

"Yes."

"Good. Now, may I see your papers?"

Hobey and I looked at each other.

"Maybe we should see yours first," said Hobey. "How do we know you are who you say you are?"

"Ah. I see you have been to the cinema. Perhaps a little too often."

"As it happens, I'm in the Business. A writer. In fact, I have just finished working on *Gone With the Wind*. I suppose you've heard of it."

Actually Hobey had been fired from that picture after two weeks, but he did get a check for his work, so his claims were legitimate, if slightly misleading. I was pretty sure his name would not appear in the credits.

"*Gone With the Wind*? No. I cannot say I have heard of it," said the Inspector. "Hmm. What can it be? An advertisement for a digestive remedy, perhaps? '*Use Gas-O Lozenges and be gone with the wind?*'"

Despite himself, Hobey had to smile. I could see him filing the joke away to use on a producer he didn't like, which included most of them in Hollywood.

"No. It's a major motion picture."

"A *major* motion picture? Really? Well, that *is* very interesting. I am suitably impressed. Yes, suitably. I look forward to reading your memoirs. Now, may I see your papers?"

He was taking no guff, apparently, so we handed over our passports. He studied them for a few minutes, nodding his head in appreciation.

"Excellent work," he said. "Who is your forger? An American, I suppose."

"Who says they're forgeries?" said Hobey.

"I do, messieurs. I do."

"Well, they might be," I said.

"'Might be.' 'Are.' These are semantics, I believe. You say tomayto and I say tomahto. Perhaps you would like to come clean, as they say in your films. To sing like the canary. I assure you it will make no difference to you in the long scheme of things. But what does, eh?"

I didn't know what he meant by that last bit, but there was obviously no use denying anything with this little man.

"Suppose they are," I said. "Maybe you'd also like to see letters from our police and FBI."

"I should be charmed. Are they forgeries, too?"

"No. They are real," I said.

I gave him the letters.

"Ah. You are here on business. Would you care to explain?"

So I told him Marvin's sad story, figuring it would appeal to his Gallic romantic streak. But it didn't.

"Ah! An *amour fou. C'est classique.* You have a fool for a client, it seems," he said.

Did I? I suppose so. But one part of me had been wondering about that. Was what Marvin Ginsberg experienced all that common? Was it just a middle-age infatuation, the commonest of clichés? Or was it something rare, an emotion most of us never feel but have heard about and sometimes wish for? Was it all only a matter of degree, with silly infatuation at one end of the spectrum and genuine ... what? – love, I guess – at the other? Poets didn't write lyrics about middle-age puppy love, but they did write about that other thing, whatever it was. Well, all that was in

Hobey's field. I couldn't explain it. Maybe he could. God knows he kept trying. He hardly ever shut up about it.

"A fool? Maybe," I said. "But not anymore. He's dead. That's the murder referred to in the LAPD letter."

"Ah. *Bon.* His troubles then are *finis.* Perhaps we will be able to cooperate, if you should find the girl and if she should be in any way implicated in your client's unfortunate demise. Do you by any chance have genuine papers? Indicating your real names?"

"Yes."

"Perhaps I might have a look." We handed them over. "Ah! These are much better. Are these your real identities?"

"Yes."

"*Bon.* I suggest that the next time a member of the Sûreté requests to see them, you show these real ones. We are adept at spotting falsies. Is this a correct word?"

"It can be. It depends on the context."

"Most things do. Of course, your falsies are perfectly fine for local police. They are mostly ignorant peasants. But do not try to fool the professionals. Well, I must be going. There are not many others on the train, but I shall have to examine them. Not many people are trying to sneak *into* France these days, but the ones who are trying to do so are precisely the ones we don't want. Like distant relatives who need money."

"Meaning?"

"Meaning the wretched refugees from the Spanish war, recently concluded. An army of mechanics and farmers and bus drivers and assorted communists were no match for Franco's collection of Moors. Of course, the Italian and German bombers helped, too. So the refugees have come here in their thousands. We have put them in detention camps until someone can figure out what to do with them. If we send them back, they will all be shot. Too bad for them, of course. But we don't want them here, either, and we certainly don't want any more."

"I thought you would be worried about spies, what with all this war talk."

"Yes, of course, from our neighbors to the east. They are lurking here and there like wolves 'seeking whom they can devour,' when the time comes. So we keep our eyes open for them, too. Although, I must say, the German spies are easier to detect than their Italian cousins. The Germans are so serious, you see. Their true belief gives them away. No spy can be effective without charm, and no zealot has charm. They have no *sprezzatura?* You know this word?"

"Not really," I said.

"You should. I suggest you look it up."

"Where does all this leave us?"

"You? Well, since you gentlemen are neither zealous Germans nor charming Italian spies, and since you are not wretched Spanish refugees, and since you have no intention of staying once you have completed your romantic mission — you don't, do you?"

"No."

"*Bon.* Then I will overlook your forged papers. I am perhaps getting too soft-hearted in my old age. It comes of too much red wine and *bouillabaisse.* It is a Corsican passion. But ... I will give you my card and expect you to stay in touch. Don't be a stranger, as you say in the cowboy films. *N'est-ce pas?*"

"Of course. It will be our pleasure."

"I doubt it, but do it anyway."

He got up to leave and said, "I bid you good day," but then turned around at the compartment door.

"You say you're a writer, Monsieur Baker?"

"That's right."

"Then you must be familiar with the Frenchman who said 'I prefer a pleasant vice to an annoying virtue.'"

"Sorry," said Hobey. "I can't place it. It's a good line, though. I wish I'd written it."

"I suspect you will, someday. It is from our greatest dramatist – Molière."

Then he smiled and left.

Hobey and I stared after him and then at each other.

"Can't be a coincidence," I said, after a moment of shocked silence.

"Can't be. Do you suppose he's the friend of our friends?"

"He said he was Corsican. Aren't all the gangsters in Marseilles Corsicans? I think I read that somewhere."

"Could be," said Hobey. "Napoleon was a Corsican."

"I didn't really think this guy was a cop. But he didn't look much like a gangster, either."

"No. More like a prosperous pimp. But as the real Molière once said – 'never underestimate a guy in a derby.'"

"Really?"

"It sounds better in French."

Chapter Eleven

It took longer than it should have to get to Lyon. We stopped at every station along the way. Not many people got on, although each station was crowded with people wanting to go south.

"They know something we don't know," said Hobey.

"Speaking of that, I've compared the phone number on the card Molière gave us to the number Catherine gave me, and it's not even close."

"Probably a Chinese laundry. My guess is that Catherine's number's the right one. If he's really a gangster, he's not about to have his number printed on a business card. When we get to Lyon we can try it and see who answers."

Which we did. The Lyon train station was as crowded as all the others, but once again not many were going north. Hobey understood how to use the French telephone system and called the number on Molière's card, while I stood at the buffet and had a glass of wine.

"Like I figured," he said, when he came back, "a phony. A butcher shop in some small town south of here. They specialize in sausages for *choucroute garnie*."

"Another of his jokes?"

"Could be. You can make sausage out of anything, including rival gangsters, I suppose. Anyway, then I called Nicole's mother and introduced us as talent scouts from the US looking for a fresh face to play a romantic interest in a novel being made into a movie."

"*Gone With The Wind*?"

"No. Something about love on the Riviera. I told her we'd seen Nicole somewhere and she seemed perfect, and we wanted to get in touch. Anyway, mama got very excited and said to come right over."

"Did you mention Marvin?"

"No. For some reason I thought it might be better to keep his name out of it. Suppose the girl was involved in something nefarious."

"Very possible."

"And suppose mama knew something about it. Then we'd never get anything out of her."

"Good thinking. But we probably should have some story about where we saw her."

"I'll think of something once we get there."

"What if nothing comes to you?"

He looked at me with a smirk. "Something always comes to me. Whether I do anything with it is a different question."

We checked into the hotel across from the station – a moderately comfortable place with a depressing color scheme of shades of brown and green – and then went downstairs to get a taxi over to the suburb of Villeurbanne.

EPITAPH FOR A DREAM

We crossed over two rivers, one small and the other the Rhone. The cabbie wore a leather hat, leather vest, a cavalry moustache, and a cigarette behind his ear. He was somewhere in his early middle age, and he seemed glad to see us.

"You are Americans? I speak good English. I was with the American Marines in the last war. I was a scrounger. You know this word? It means someone who goes around and gets things. A military businessman. Fine fellows, the Marines. Very generous with their tobacco and chocolate. *Semper Fi!*"

"What do you think? Will there be another war?"

"Will there be a war, messieurs? Of course. The Boches will come again, and we will give them a kick in the onions again, and they will go home singing Wagner in soprano. You know what Rossini said about Wagner – that you could not understand it the first time you heard it, and he did not intend to hear it a second."

"I hope you're right."

"Of course – ha! No one likes the Boches, not even the Italians, though both like to dress up and wear shiny boots. You are here on business?"

"Yes. Of a kind."

"Monkey business, eh? I understand. Our women here are the most beautiful in France, and all of them are virtuous except the interesting ones. Perhaps you would like a recommendation. I know of a very good house. It is run by a woman of refined taste who goes by the name of '*La Grande Horizontale.*' She has cultivated an enormous *derrière* over the years. It is a popular sight for tourists, mentioned in the Michelin Guide."

"How many stars?"

"The maximum – three. Three stars for one full moon, eh? I make the joke. Impressive. That is the word for it. And her girls are all fresh from the convent. They have no bad habits. Ha! Again I make the joke."

"Perhaps another time. We're in a bit of a hurry."

"Too bad. Life is short and nights are long, when you are alone, *n'est-ce pas*? I am a *philosophe*. Well, here we are – 122 Rue Hippolyte Kahn. I will be happy to accept payment of the fare and perhaps a trifle in addition – what you Americans call a 'tip.' Do not believe the *canard* that ten percent is the standard. Only a German would consider that sufficient. *Bon. Merci,* messieurs."

The building was a five-story apartment house. There was a concierge sitting in a little room just off the lobby. She looked like a massive frog in a flowered dress but she had a warm smile for us. Maybe Madame Bertrand had told her we were emissaries from the magical world of Hollywood, so we were expected and welcome. She told us Madame Bertrand's apartment was on the second floor, so we took the tiny birdcage elevator up and knocked on the apartment door.

Madame Bertrand opened it. She was a tall woman with very dark hair and lively blue eyes, and she smiled with what seemed like actual sincerity, rather than salesmanship. She could not have been much past forty, and she was, in a word, breathtaking. I glanced at Hobey, and it was clear that he was instantly smitten. I recognized the signs, because I had seen them before, and more than once. Well, I could hardly blame him.

"Gentlemen," she said, in English. "Welcome. Please come in."

She was slim and elegant and she wore almost no make-up except a little lip rouge and something that accented her lovely blue eyes. She didn't need anything more. Her skin was flawless, her features perfect, and she moved gracefully and smelled like morning in a flower shop. The whole room smelled good, as a matter of fact. The dress she wore was black and silky and clung to her in the way I imagined the couturier intended.

"You are looking for Nicole?" Her English was charming, and I began to regret having brought Hobey as a translator. Impure thoughts floated to the surface like bubbles in champagne. Or Budweiser.

"Yes," I said, as Hobey stood staring at her.

I introduced us both, using our traveling names, and she shook hands with a good firm grip and asked us to sit down. Her main room was very comfortable and tastefully decorated. It looked like one of those Fred and Ginger sets – art deco, and mostly blacks and whites, which fit well with Madame Bertrand's personal color scheme. This was by design, of course. There were fresh cut flowers in crystal vases and a shining black grand piano in the corner. The paintings on the wall seemed original, and I thought Bunny would approve. I hoped that Hobey would not go over to the piano and offer to play one of his comic songs. But he was far too distracted to think of that, although the piano did attract his attention.

"Do you play, madame?" he said, gesturing to the piano.

"Please, you must call me 'Rosemarie.' And, yes, I play. Now and then I still sing professionally, in the cabarets. Nothing too grand. But fun, you know?"

"Like what's her name -- Edith Piaf?"

She laughed.

"Oh, no. Nothing at all melancholy. Her sad songs make me laugh. Sometimes lost love can be a good thing, you know? Good riddance. May I offer you some cognac? It is not too grand, either, but very nice, I think."

She could have offered Hobey a cup of hemlock, and he would have taken it gladly. I wouldn't have minded either. She had no maid, at least not one there at that hour, but the apartment looked like the kind that would have one. She poured our drinks and one for herself, and we all sat around enjoying the glow. At least Hobey and I did.

As I looked around I wondered who paid the bills. Better not to know, I suppose.

"Is this your first visit to France, messieurs?"

"Not for me," said Hobey. "I spent quite a bit of time here in the Twenties."

"Ah, yes. The good times. Oh, well."

We sat there thinking over the good times, but finally she was ready for us to get to the point.

"So you want to find Nicole for a picture? The cinema?"

"Yes," said Hobey.

I was interested in the story he would come up with and sat back to listen.

"I'm a writer, actually," he said. This was true, of course, but Hobey also believed that saying it was the quickest way to arouse a woman's interest. "In fact, I just finished with the script for *Gone With The Wind*." I admired his choice of words – "finished *with* the script," not "finished the script." "Have you heard of it?"

"Oh, yes," she said, enthusiastically. "I have read they are making that movie. The newspapers say Katherine Hepburn is being considered to play Scarlett? I hope not, if you'll forgive me."

"No. We rejected her. Too ... too Hepburn-ish, if you know what I mean."

"Yes. I do. Who is to play her? Scarlett, I mean."

"We're still looking."

"Well, that is very exciting. Are you thinking of Nicole for that picture?"

"Ah, no. For another one. Set on the Riviera. A romance."

"Ah, well that is more appropriate, yes? How did you find her? I mean, what made you think of her?"

"Well, I'm writing the screenplay – an adaptation of a novel of mine ...." This was Hobey's wishful thinking in full flower, but it made a good story.

"You have written a novel?" she said. "How wonderful!"

He almost blushed.

"Yes, well, it was only a small success."

"A *succès d'estime*, I am sure."

"Well, perhaps. But anyway, the producers asked me – us, I mean – to help out with some of the production. To scout some locations and think about some casting. And I remembered seeing a publicity picture of Nicole. You know, there are hundreds of these things floating around in Hollywood. Casting directors are always sending us photos to evaluate. And there was something about Nicole that just seemed perfect. So I called to see who her agent was, and no one seemed to know. They only knew she had gone back to France and had left this address. So, since we were coming here anyway, to scout locations, as I said, the producers suggested we try to find her. And so, *voilà* – here we are!"

"It is incredible. I did not know she had even taken publicity photos. I did know she had met some people from the cinema when she was in America. But I had no idea ...."

"Well, that is fairly common. That's how stars are often discovered. Many times it's just an accident. Just a matter of luck. Someone sees a picture and says – 'That's the girl!' You've heard of Marion Davies?"

"Yes, I think so." Clearly, she had not.

"Well, there you go."

Rosemarie Bertrand wrinkled her forehead just a bit as she wondered what 'there you go' might mean and just who Marion Davies might be, but she let it pass and just smiled.

"I suppose I should not be too surprised. For a time there she was receiving letter after letter from a man in Hollywood. I don't know what was in them. I just sent them along to Nicole wherever she happened to be at the moment. She was – and is – like a firefly, you know. Flickering here, flickering there, always floating from one place to another. I sent them all *poste restante*, because she never had a permanent address until recently."

"*Poste restante*?" I said.

"Like general delivery at the local post office. To be picked up," said Hobey.

"I don't suppose you know if she ever picked them up."

"No. She never mentioned anything."

"There was some rumor that she'd come back to France to get married."

"Nicole? Oh là là! No. Not at all. She is not the type. She gets that from her mother, I suppose. *La mère et la fille – Les Deux Bohèmes*, you could say. But not tragical. Is this a word?"

"It is now," said Hobey, gallantly.

"No, she will not get married. She is an artist and artists who marry are always unhappy, so why bother?"

"Do you speak from experience?"

"Of course. Has it been the same with you?"

"As a matter of fact, it has."

"Well, *c'est ça*." Which, I came to learn, was French for "there you go."

"We were told she was engaged to someone – someone in the grocery business, maybe."

"Really? Ha, ha! I think someone is playing a joke. It is possible that Nicole got engaged, but it is impossible that it was to someone like that. And it is equally impossible that she intended to go through with it. A moment of madness or fun – yes. Something more permanent and official, no. Besides, she is involved with another man now. A sort of artist, too. And I am sure *he* has no plans to marry Nicole, or anyone else."

I figured it was time to get to the point. Hobey would have sat there quite happily for the next several days.

"Would you mind telling us where she is living? It's possible our paths will cross, and it could very well be to Nicole's advantage. Of course, if you'd rather not, we'd understand."

"Oh, of course. She is working in Cannes, at a gallery there. I have the gallery's card with their address." She went to her desk to get the card. "But she is not living in Cannes.

TERRY MORT

She is just down the coast in a little place called Cap
d'Antibes. Do you know it?"

"Yes," said Hobey, wistfully. "I spent some time there, a
while ago."

"It has become *très chic*, no? It did not used to be, but
some people have discovered that it is very pleasant there in
the summer."

"Who is the artist she's living with? Anyone well known?"

"Oh, no. He is young. But he has talent. So, who knows?
He is also wealthy, so it doesn't matter in the long run. But
what does, eh?" She favored us with a knowing smile. Some
might describe it as charming, but it was more than that.

I could see Hobey melting. To him there was nothing
more seductive and alluring than a beautiful woman with a
sense of humor and the knowledge – or at least the belief –
that in fact nothing did matter in the long run, so why deny
yourself anything, either this day or the next? I found it kind
of attractive myself. By comparison to Hobey's gum-chewing
girlfriend, the Miss Lonleyhearts of LA, Rosemarie Bertrand
was from a completely different species. Or was it genus?

Well, we had the information we had come for and there
was no reason to stay. And even though Rosemarie was
more than cordial, we began to notice the slightest little signs
that the visit had reached its logical conclusion.

"Well, we must be going," I said. "I wonder if we could
ask you a favor, though."

"Of course."

"We can't be sure that we'll be able to meet Nicole. I
mean, we might get a telegram from the studio sending us off
in a completely different direction. So it would be better if
you didn't say anything about this – until we contact her, I

mean. There's nothing secret about it all, of course, but it would be a shame to raise her expectations and then have us disappear or, even worse, never show up. That sort of thing happens all the time in Hollywood. It is one of the town's worst features."

Aside from Jimmy Durante's nose, that is. I thought of saying it, but puns don't travel across borders very successfully.

"That's quite true," said Hobey. "People there are always making promises that they never mean to keep. And even if they do mean to keep them, most of the time they don't, for any number of reasons. Disappointment is chronic. Even I have experienced it."

"Really? That is difficult to believe." Was she teasing? It was hard to tell. Did Hobey care? Not in the least.

"Sad, but true," said Hobey. "Anyway, I agree. It would be best if this remained between us until we can talk with Nicole."

"Yes, I understand. Our secret will stay with me." She stood up to walk us to the door. "I am so happy to meet you, both. Thank you for coming by. And if you find yourself in Lyon again, please call on me."

"You can count on it," said Hobey. "And thank you."

And so we left.

"I think I'm in love," said Hobey.

"What else is new?"

I was, too, a little. But, unlike Hobey, I could control it. Pretty much.

Chapter Twelve

When we emerged we were surprised to find the same cab standing in front of the building. The driver was leaning against the front fender, smoking.

"I have waited for you, messieurs, because I do not think you will find a taxi very easily in this part of town."

"Well, this is convenient," said Hobey. "Back to the hotel, if you please."

"*Bon.* We go. My name is Jean-Baptiste Poquelin. I always introduce myself to people the second time I pick them up. Not the first, for we French are very reserved. Perhaps you would favor me with your names? For politeness."

We told him our travelling names.

"Ah, good," he said. "My name, Jean Baptiste, is very grand and I admire it, but I do not use it very often, except when I am having a drink with the president of the Republic or the Pope. Special occasions, you see. But normally I go by the *nom de taxi,* 'Klep.' You know this name? The Marines gave it to me in the war, because I was so helpful to them getting things they wanted. A little wine. A little cheese. A little souvenir, although sometimes the souvenir was not something to be taken home to the sweetheart. They told me the name was a compliment. So now everyone calls me Klep, even though no one knows why, or what it means exactly, including me. But I like the sound. Like something from your western films. *'Howdy, Klep.' 'Howdy, pard. Where are the cows?' 'I don't know. Where is my horse?'* – that sort of thing."

"You should go to Hollywood and be a writer," said Hobey. "There are people doing it with far less talent for dialogue."

"I was thinking of doing that, but my old mother got sick. The doctor told her that if she didn't stop drinking absinthe, she would never see ninety."

"I thought absinthe was illegal these days."

"Yes. It is. So, where are you gentlemen off to next?"

"Cannes."

"Holy *merde,* as the marines used to say. How are you thinking of getting there?"

"By train, of course."

"Ah. Well, I must disappoint you. The trains going south are impossible. Many people remember the last war, and many do not want to stay and see what happens this time. Once is enough, as the old man said to his mistress. Do you know that the Boches have a cannon mounted on a railroad car that can shoot almost forty miles?"

"The cannon or the railroad car?"

"Ah! You make the joke, too. *Bon*! The gun. It is the Big Brunhilde, named after Goering's mistress. Her caliber is enormous. Ha! But you will find the wait for a train may be several days. Perhaps more."

I could well believe it, based on what we'd seen coming north.

"I tell you what," said Klep. "I make you what the Marines called a deal. I will drive you to Cannes for the price of two train tickets. I know a girl there that I have been meaning to visit. She will be happy to see me. What do you say, eh? It is a very pleasant drive, and it will take no longer than a train that stops everywhere, like a milkman with a *braquemard* – what you would call the *bonaire* or a stiffy."

We thought about it for a moment.

"How far is it?" I said.

"About five hundred kilometers. In miles I could not say. Maybe a hundred or so."

"It's more like three hundred," said Hobey. "But it's the same whether we go by car or by train. And it might be useful to have a car when we get there. Would that suit you, Klep? To hang around for a few days and drive us where we need to go?"

"Suit me? *Oui. Superbe.* I make you a special deal. For the trip down, the cost of two train tickets, as I said. Once we arrive, I will ask you for so many francs per day with no question of how far we go that day or how long it takes to get there. I will think about that fee for the day, but it will be reasonable, I assure you. If not, you can always tell me to go to the devil. I know the way. *D'accord?* OK?"

"OK," I said. "Take us back to the hotel, and we'll plan to leave first thing in the morning."

"OK, boss. You won't be sorry."

"What about your mother? Can you leave town for long?"

"I lost her last year. Very careless, eh? Ha, ha! I make the joke. She lived past ninety, though. Doctors don't know everything. Absinthe had nothing to do with it. She died from what's called *la gueule de bois*."

"I'm familiar with that expression," said Hobey.

"What is it?" I said.

"A hangover."

We had dinner that night in a small restaurant near the hotel. Hobey ordered roast chicken with truffles, lyonnaise potatoes and a bottle of Macon. It was good, but nothing to go into ecstasies over. But then in my opinion, when it came to food, nothing was.

"What do you suppose Rosemarie does for a living?" Hobey said.

"Being herself, I imagine."

"Yes. I think so, too. Charming woman. She reminds me of someone."

"Hedda?"

"No. Someone from the past. Oh, well."

The next morning bright and early I knocked on his door, expecting him to be ready to leave. He opened the door in his rumpled pajamas. His hair was sticking on end and he looked bleary-eyed, even though we had not had much to drink the night before. It could not be *la gueule de bois*. Then again, maybe he had a private bottle.

"I'm sick," he said. "I don't think I'm in any condition to leave today."

Well, I could almost believe that from looking at him.

"What's the matter?"

"A cold. But you know, these things can become serious." He coughed unconvincingly. "There is such a thing as congestion of the lungs."

There is also such a thing as bullshit, I thought. But I played along.

"Maybe you should stay in bed today."

"Do you think so? Could be. Yes. I think you're right. I think I'd better. Maybe a hot whiskey and lemon or two would help, too."

"Can't hurt."

"But I feel terrible about holding you back."

"That's all right. I'm not in any hurry."

"I was thinking as I was lying here, now that you have Klep to drive, you don't really need me. You won't have any trouble with the language. You could go on ahead and find Nicole. Maybe I could meet you in Cannes, once I... recover."

I knew that what Hobey had was incurable, but it didn't really matter to me.

"You could call me to let me know where you are," he said, "and I could take the train there. I know it might be a little difficult, but I don't mind."

"Good of you."

"Well, you know how it goes."

Yes, I know exactly how it goes, but in fact it was quite all right with me if he wanted to spend the next few days wagging his tail around Rosemarie Bertrand. I had a job to do, kind of. And he was right – having Klep as a driver and translator would make life relatively simple. So I agreed to the proposition and left him there with a silly grin on his face. I assumed he had enough money to last for a while. I knew his next move would be to bathe, dress and call Rosemarie and ask her for lunch. And as he was brushing his teeth he would be reciting to himself his favorite lines: *"Away! Away! For I will fly to thee, not charioted by*

EPITAPH FOR A DREAM

Bacchus and his pards, but on the viewless wings of poesy."
Well, maybe he'd need a little help from Bacchus.   But even
so, I knew he was already picturing the scene – a sidewalk
café, a bottle or two of wine, an elegant and beautiful woman
sitting across from him, and plenty of time to tell her about
life as a writer in Hollywood. It was a scene often imagined
and maybe even played before. Now he was going to play it
again. Well, who could blame him for wanting to do it? Not
me.

And if you're wondering how a 25–dollar–a–day private
dick knows those lines from Keats, well, Hobey rarely went a
week or so without quoting them, so they stuck like Scotch
tape. Besides, I read a lot.

Chapter Thirteen

I collected my suitcase and went downstairs to the lobby. Klep was there chatting with the receptionist, who seemed to be responding. He was dressed in what appeared to be his Sunday best suit and a hand-painted necktie picturing a South Seas island. His luxurious moustache was waxed at the tip and he smelled strongly of what I learned was Lilas Végétal. His hair was brilliantined and shone like a raven's wing.

"Ah, *bonjour*, boss. All set? Where is Monsieur Hobey?"

"He's not going. He's sick, sort of."

"Oh, that's too bad. Do you still want to go?"

"Yes."

"*Bon.* Well, since there is only one of you, I will take you for the price of one train ticket. It saddens me to do it, but that is only fair, no?"

"No. We agreed on the price of two tickets, so we'll stick with that."

"Ah! *Superbe.* Well then, let us go. *Semper Fi.* Goodbye, Lucille," he said to the receptionist. "I will return in a few days, and by then perhaps you will be feeling better."

She stuck her tongue out at him and shrugged.

"She is indisposed because of an indiscretion," he said to me. "These things sometimes happen. I do not judge. I simply wait until everything clears up. The car is just outside."

I got in the front seat of the cab.

"We go, eh, boss? Over the top! Follow me! Remember the Maine!"

And soon we were underway, south along the main highway, a road that paralleled the Rhone River.

"How long do you think it will take us?"

"It is difficult to say. So many factors. Traffic. Weather. Herds of sheep in the villages. Probably two days. Maybe three. I know the best little *auberges* along the way. You know this word? It is like the English inn. We can stay there for next to nothing, because the owners are friends of my friends. Are you in a big hurry? Is there some woman in Cannes waiting?"

"Well, there is a woman, but she's not waiting. So there's no particular hurry. Why?"

"It's just that this trip presents a happy coincidence to me. I can stop here and there along this very road to do some favors for some friends of mine. It will take only a few minutes each place. A quick stop and hello and thank you and then on again. OK?"

"I suppose. What kind of favors?"

"Just to pick up some payments. You see, my other job is a collector for an insurance company. We insure many of the vineyards in the Rhone Valley. This valley is famous for many wines. I'm sure you know that."

"Not really."

"No? Well, perhaps you will learn something along the way. Anyway, these vineyards buy our insurance, and every once in a while their premiums come due, and if I happen to be in the area, it becomes convenient for me to stop and say hello to our clients – to give them the glad hand – and also to collect the fees. Yes?"

"So the timing of this trip worked out well for you."

"Yes. *Superbe.* Sometimes good things do happen."

"What kind of insurance does a winemaker need? Something to protect against bad weather? Crop failure?"

"Oh, no, boss. There is nothing anyone can do about that. Mother Nature does what she pleases, like most women. But unlike most women, she cannot be reasoned with. Her knickers remain firmly in place. You know this word? Knickers? I love this word. I learned it from the British Tommies."

"Pants that stop at the knees?"

"Ah. Not exactly. These knickers are a woman's underpants, sometimes silky, sometimes wooly, sometimes nothing more than a zephyr of wind, sometimes like a two-man tent - but always inconvenient to the man with an idea. Yes?"

"I see."

"So – our insurance does not protect against Mother Nature, but against mishaps. Once the wine is made and in bottles, it must go to market, of course. This is where we come in, like the Marines said to the madam. We protect the *camions* – the trucks – and the drivers."

"Against accidents?"

"Yes. Of certain kinds. It is very convenient for everybody."

"What's the name of your company?"

"My company? Why, 'Tartuffe et Compagnie.' Have you heard of it?"

"No."

"I am surprised."

"You must be a busy man, having two jobs."

"Yes, it's true. That is why I look so haggard and fatigued." He grinned at me, for he was the picture of health. "It all started when my dear old mother began her slow decent to the hereafter, and I needed extra money. Absinthe is expensive, because, like you say, it is not very legal. When the people like something, the politicians make it illegal or tax it. But someone will always find a way to provide it, and because the supply is limited, they charge more money. It is simple. Nothing more than supply and demand, isn't it? So I got into the insurance business on the side simply to make my old mother's final days agreeable to her. Now that she is gone, well, I don't need so much, because I don't like absinthe, but I do like the extra money, so why stop?"

"Why indeed?"

"You said it, boss."

And so we headed south, down the Rhone Valley. It was a beautiful day, sunny with high clouds, and the road through the countryside was decent. I figured we would make good time if it stayed like this, but it didn't. Every so often we would come to a small village and the road would narrow to a single lane, and we would have to go creeping through the center of town, avoiding pedestrians who in their time immemorial fashion considered they had the right of way, they and their animals. And Klep gave one and all a hearty greeting, and now and then stopped to have a word with a goat girl or a milkmaid. It didn't matter if the women were good looking. He was a small "d" democrat when it came to them.

When I made some remark about this, he smiled and said, "Do you play golf, boss?"

"No."

"Too bad. It is a game *magnifique*. But *très difficile*, you know? So you go to the driving range to practice your shots. You hit many balls, over and over, so that when the time comes to play on a real course, your stroke is *superbe*. It is the same with homely women. The more you talk to them, the better you are prepared for meeting one who is not so homely. And in the meantime, you make the homely ones happy, and what is life all about, except to spread happiness, eh? Ha! I make the joke."

"You don't believe that?"

"Do you?"

"No. But I'm not a philosopher. So what is life all about?"

"You tell me, boss. You tell me."

That afternoon we came upon the first of the vineyards where Klep needed to stop.

"Ah, *bon*! Here is one of our new clients."

"It doesn't look like much." There were only what seemed like a hundred acres or so of vines terraced on a small hill, and a large barn-like building and small house that was the office.

"They are a small business. But looks can be deceiving when it comes to wine, although in this case they are not. Still, they are one of our new clients. We seem to specialize in the smaller vintners.   The big boys have too much influence, you know?"

Well, I didn't quite understand what he meant, but I let it slide.

We pulled up in the dusty driveway, and a gloomy-looking man about fifty came out from the house. He was wearing the inevitable beret and shabby work clothes – soiled white shirt, black pants held up by suspenders – along with a pot belly and a scowl.

"Ah, here is the owner. A Monsieur Hébert. A tough cookie, as you say in the cinema. Reach in that compartment in front of you."

I did, and found a .45 Colt automatic.

"You want this?"

"Yes. It is a question of persuasion sometimes. I got it from the Marines in exchange for something. It is a gun *superbe*, although it is sometimes difficult to get bullets for it, because it is American. But with a gun like this, you don't really need many bullets. The client sees that you have it and knows that only one bullet will be sufficient to do the business, and events proceed pleasantly from then on."

Klep took the pistol and shoved it in the front of his pants.

"It is not loaded," he said with a grin. "If it was, I would put it somewhere where it could not accidentally go off and cause tragedy to Dick, Tom and Harry, my three musketeers, as the Marines used to say. It is merely for the drama."

So now I knew what kind of insurance business Klep was in – which made me wonder just how accidental this whole encounter really was.   And didn't the real Molière write a play called Tartuffe? I wasn't sure, but I'd ask Hobey, when and if I saw him again.

Chapter Fourteen

I didn't bother asking Klep whether he was assigned to look after me by the "friends of our friends." It didn't really matter. Having him along as a driver and interpreter was good enough. Besides, I was pretty sure I wouldn't get a straight answer.

We stopped a half a dozen times at different small vineyards along the way, and Klep repeated his friendly extortion. He never drew the pistol and never threatened anyone. In fact, most of the conversations were pleasant, at least on Klep's part. The various clients, though, were never very glad to see him and forked over their premiums with Gallic shrugs and sour expressions. Once or twice they pleaded poverty, but Klep was not dissuaded. "In the future you must learn to economize," he would tell them. "Cut back on women and song, but never let your insurance lapse. It would be dangerous to do that."

On the road we did talk about the kind of risks Tartuffe and Company insured against.

"Oh, we cover everything except actual accidents. If a driver legitimately goes off the road and tumbles down a ravine, because he is a bad driver or because he turned sharply to avoid a sleeping dog – well, too bad. We will send flowers and condolences. But with our insurance, no one will ever dare to highjack a shipment or sabotage a truck by putting sand in the gas tank or slashing the tires, and no one will snatch a driver and leave his truck alongside the road to be picked over by criminals and sold at a discount. But the people who do not have our insurance often experience these sad events. You see?"

"Yes."

"We are like the *prophylactique*. You know this word?"

"Yes."

"*Bon.* We prevent unwanted events, like the famous American Trojan. The Marines in the war were well supplied with them, and it was a good thing, too, or else there would be many little half-Yankees left in France and many American girls feeling an unwelcome sensation and asking embarrassing questions just after their men came home. Isn't it?"

"Yes, it is."

"It is the same with our insurance."

"I understand." And I did.

On the second day we traveled through the southern wine-growing areas of the Rhone Valley.

"This is one of my favorite regions," said Klep. "Tavel. Do you know of this wine?"

"No."

"You are very ignorant about wines, *n'est-ce pas?*"

"Very."

"That is a shame. It is too bad we are on a mission, or we could spend several weeks stopping here and there and

111

learning something. But ... so it goes. Anyway, this Tavel is the only rosé wine that is made as a rosé. All others are blends. Do you know of the writer, Hemingway?"

"Yes, as a matter of fact."

"*Bon.* I have read many of this Hemingway's stories. Not many laughs. But he did say that Tavel is the wine that goes best with love. He is right about that."

"You speak from experience?"

"Of course. I once knew a woman named Clothilde. She was only interested in going to bed with me – just that one thing. Nothing more. You might say that she was very miserly with her emotions. She never spoke of love and was also very severe and specific in her instructions. She had been a nun. And afterwards she would smoke a cigarette and then begin to read a book or turn on the radio for the evening news."

"It's a sad story."

"Yes. There were times that I felt I was just a two-legged dildo."

"How many legs does a dildo usually have?"

"Eh? Oh. You make the joke. Ha! I do not complain, you understand, but I felt it was all a bit mechanical-istic. You know this word?"

"I do now."

"*Bon.* And so I decided to try an experiment with her. You see, I had read what this Hemingway said, so one night I bought two bottles of Tavel – well, I didn't exactly buy them. A friend of a friend gave me a case that he had come by. Actually he had come by a whole shipment, but that is another story. So I brought two bottles to Clothilde's house, and after a few glasses, I noticed a certain expressiveness in her eyes. Nothing too serious, you understand, but definitely there. A *soupçon* of tenderness, you might say. Then I did the same thing the next night, and I could see an even warmer glow in her eyes, even though afterwards she turned on the radio, as usual. But on the third night, after now a total of six bottles of Tavel, her resistance definitely softened, and she began to realize that she actually cared for me a little. And after two more evenings she was almost in love and even refrained from turning on the news of the world. And from then on the shagging was more and more affectionate, until it became too much. The pendulum had swung the other way, you see, and I had to ride off into the sunset, like they do in your western films. You know this word? Shagging? It is something the English say."

"Yes, I've heard it." It was one of Amanda's favorite expressions. Well, she was a Brit. On the day we'd said goodbye, she'd told me not to look glum, because we both knew what we'd had was just a harmless bit of shagging. I agreed. Sort of.

"So, you see, this Hemingway was correct about Tavel, even though his stories do not raise many smiles. I remember the story called 'The Gambler, the Nun and the Radio.' I thought it could be about me and Clothilde, although she was no longer a nun. But of course the story was about something else, which I forget."

"Are you a gambler?"

"Life is a gamble, boss. I think you know that."

"Whatever happened to Clothilde?"

"Sometimes I wonder."

Because of the various stops to see Klep's clients and the meandering nature of the road which went straight through every town and village, and because Klep had the habit of stopping here and there to point out something of interest, like the spot where he once ran over a goat, it took us three days to get to Cannes. We spent the two nights in country inns that Klep knew about. The proprietors in both cases seemed to have mixed feelings about whether they were happy to see Klep or not. But when I told them I would insist on paying the full rate, they brightened up.

About midday on the third day we arrived in Cannes.

Coming down from the hills into the town was in some way like returning home, for both Cannes and certain sections of southern California, like Malibu, had that magical feeling of a Neverland where the gritty details of everyday life were banished. If there was any grit here in Cannes, it was well hidden. There was only the sun and the sea and the beaches – along with the elegant yachts moored just offshore and the casino and the creamy white hotels that lined the main road, the palmy *Boulevard de la Croisette*. The views along the boulevard were of the crescent-shaped blue harbor and the beach. The air smelled of the sea, of course, but the air also smelled of perfume, the kind that comes in cut glass bottles and costs what a shop girl earns in a year. There was something else, too. Hobey once quoted a line about a woman with a voice that was full of money. You knew the voices of Cannes were sultry with the same sounds. The women's voices, I mean. You could see these women languidly arrayed on the beach, each one brown in the sun and each one slim and as elegant as the white-hulled vessels riding easily at their moorings.

"*Superbe,* eh boss? This is the place – from here to the east and Antibes and beyond, all the way to Nice – where you will find the most beautiful women and the baldest men, and what makes this place a paradise is that many of the beautiful women and the bald men are together. If they did not arrive together, they find each other here, even though they came following different scents – the women, the scent of wealth, the men, the scent of the women. Even better, some of the men are *très* fat, and smoke disgusting cigars. It gives the rest of us great confidence and hope. Just think what men like us who are neither bald nor fat can do here. It is like the promise of heaven, except that you don't have to wait. And what's more, it is a heaven that you can actually see, and you never have to wonder whether it is really there."

"I assume the bald, fat men are the ones with the yachts."

"Of course. Otherwise they would be at a disadvantage, and it would be unfair. Where do you propose to stay?"

"I don't know. Where do you suggest?"

"Why not the Carlton? It is one of the best."

"Sounds good." I had long since decided that the more of the five thousand I spent, the better I would feel about using any of it. That way, when I went home, I wouldn't feel I'd made a profit out of Marvin Ginsberg's doomed fantasy. As I said before, when you want to sell yourself a story, you have a sucker for a customer.

"How about you? Where are you going to stay?"

"Ah. I told you there is a woman here who will be glad to see me. I will take you to the Carlton and then make her day a happy one by appearing as a surprise, like Napoleon returning from Elba."

"That didn't end well, the way I remember it."

EPITAPH FOR A DREAM

"No. But history does not repeat itself. It only seems to. Besides, this woman is no Duke of Ellington. She has no resistance and does not want any."

When we pulled up to the entrance of the massive birthday cake known as the Carlton, no one seemed all that excited to see us. No doubt Klep's ancient Renault taxi had something to do with it, along with the fact that I didn't have piles of Vuitton suitcases and trunks. I carried only one serviceable valise made by someone anonymous. But when I walked into the massive marble-floored reception and asked for a suite with a view of the sea and didn't ask how much it cost, the man at the desk became friendlier.

"OK, boss," said Klep, after I checked in. "I will be close by, if you need me. Here is the telephone of that lady I mentioned. If I am not there, she will know where I am."

Then he left.

They gave me a suite on the third floor. It was decorated in lavish, overstuffed style, mostly in white, and had a balcony with filigreed iron railing. It looked out over the main road and the beaches and the turquoise Mediterranean. A nice breeze that ruffled the sheer drapes, and the air smelled of yachts and well-kept women. The management had provided a chilled bottle of Veuve Cliquot '26 in a silver ice bucket, along with two crystal flutes. Someone apparently assumed I'd be having company. I opened the wine, poured a glass and went out on the balcony to enjoy the view. *A man could get used to this fast*, I thought. *Bless you, Marvin Ginsberg, wherever you are. The profits from your latest and last musical are not going to waste.* I did wonder how much these rooms cost, but it was only a matter of curiosity. Management obviously felt secure in giving me a suite, even though I was a stranger, because I had turned over my passport when I checked in. They therefore assumed I couldn't disappear after staying a few days while living on room service. I had no intention of doing that, but I had to smile when I thought that my passport not only identified me as "Bruno Feldspar," an entirely fictitious character, but also wasn't even a real passport, just one of Blinky Malone's better efforts. And I wouldn't have to go through the bother of replacing it, because I had a duplicate sewn in the lining of my valise. Blinky had recommended doing this, because, as he said, "You never know when you'll get the urge to skip. Or need to." I also had my real passport in my pocket, just in case someone with Inspector Jacques Montpelier's keen eyes for forgeries showed up and asked to see my "papers."

I sat on the balcony and surveyed the perfect view, finished the bottle and remembered, not for the first time, the Biblical phrase "And it was good." Then I took a shower and changed into something more appropriate to the scene. I went downstairs to ask the concierge how to find the gallery where Nicole Bertrand worked.

I hadn't worked out what I was going to tell her, even though I'd had plenty of time to think about it. Like Hobey, I trusted my ability to come up with a plausible story on the spot and in the moment. Often that's the best way, because you can react to situations that you couldn't anticipate. One thing I didn't want to do was just give her the bad news about Marvin right away. There were several reasons for that, most of which revolved around the fact that I remembered how she looked in the painting.

Chapter Fifteen

Nicole's gallery was a short distance up the hill, in the old district of town called Le Suquet, a collection of shops and cafes arranged along ancient winding streets and narrow staircases. Here and there an iron gate led to a courtyard filled with flowers and fruit trees, with now and then a discreet fountain. At the top of the hill was an old tower built in the days when life was "nasty, brutish and short." But I had to think that, even then, life had still been more pleasant here than in most of the other muddy settlements of the Dark Ages. There were a few tourists strolling on the narrow streets, not all of them bald, fat men with slender, elegant women. But some. And on the Rue d'Antibes, the main street of the district, I found the Gallerie Provna.

The gallery was owned by a Polish sculptor, the son of an aristocrat. He worked in cork and aluminum and old tin cans and created shapes never before seen or previously conceived. Or wanted. I thought of Mark Twain's comment about Wagner's music – it was not as bad as it sounded. He might have said these works of art were not as bad as they looked. But I doubt it. As I stepped in the door and surveyed the exhibits, I thought I had never seen so many profoundly ugly works of the imagination, not since my last really bad dream.

And then she came out from behind a tall desk in the back, and all of a sudden all the hideous art objects were blotted out, order was restored, and life regained its balance.

"*Bonjour*," she said, with a friendly smile. "*Puis-je vous aider?*"

"I'm sorry," I said. "I don't speak French."

"No?" She said, laughing. "Well, are you lost? This *is* France, you know."

"Lost? Yes. And very suddenly."

"You are American."

"Does it show?"

"Yes, of course. Are you interested in art?"

"Certain kinds, yes."

The certain kind was standing in front of me. One of nature's finest efforts. She was her mother's daughter, for sure, and even more breathtaking. She was just an inch or so shorter, but just as slim and graceful. She was wearing a black dress and no jewelry. She was tanned a rich, reddish brown, sort of the color of autumn apples, and her lips were the same color, just a shade darker. She wore no makeup at all and didn't need it. The blue of her eyes was the blue of the sea on days when it was calm and sunlit – an obvious and maybe banal image, but inescapable in this setting. Her dark hair tumbled around her shoulders and over her forehead in a way that suggested elegant carelessness, as though she had just stepped off the beach. She looked like the girl in the painting, all right, only more so. And my heart went out to Marvin. Poor, sad fool. I could understand.

"Are you looking for something in particular?" she said.

"No. I've found it."

She looked at me with amused disapproval.

"Oh, monsieur. Do you really mean to use that line?"

"I'm afraid so. It's the best I can do on the spur of the moment."

"Perhaps you will think of something better when you have had time."

"Let's hope so. But the fact is ... I have come looking for you."

Now, I thought, I hope the story comes.

"Me? Whatever for?"

How about the truth, I thought? The truth minus the sad news about Marvin? The truth about the painting? Was it a copy or was it a genuine Picasso? That was certainly what we wanted to know, but at the moment I couldn't see how to raise it without tying it to Marvin. Maybe there was no other way around it. And wasn't the other purpose of this whole trip to find her and tell her what happened to Marvin? That's the story I had sold myself, after all.

"It's kind of a long story."

"Is it a good one?"

"Maybe. I don't suppose you'd like to go to one of these very nice cafés and have a drink."

"With you, monsieur?"

"Yes."

She thought about it for a moment or two and, quite naturally, looked me over.

"If I have a drink with you, will that help you think of something clever?"

"It could."

"Do you have a name?"

"Bruno Feldspar." I could have gone with the truth, I suppose, but reality seemed inappropriate just then. Plus, there was the lurking feeling that I might want to disappear suddenly. I often felt that way. It was a character flaw, I suppose. But I could live with it.

"Oh. 'Bruno.' *Très drôle.*"

"Yes, I'm afraid so. But the rest of me is serious."

"Too bad. But ... no one is going to buy anything today. No one ever does. Who would?" She cast a dismissive hand at the strange shapes. "So it will be all right to leave for a few minutes. There is a place round the corner."

She got her bag from behind the desk, and as we went out the door she put a sign in the window – "*Fermé.*" Closed.

"Apparently you're not afraid of losing business."

"I just work there. And because I work there, I know that no one will buy anything. A few may come through to gawk and gasp, but the gallery is the plaything of a strange man who thinks he is an *artiste,* and because he has the money to have this gallery, he can tell himself that he is. He pays me, because I am beautiful." She said this casually, as if it was so obviously true that there was no reason to be coy about it. And she was right.

"I can understand that."

"He thinks that someone will buy his ugly trash so they can flirt with me. No one is that beautiful." We walked around the corner and came to a small café. "Here we are. Does this suit you?"

"Perfectly."

There were only three tables on the sidewalk. No one was sitting at them. There was a large sparkling plate glass window with the words *La Truite d'Argent* in gold letters. "The Silver Trout."

"Let us sit outside. It is a beautiful day." She pronounced "it is" as "it tis." As Klep might say, *"superbe."*

The waiter came and greeted Nicole with a small bow and a smile.

"What would you like?" she said to me.

"A friend has been telling me about Tavel. I've never tried it. How does that sound to you?"

"It sounds to me like it is past time for you to have some. Good. I like it, too. Especially on a warm day." She ordered and the waiter smiled again and glanced at me. He didn't wink, but he looked like he thought about it.

"So, monsieur, you have come looking for me. Why? And how did you find me?"

They say when you're telling a lie, the best thing is to stick to as much of the truth as you can. That's usually wise, because later it's easier to remember the things you've said. But I didn't think that would work in this case. As I sat there looking at her, I thought again that there was no way to bring up the painting without somehow bringing up Marvin. So it was either tell her about his death right away or take a back door in. I didn't want to tell her. Not yet. I wasn't sure why. Not exactly, anyway. Marvin may have been telling the truth. She might actually care for him, in which case, my news would be very bad news indeed. It was not the sort of start I was looking for. So I thought I'd try the back door first.

"Do you go to the movies very often?" I said.

"Yes. Now and then."

"There's a scene in one of my favorites – it's called *Rendezvous on a Train*. Do you know it?"

"No, I don't think so."

That was not surprising. No one else had, either. I was making it up as I went along.

"Well, there's a scene in it when the star, Clark Gable, meets Zephyr Prudomme on a train."

"I have not heard of her."

"She's new. Anyway, Gable is sitting in the dining car and this beautiful woman played by Prudomme comes up and asks 'Is this seat available?' And Gable says, 'I've been saving it for you.' 'Really?' she says. 'Yes,' he says. 'All my life.'"

"Oh là là. *Très* corny, I think."

"Well, it plays better than it sounds. Gable can pull it off."

"I would hope so." She smiled slyly and with a trace of amused disapproval. "Is this part of your clever story?"

"Not working?"

"Not so far."

What the hell, I thought. This wasn't going anywhere.

"No, I guess not," I said, finally. "The truth is, I was looking for you because I was asked to find you."

"Me? Truly?"

"Yes. I have some bad news. I'm sorry to have to tell you, but Marvin Ginsberg is dead. Just before he died he told me about you, and afterwards I felt I should at least let you know that he was thinking of you. And he wanted to find you again. I wouldn't want you to think that he ... just forgot about you."

"Marvin Ginsberg," she said, quietly, almost to herself. Was she remembering those soft nights aboard the *France*? Those nights in Paris? It looked like she might be.

"Yes," I said. "Marvin Ginsberg."

She looked at me for a moment. Then she said:

"Who's that?"

Who's that?

I don't mind saying I was confused. After a moment, I said:

"You are Nicole Bertrand, aren't you?"

"Yes."

"And you were recently in the US and returned to France on the SS *France*?"

"Yes, that's true."

"But you didn't meet someone on the voyage home? A Hollywood producer named Marvin Ginsberg? And you didn't have an affair with him?"

"An affair? *Mais non*. None of that. It was a very rough voyage, and I am a very bad sailor. I was sick in my room almost the whole time. I was not fit to have an affair with anyone, and, believe me, no one would have wanted one with me. *Mal de mer* is not a pretty thing. And I never heard of Marvin Ginsberg. The only man I met on board was the ship's doctor, and he was old and fat and had hair in his nose and ears."

I stared at her. That was easy enough to do. But it wasn't easy to figure out what the hell was going on.

"And you never received any letters from him? They were forwarded *poste restante* while you were travelling." Forwarded by her mother, in fact.

"Letters? No. Of course, I never went to the post offices, anywhere. Why would I? I didn't expect anyone to be writing to me."

What the hell?

"It's all very puzzling," she said. "I wonder how this man Marvin... Is it Marvin?"

"Yes."

"I wonder how he knew to send you to here. To find me here."

"I don't know. He gave me your mother's address, and she sent me here."

"Yes. I use my mother's address as my home. It is on my documents."

"Is it possible he saw you on the ship and maybe even met you briefly and wanted to follow up, somehow?" A strange and sudden obsession with a stranger?

"I suppose. But I was sick so much of the time... I just don't know."

"Well, poor old Marvin got his wire crossed up somewhere. Maybe he got your name and address from the ship's passenger list. Thought you were another woman he really did meet. It seems unlikely, but there's really no way of explaining it otherwise."

"Now that I think of it, there was a young woman in the cabin next to me."

"Was she beautiful?"

"Not very. But she was attractive, you know? Very chic. And I remember now, her name was Nicole, too. Could that possibly explain things? Perhaps it is a mix up of identities. Like a Hitchcock film, no? Like *The Lady Vanishes*?"

EPITAPH FOR A DREAM

It was easy to believe her. But I didn't. I didn't even especially *want* to believe her. But I did want her to believe I believed her. For more reasons than one.

Fortunately, the waiter arrived with the wine and gave me a chance to think. He poured some for me to taste. It was exquisite, and I nodded appreciatively.

"Do you like it?" asked Nicole.

"Yes. Delicious."

"*Bon*. You have good taste."

"I wonder, are you familiar with Hemingway, the writer?"

"Yes. Why?"

"Just curious. He mentioned this wine, somewhere."

"I know. He said it is the wine that goes best with love. Did you know that?"

"Yes, as a matter of fact, I did." There was no sense telling her I'd just learned it from a minor French criminal with the nom de guerre "Klep".

"What do you think?" she said.

"I think Hemingway knew what he was talking about."

"*Bon*. Then what shall we drink to?"

"Well, there seems to be some kind of mystery here. Shall we drink to that? To mystery?"

"All right. Yes. To mystery."

We clinked glasses and looked in each other's eyes. As usual in these kinds of situations I asked myself *Is anything happening?* Possibly. She was friendly and at ease, not overtly flirtatious, but not indifferent, either. And she was stunning. But then I thought again about what she'd said: "*Who's that?*" – "*Who's that?*" It was a hell of an epitaph for Marvin's dream. And I couldn't help feeling sorry for the guy, couldn't help thinking they were pretty damned sad words to go out on.

And I knew those two words applied to more than just poor, old, love-sick Marvin Ginsberg, deceased. I'd already pretty much decided that Nicole was lying. Why? I didn't know. Who was she, really? That wasn't clear, either. Did I care? That was a different question.

Chapter Sixteen

We finished our first glasses and the alert waiter came and refilled them.

"So how did you know this man? Marvin Ginsberg?" she said. "Are you in the film business, too?"

"Yes. Marvin told me about this girl he met on the *France*, and since I was coming here on a project, he asked me to find her. I thought it was you."

"I'm sorry to disappoint you."

"You haven't. In fact, I'm kind of glad you're not the one. I mean, I must have made some mistake, but I'm glad I did. I wouldn't want to start out by giving you sad news."

"Start out?"

"Yes."

"Ah. I see. Well, then, since we are starting out, as you say, why don't you tell me about yourself?" She leaned forward a little and adopted a look of genuine interest. She was very good. She seemed sincere. "Why are you in France? Are you working on a film? Are you an actor? I would not be surprised if you were."

This was intended to be a compliment.

I took it as such with a debonair but modest gesture, as though such things were normal.

"I used to be an actor," I said. This was only a little short of the truth. I was a bit player in one movie when I first came to LA. One movie and three seconds of screen time. That counts, though. I got paid. "But I realized the best jobs were on the other side of the camera. More interesting, and, as a rule, more money. So now I'm a writer and producer. I'm here to scout locations for a movie about the Riviera."

"How interesting. What is it about? Or is it a secret?"

"Are you really interested or just being polite?"

"No, I am interested. All French people are interested in the cinema."

"OK. Well, it's the story of a man, an American who meets a girl, a French girl. She lives in a villa somewhere on the Riviera. They fall in love and have ups and downs – the usual thing, with good scenery. I'm here to find the right scenery."

"Are you the writer, too?"

I remembered Hobey's philosophy.

"Yes. But I haven't quite finished the script yet. Finding the right location will help."

"*Bon*! I know just the place. Cap d'Antibes. It's where I live. There's a villa that belongs to a friend of mine. I am staying there – until I can find a place of my own. It may be just what you are looking for. Would you like to come and see it this evening?"

"That sounds like a very good idea." And it did, too.

"Good. I will write down the address for you. It's called Villa Americana. *Apropos*, no? Any taxi can find it. It's not far. A little over ten miles. I would drive you myself, but I have things to do in the gallery. Is that OK?"

"Perfectly."

"Good. Let us finish the wine, and then I will meet you there tonight. Shall we say 7:30? I will give you dinner. Nothing too fancy, but good. *D'accord?* OK?"

"Yes."

We finished the bottle, and I walked her to the gallery.

"Well, monsieur, what did you think of the Tavel? Very good, *n'est-ce pas?*"

I thought of saying something about Hemingway being right, but I remembered her comment about Clark Gable's fictitious line. *Très* corny.

"I liked it very much."

She smiled, as if she knew what I had been thinking and knew I'd rejected the Hemingway line as being too obvious. Obvious is never good. Like corny.

"See you at 7:30," she said.

Well, she was gorgeous and charming, and I was pretty sure she was a liar. And I wondered again – did I care?

No. Not for the time being.

I went back to the hotel and asked the concierge how to send a telegram. He told me he would take care of it for me if I liked, so I wrote three short messages, one to my buddy Frank Kowalski at LA homicide, another to Bunny at UCLA, and the third to Hobey, telling him where to reach me. Next, I asked the concierge to call Klep at his girlfriend's number and tell him to pick me up at 7:00. Then, since it was only four o'clock, I went to the room, changed into a bathing suit and hotel robe and went to the beach.

The afternoon air was cool, and the beach wasn't very crowded. There were a few holdouts for the last of the sun. I waded into the warm water and then swam out to the raft that was about fifty yards offshore. I was pretty sure there would be a beautiful woman out there, probably one who was interested in meeting a dashing young private eye from California. Or maybe I'd continue being a writer. Who were the Greek nymphs that hung around the sea? Nereids? Something like that. As it happened, there was only a bald fat man there. Well, I thought, how many dream girls can you meet in any one day? I'd had my quota. It's best not to be greedy. I swam back to the beach, dried off and went to the hotel. Perhaps a little more champagne was in order.

That evening Klep arrived right on time.

"Hello, boss," he said, cheerfully. "Where are we going?"

I gave him the slip of paper with the address.

"Ah! Cap d'Antibes. *Superbe.* I know all about it and will fill you in on the way. Do you have a date with a beautiful, rich girl?"

"She's beautiful, but I don't know how rich she is. Not very, I suspect."

"Well, as the old man said to his young mistress, money comes and goes, but beauty only goes, so it's best not to waste it."

"What did she say?"

"She agreed and said let's not waste this beautiful day – let's go shopping."

"I'll go you one quotation better."

"Yes?"

"'Beauty is truth, truth beauty, that is all ye know on earth, and all ye need to know.'"

"Who said that?"

"An Englishman named Keats."

"He doesn't know much, does he?"

"Well, he was young."

"He'll learn better as time goes on."

"I doubt it. How long a trip is it to Cap d'Antibes?"

"Oh, not much more than thirty minutes. The road and the countryside are *très* scenic. That is why so many artists have come here. Picasso comes now and then. For many years he has come here to various houses. He flits here and there. I believe he had difficulties with his first wife. Or second. Or some girlfriends. Or all of them at the same time. I can't remember. They say his domestic life lacks serenity, that he lives with a flock of ptarmigans. That could explain many things, such as his painting and why he's always running away."

"Do you mean termagants?"

"Them, too."

"Do you know anything about the owner of this place we're going to?"

"Villa Americana? A bit. He's very wealthy. His father was a profiteer in the last war. Very canny man. Sold canned fish to the army. Ha! I make a joke, accidentally. Anyway, his name – the son, not the father – is Jean Marc Dufresne. He is a painter and there is talk that he's a protégé of the great man himself."

"Picasso?"

"The same. But I cannot say that is true for sure. A man like Picasso acquires many friends and protégés, whether he wants them or not. And whether he even knows it. Anyway, some say Dufresne has talent. I am no judge. All this modern painting looks unnatural to me. I like to see women with two eyes and one nose where they are supposed to be. And I prefer two breasts in the front."

"How is it you know so much about this Jean Marc? Have you met him?"

"Oh, no. But friends of mine and their friends knew his father during the war and after. Besides, word gets around, you know? And there is my lady friend in Cannes. She has her ear to the ground."

"What does she do?"

"She keeps her ear to the ground."

"Does that pay?"

"Of course. Otherwise, why do it? It is not because of natural curiosity. How much it pays depends on what she does with what she hears. But you know the fat bald men we saw here there and all over the place? They often are anxious to buy what she hears so that it does not reach the wrong ears. She is like a negative newspaper. All the news that should never get printed. For a price, always for a price."

"Good line. I'll remember it. I'm surprised you're comfortable being with her."

"Me? I have nothing to hide, boss. You know that. Ha! Besides, she is *magnifique*. Such a body! Everything is where it should be – and abundant. This is the word I want? Yes, I think so. It's no wonder she hears things. And besides, her other business is just made for gathering information. She is much in demand."

"A prostitute?"

"Oh, no, boss. A *courtisane*. There is a difference, no?"

"Is there?"

"Of course. If there was not a difference, there would not be two different words. The great Flaubert talks of *le mot juste.*   Which means the precisely correct word for each situation. Which also means that no two words mean exactly the same thing."

"I'm impressed."

"Yes.   I do not spend all my time collecting insurance premiums or going to bed with *courtisanes*. When you drive a taxi, you have lots of time to read and think about things. But I tell you this – I am glad the women I meet are not like Madame Bovary. She makes heavy weather over trifles. *Très fatigant.*"

"I admire your interests. I read a lot myself."

"*Bon*! We are birds of a feather, eh, boss?"

That was truer than he knew.

"How did this Jean Marc come by the villa?"

"Come by?

"Acquire it."

"Ah.   Well, the story goes that it was built by a wealthy American, maybe just before the war. Maybe just after. I forget. In those days, no one came to Antibes. But this man liked the scenery and the weather, I suppose, and so he built the villa. Before, it was a collection of small houses – almost like a tiny village. So he connected them up and put in bathrooms and made something new, so that the house was on many levels, all perched on the cliff above the sea. And he built gardens and patios on the terraces. And put in some fruit trees. Then he built a stairway to the beach and cleaned up all the seaweed and rocks and made it a place for parties. And because he was rich, he had a lot of rich friends and a lot of other friends who liked free dinners, meaning artists and writers and musicians and that sort of people. In the years after the war they came to visit, and there was always a party.

And then the French people of a similar class no longer thought of this country as a place to stay away from and started to come, and someone built a casino, and the small hotel began to stay open in the summer again, and *voilà*: it became fashionable. But then the Great Crash happened and everyone lost money and all the Americans went home and things became sleepy again. But it is still *très chic*, and many who were able to save their money, or find a way to make more, have stayed. And this includes Jean Marc's father, who made such profits in the war that even though he lost half his money in the Crash, he still had plenty left. And he had branched out into other things, also fishy. Ha! So he bought the villa from the Americans."

"What's he doing now?"

"The father? Feeding the fishes. *Très ironique*, no? They say he made enemies of the wrong people, and what 'they' say is usually how it was. This was only a few years ago. It was in all the papers."

"I missed it."

"Too bad. It was *sensationnel*. Of course, no one was caught. Whoever did it knew their business. Now the son lives in the villa and presents himself as an artist."

"Is he, or was he involved in the family business?"

"Not that I have heard."

"And you would have heard."

"I think so."

"Klep, I think you are like your lady friend, the courtesan – well connected."

Klep grinned and shrugged.

"That is *le mot juste,* boss. *Le mot juste.*"

Chapter Seventeen

The scenery on the way to Antibes and then down along the cape was as advertised. On the right side the sheer cliffs dropped away to the sea, while on the left they rose high enough to cast shadows over the road. Here and there, a villa was perched on the side of a hill, white and gleaming in the fading sunlight. The cliffs and mountains were an artist's dream – gray rock mixed with green pines and cypress, and beyond, of course, was the sea, an avenue of history, both real and imagined, tragic and mythic, romantic and treacherous – the graveyard of heroes and villains, including Jean Marc's old man, apparently.

"Didn't I tell you, boss? The view *fantastique*, no?"

"The view *fantastique*, yes."

"I have an artist's eye. If I could paint, I would be renowned."

Klep had no trouble finding Villa Americana. It was at the very tip of the cape, and, like others we had seen, it was set on the side of a sloping cliff. The various small houses that had been converted and connected were all painted a brilliant white and their roofs were red tiles of the kind you see everywhere in the Mediterranean. You could see the terraces and gardens arranged around the houses and down the cliff side, and you could see the steep staircase down to the beach. We drove up to the front of the house. The gravel driveway was smooth and well kept.

"Good luck, boss. I say that only for the sake of politeness, not because you will need it."

"Just wait a minute until I make sure this is the right place."

"OK."

I don't know what kind of wood the front door was made of, but it was heavy and massive. I banged the bronze knocker. It was some sort of grinning gargoyle.

The door swung open slowly, because of its great weight, I suppose, and also because the man who opened it was small and slight and looked older than he probably was. The word "gnome" seemed to fit, almost. I assumed he was some kind of servant. I had fully expected the owner of this place to show up in an ascot, blazer, white flannels and amber cigarette holder. This old boy was wearing canvas shorts and a sleeveless T shirt of the kind sent into fashion oblivion by Clark Gable, when he went shirtless in "It Happened One Night." He had a nasty-looking French cigarette dangling from his lip, peasant style.

"*Oui?*" said the little man.

"I'm sorry. I don't speak French. But I'm here to see Nicole Bertrand. I am Bruno Feldspar."

He smiled and switched to English.

"You are American?"

"Yes."

137

"I know many Americans. There are not so many here as there used to be. No one misses them. Only the wine merchants. But I remember some of them fondly. They gave good parties. Please come in."

I thought it would be polite to ask for the owner.

"Is Monsieur Dufresne at home?"

"Yes, of course. I am he. Or should I say him? I sometimes mix up my pronouns."

"You are Jean Marc Dufresne?" It wasn't easy to keep the surprise out of my voice, and in fact I couldn't.

"Oui. Who were you expecting? Or should I say whom? English is very confusing."

"Oh."

"I am sorry to disappoint you." There was a glitter of humor in his very dark eyes.

"Oh, no. I was just expecting ... Nicole." It was lame, and he knew what I was doing, but he let it pass.

"Nicole. Ah, I see. Did she invite you?"

"Yes. For dinner."

"She is very sociable. I admire that. I am too much a recluse. I wish I could have her gaiety. What time did she ask you to come?"

"Just now – 7:30."

"Well, I would like to say that it is strange, because she is not here, but it is not so strange, because she is like that. Unpredictable. This is the word I want?"

"Apparently, yes. When do you think she will return?"

"That is difficult to say. You see, she gathered up all her things and moved out. She and her boyfriend. They drove away in his little car. A Citroen TPV. This car does not go very fast, but it is reliable, which Nicole is not. She may come back someday, but you never know with her. I like her, but, as I say, she is not dependable."

"Moved out?"

"Yes. She seemed to be in a very great hurry."

"About what time was that?"

"About four thirty, I would say. I rarely pay attention to the clock. It goes, and I ignore it. Or I should say we ignore each other. I reject the idea of time. One day I will be proved wrong, but until then I resist the whole notion. Have you known Nicole long? If so, you will not be surprised by this, I think."

"No. Only a few hours."

"Oh. Then you probably are surprised."

"Yes. Very."

"Well, since you are here, let me offer you a drink. There was a time when Nicole's behavior surprised me, too. We will commiserate. Is this the right word?"

"Yes. And thank you. But my driver is outside, waiting .... Perhaps I had better not ...."

"Oh, have him come in. I am a recluse, as I said, but now and then it is pleasant to have company. I will show you around the villa, if you like. It is very interesting, I think."

"Well, yes, then, thank you. I'll just call my driver."

I was confused, to say the least.

"What's wrong, boss?"

"She's flown the coop. For good. Or at least the foreseeable future. With a boyfriend. In a Citroen."

"Truly? That is very strange, no?"

"Very strange, yes."

"Well, this is what dream girls do."

"This one seems to make a habit of it. The ones the poets write about don't have boyfriends, and they don't vanish in Citroens."

"Was it a TPV?"

"I think that's what he said."

"Then they are vanishing at a very slow pace. But they will get there eventually. It is curious that she has one, though. They are very new. She must know someone."

"I wouldn't be surprised. And Jean Marc Dufresne turns out to be an older gent, kind of like Peter Lorre twenty years from now."

"Hmm. Some people do not age well. It is exposure to the sun. It is *très fort* on the *Côte d'Azur*."

"You don't seem surprised – about Dufresne."

"Well, boss, surprise is not my *métier*."

"Anyway, he's invited us for a drink. I couldn't think fast enough to come up with a reason to say no, but now that I think of it, it might be a good idea. I need some information on a painting, and he just might have it. So come on in and join the party."

We went back inside and I tried to introduce Klep, but I couldn't remember his real name. He offered his hand to Dufresne and introduced himself.

"Good, evening, Monsieur Dufresne. I am Jean Baptiste Poquelin, at your service."

Dufresne looked at him a moment and then smiled.

"You have a famous name, monsieur."

"So I am told. But I am not famous. I prefer it that way. If someday I become famous, I'm afraid it will be for the wrong reasons."

"I understand. Please come in, gentlemen. I always drink champagne at sunset. Perhaps you would like some, too."

"Yes. Thank you."

The main room had a stone floor, a high, beamed ceiling and large plate glass windows in the rear. The windows overlooked the gardens below and, beyond that, the sea. There were a few handsome handmade tables and benches and a scattering of comfortable chairs. The walls were brilliant white and almost completely covered by paintings of different sizes and styles, some depicting geometric shapes, others random daubes of color, and still others actual humans, including several quite graphic pictures of a couple entangled with each other in various erotic positions. The women in the pictures all looked like Nicole, and in every one Nicole's expression was ecstatic, although in slightly different and very interesting ways. The man's face was never shown. They were all variations on the painting over Marvin's fireplace.

"Nicole was your model," I said.

"Yes. And more than just mine. She is, or should I say "was," very popular with the artists in the area, including the maestro himself."

Of course. It would be too simple if Dufresne and Dufresne alone had painted her.

"By 'maestro' you mean Picasso?"

"Naturally."

"Are all these paintings your work?"

"Oh, no. Some are, but many are by my friends who live here at least some of the time. At other times they live in Paris or places in Spain. All over. We are quite an

141

international brotherhood, you see. I sometimes forget who did which paintings. Sometimes people don't bother signing a piece of work. Most artists are often quite indifferent about a painting once it is finished, especially if it is dashed off in the heat of a moment. It is the act of creation that matters. The thing created becomes almost irrelevant once it is done."

"Truly? I mean, that seems surprising."

"Does it really? Do you think God cares about this world now that He has finished making it? Not according to the evidence of my eyes. He has moved on to other things. Somewhere else. Perhaps He views Man and this world as a failure. I would, certainly. Perhaps it was merely an experiment or like a sketch for a painting. Unfinished. Discarded."

"Mark Twain said God invented man because he didn't like the way the monkey turned out."

Jean Marc grinned and slapped his knee.

"Ah! That is very good! *Bon.* It is the same with the artist. We are almost always dissatisfied with a work. It never quite matches the vision in our heads. And so, we forget about it and start again. Bérénice!"

An ancient, wizened woman emerged from another room.

"What do you want?"" she said irritably. She was every inch the Mediterranean peasant woman, with black, evil eyes and a black headscarf.

"Bring us champagne."

"You drink too much. And who are these people?"

"My guests, you horrible old crone. Now bring the wine and be sharp about it." He said this with a smile. And she shuffled off, muttering. "Bernice has been with me since I was a child. As a housekeeper and servant she is a disaster.

She does almost nothing and takes liberties and complains. I tolerate her because she is an excellent model. Such a face. No prune in the world can equal it. No old crow sitting on a fence can match her glare for menace. She is the essence of malevolence. This is the word, *n'est-ce pas*? I love her. And she makes me laugh. Shall we sit on the nearest patio? We can watch the last of the sun."

We sat around another table that was made of the same wood as the door. The top was unpolished but sanded and smooth. It was obviously the work of a craftsman.

"Did you make the furniture?" said Klep. "I ask because I have an interest in such things."

"Yes. It amuses me."

"My compliments. If you ever need specialty tools, I have a very good source."

"Truly? I will remember."

Were they talking a secret language, somehow? I couldn't tell.

"I wonder if you can tell me something about Nicole and this boyfriend," I said. "It seems very strange that she should leave like that. It almost seems that she has something to hide."

"Who doesn't?" said Dufresne.

Bernice arrived with the champagne and three glasses.

"Thank you, my love," said Dufresne.

"*Vafanculo*," she said under her breath. She went back to the house.

"Bernice is Italian," said Dufresne, by way of explanation. "So, you want to know about Nicole. Well, what's the expression you Americans use? The line forms in the front?"

"In the rear, usually."

143

"Ah, yes. That makes more sense, I think. But I will tell you what I know."

He poured out three glasses of champagne.

"*Santé*," he said. We each took a drink. The wine was icy cold and delicious. "So. Nicole Bertrand. Who is she? Well, part of the story is unexceptional. She almost grew up here, in the Villa Americana. Her mother is a very beautiful woman. An actress. Or at least she used to be."

"I know. I met her in Lyon."

"Yes? Then you will understand that she was a great favorite of the American who owned this house before my father bought it. The man who built it, in fact. His name was Richard Bloom. He had a difficult wife. She was richly endowed with personalities, so you could never be sure of who you were talking to. Or should I say 'whom?' Anyway, sometimes she was charming and sometimes she was irritable and sometimes she was as silent and unreachable as a stone, and sometimes she was madcap and liked to jump off these cliffs into the sea, even though it was foolish to do so. Very dangerous. But she never hurt herself doing it, much to everyone's surprise. But this kind of behavior was very tiresome to those around her all the time. Only weekend party guests enjoyed it, because she was so gay, usually. But her husband grew weary of it, and when Rosemarie Bertrand came to a party with a friend of a friend, it was love at first sight for Richard Bloom. *L'amour fou*, as we say. They went off together, and Richard's wife went off with a Frenchman who said he was in the Foreign Legion, but that may not have been true. It is an easy thing to say and all you have to do to prove it is to have a Legionnaire's tattoo, and these are easy enough to acquire. Anyway, the affair between Richard and Rosemarie resulted in Nicole, and ever since she has thought of this villa as home, so she comes and goes as she pleases. I have been glad to have her. There is plenty of room. For about five years she lived here and posed for all of us, as I have said. She has a beautiful body, as you can see. And the face of a goddess. She met some men, but they have come and gone, too. This latest one is a painter. He is Italian. From somewhere in the south. A silent, sinister fellow. But very handsome. We call him Don Giovanni, as a joke, although that is his name as it happens. Giovanni-something. Martini? Yes, I think that's it. Like the vermouth. And so she has gone off with him. Where? Who knows? Will she come back here? Probably. When? No one can say."

"Whatever happened to Richard and his wife?"

"He more or less disappeared into the hinterlands. She drowned. Not here. But in the sea off Long Island, New York. Sad, really. But I never knew her. Or him, for that matter. He had money, so he could do as he pleased. I have heard that he became a fishing guide in some place called Idaho. Is there such a place?"

"Yes."

"Well, perhaps it's true. But I can't be sure. You know how you hear things."

"I wonder – do you think it's possible that Nicole might have 'borrowed' any of these paintings? From time to time?"

"Borrowed? It is possible. Look around the house if you like. Paintings are everywhere. I have stacks of them in my studio, too. As I said, I do not care about them once they are finished. So it is possible."

"How about the ones given to you by other artists?"

145

"It is the same. If they gave them away, they did not care about them. And I don't either, although I appreciate the gesture."

"Some would be valuable, though."

"Yes. But such things don't matter to me, really. The price that some people put on a work of art has nothing to do with its merit. The price goes up or down based on the whims of some silly people who are paying for the name at the bottom, or on the advice of a so-called critic. Picasso could sign a blank canvas and someone would buy it, and some journalist would extoll its brilliant negativity. But to an artist, genuine merit is either there, or it is not. And, as I said, usually it is not. Usually, it is a failure. Besides, my father, poor man, left me very well off. So I have the freedom to care about what matters and ignore everything else."

An hour later, in the car on the way back to the hotel, Klep said, "I am wondering about something, boss."

"What is it?"

"You know when you asked him whether Nicole ever borrowed some of the paintings."

"Yes. And?"

"Well, do you think 'borrow' was *le mot juste?*"

Chapter Eighteen

"What did Jean Marc mean when he said you had a famous name?"

"I don't know, boss. I was just being *aimable*."

I didn't believe him, but it didn't seem worth getting into.

"Well, that was an interesting visit," I said. "What did we learn, do you think?"

"Learn, boss? Well, not too much. First, Nicole tells fibs. That is not so bad or unusual. A beautiful woman cannot be expected to tell the truth. Some of the time, maybe. But as a rule? No. Second, she steals paintings. But she steals them from a man who doesn't care. Or even notice. So I ask myself – is that really stealing? This is a question for a *philosophe*. If a tree falls in the woods and no one hears it, did it really fall?"

"You are an empiricist."

"If you say so, boss. I quote you a line: 'It's public cry that gives crime its origin; if you sin in silence, then it's not a sin.'"

"What's that from?"

"Molière's *Tartuffe*, of course."

147

"I should have known." Molière's collected works were probably required reading for budding gang members.

"Or suppose," he said, "one day Nicole noticed a pretty stone in Jean Marc's patio and put it in her pocket, would anyone consider that theft? No one noticed, but if they did, no one cared. How is that different? Jean Marc's ideas are very interesting to think about, especially for someone in my business. But that is for another time."

"All right. What else do we know?"

"We know that Nicole goes with a sinister Italian, which could mean something, or nothing. Most Italians from the south are dark and sinister-looking, even though they may actually be meek, mild and henpecked. Looks can be deceiving, no? *Regarde-moi, par example.* Someone might say I look like a film star, no?"

"But which one?"

"Ah, boss, that is the question."

"What do you make of the car they drove away in? Any significance?"

"Well, we know it is a Citroen model that is still what is called a prototype and not available on the open market, which means that one of them has very good connections with the people at Citroen, and, if so, that it is probably Nicole, because why would an Italian know anyone of importance? Of course, it is possible that they stole the car from someone, but it is very easy to recognize. It has only one headlight like the famous monster, Cyclops, so I doubt they stole it. Any car thief who understands his *métier* steals a car that is like many others, so that the cops become confused. Or more confused than normal. A mere switching of the license plate is all that's required to send them into a muddle."

"You would know."

"Of course. I read things. That's all we learned, I think."

"I agree with all of that. So where do you think she has gone? Back to Lyon? To her mother's?"

"Well, let us assume that she ran away because you showed up and started asking questions, and she did not want to give you the right answers, only little fibs. And you showed up in Cannes because her mother told you where to find her. In that case, would you go to the mother?"

"No."

"Me neither, pardner, like they say in the cowboy flicks. She could be anywhere in the world *except* her mother's."

"That leaves a lot of territory to vanish in."

"Well, boss, like we said – that's what dream girls do. If she was homely and fat, she would never vanish, despite your hopes. As it is ..."

"Are dream girls ever homely and fat?" I knew I was descending into the role of straight man, but I didn't mind.

"I couldn't say, boss. I don't usually dream about anything. It comes from having a conscience *sans* spots. Ha!"

"You mean 'spotless'?"

"*Exactement.*"

"I envy you."

"I don't blame you, boss. I don't blame you."

Klep dropped me off at the Carlton and went off to spend the night with his courtesan, whose name I learned was Camille. Of course.

"Maybe Camille will have heard something," Klep said.

"Maybe. But is it likely?"

"No. But like the old man said to his mistress, 'You never know; you must have faith.' *Bon soir*! See you in the morning."

I went to my room and ordered another bottle of champagne. I sat out on the balcony and watched the stars reflected off the sea and listened to the clanking of the ropes on the masts of the sailing yachts and the laughter from the late evening parties. Well, I thought, I have done my best for Marvin Ginsberg. I have found his Nicole and given her the sad news, and she has taken off again. The odds of finding her were slim, at best. Too bad. I could understand his feelings for her, but I wondered if he ever really knew what she was. Clearly, she took a painting from Jean Marc and gave to it Marvin. But the question was – who painted it? Was it a Picasso or a Jean Marc, or was it by some unknown artist who would likely remain unknown? Maybe even Nicole's Italian boyfriend? One thing seemed pretty clear: whoever painted it didn't seem to care what happened to it.

In the morning, I got a little closer to what might be the truth.

The concierge had three telegrams for me – answers to the three I'd sent. The first was from Kowalski: *Bank records show Ginsberg withdrew 20K in cash three months ago. Also, opened five thousand letter credit. All other expenditures routine. Nothing new on wife's accident.*

I knew about the letter of credit, but the twenty thousand was something else again. I igured it was a payment for something Marvin didn't want anyone to know about, but what? In his business, it might be anything. There was the unresolved case of his wife's death. It appeared to have been an accident, but that was still an open question. And her death was not only a relief to Marvin, but also a very convenient removal of an obstacle between Marvin and his *amour fou*. A perfectly executed hit and run that left no traces might very well be worth a lot of money to a rich man like Marvin. But twenty thousand seemed awfully high. I'd have to check with Tony on the going rates, when I got back. Maybe Marvin only used a piece of the twenty – say, ten thousand – for the hit. What was the rest of it for? The Picasso?

But maybe the hit and run accident had been just that – an accident. Nothing sinister at all. In that case, the most reasonable conclusion was that Marvin used the whole twenty thousand to pay Nicole for the painting – a bargain basement Picasso, a classy memento of their affair. But was it a real Picasso? Or had Nicole and her boyfriend pulled a fast one on a lovesick producer and sold him a clever forgery? And was there any connection to Marvin's untimely and very unnatural death? Dead men tell no tales, they say. Cash cannot be traced, they say. And dream girls always disappear. The Case of the Wandering Marvin had all three elements.

The second telegram was from Bunny. I had sent mine to his UCLA office, but his efficient secretary had forwarded it to him: *Still in London. No news on painting. Return date uncertain but eventual – one hopes.*

The third was from Hobey: *In jail in Lyon. Please hurry back. Need bail.*

Swell.

I called Klep and told him we had to get back to Lyon.

"Hobey's in jail," I said, by way of explanation.

He did not seem surprised.

"Ah.   These things happen sometimes," he said, philosophically. "I will be there *tout de suite*."

I checked out of the Carlton, reluctantly.   It seemed a shame to let some of Marvin's dollars go unspent in such a paradise. But there was no help for it. While I was waiting for Klep, I walked over to Nicole's gallery, but as I expected, it was dark and had a 'Fermé' sign in the window.

I walked back to the hotel, and Klep pulled up a few minutes later.

We headed north.

"Will we have to stop and collect from any of your clients?" I asked.

"No, boss. They are all up to date. What did your friend do to get himself jugged like a hare?"

"I don't know. He just said to come quickly and bail him out."

"Ah. Well, I am afraid he will suffer a disappointment. I have seen many American films, so I understand what you mean by 'bail.' Unfortunately, the French system is not so enlightened, and we do not have such a thing. The prisoner will be in police custody until he is sent before a judge. From there, who knows? It all depends on what he did. He could be off to prison as *tout de suite* as I arrived this morning."

"Uh-oh."

"That is *le mot juste*, boss. It is lucky collections are up to date. We can drive straight through. I know a faster way."

"What can we do when we get there?"

"Well, we will do what is sensible. First, we will find out how Monsieur Hobey got his *zizi* in a wringer. Then we will make some calls to friends. It is *très normal.* I would not be too worried, unless he has seduced the judge's mistress. Judges can be vindictive. But most other things can be arranged, one way or the other."

"You don't seem very concerned." I took this as an encouraging sign.

"I'm not, boss. But I am not the one who tangled up his *zizi.*"

"By the way, I don't suppose your friend Camille heard anything about Nicole."

"No, boss. She has a cold."

We drove north without stopping, except to refuel. At one point, while the taxi was getting topped off, Klep went into the service station. He was gone only a few minutes.

"I made a few calls, boss," he said, cryptically. "No reason to wait."

"A friend?"

"Who else?"

We arrived in Lyon about nine that evening. Klep drove directly to a police station in Villeurbanne.

"Are you sure this is the right station?"

"That was the purpose of the calls, boss. One of them."

It was getting late and the sergeant at the desk was sleepy. He did not welcome the new business we were bringing him. Klep necessarily took over initial negotiations.

"So, my friend, how goes it?" he said to the sergeant.

"It goes. What do you want? Your face is familiar."

"Thank you. It is good to be recognized, except when it isn't. But we are not here to spread happiness or exchange photos. We are here to inquire about a prisoner you have – a Monsieur Hobey Baker."

"The Yank."

"The very same."

"He is a poor fighter," said the sergeant, with some contempt. "He seems to be the kind who drinks and believes he is D'Artagnan come to life. Then finds out he was wrong. You should tell him to adopt diplomacy in the future. If he has a future."

"A useful suggestion. But surely there has been some misunderstanding? A case of mistaken identity?"

"He punched a policeman. The policeman punched him back and then dragged his body to the station. There is no mistake."

"Punched a policeman? Is that a crime? Some might say it was a political act allowable under the Napoleonic Code."

"Your mother should have told you: no one likes a smart ass."

This probably sounded better in the original, but I still had to smile when Klep translated it for me.

"My mother believed in tolerance. Your mother did, too, evidently."

"Eh?"

There was no telling how long this verbal sparring match would go on, but while the sergeant was trying to decide whether he or his mother had been insulted, the door to the station opened and in strode Inspector Jacques Montpelier, our dapper train companion and member of the Sûreté. Though I should have been surprised, even shocked, I wasn't.

"And who are you pretending to be, monsieur?" said the sergeant. He was clearly not impressed by the dapper little man with the waxed moustaches. Montpelier was not flustered. He was used to these kinds of comments.

"I am Inspector Jacques Montpelier of the Sûreté. Perhaps you have heard of it. Even a provincial dolt such as yourself *should* have heard of it."

"Say, who are you calling provincial? This is Lyon."

"Yes. But you are obviously just in from the country."

"How do you know that?"

"It is my business to know. Here are my credentials. And here is the order releasing the prisoner Hobart Nassau Hall Baker to my custody. Be so good as to produce him."

"Your custody?"

"Yes. As you can see. Baker is a dangerous foreign agent. If you are efficient it is possible, just possible, that I will mention you in my report. Assuming you get off your fat ass and produce the man."

"I should call my captain."

"Please do so, if you wish. He will no doubt thank you for disturbing his *tête à tête* with his mistress – the lovely Mademoiselle Elaine Dufarge – and telling him you are obstructing the national police in their duty in order to maintain in custody a man who, as far as you know, has only punched a policeman, and not very hard at that. Go ahead and call him. I will wait. One minute."

The sergeant thought better about it. How did this Inspector know about the captain's mistress? Even her name? How did he know that Hobey had been jugged for hitting a cop? Clearly, the Sûreté had eyes everywhere. It was enough to make a man nervous. So was Montpelier's no-nonsense glare and his whole demeanor, despite his dandified outfit. The sergeant studied Montpelier's credentials and then the order for release. They seemed in order. He could see no objection. And after all, Baker was really nothing to him. The crime was a minor one. The officer hadn't been hurt. Baker would probably get off with just a fine, anyway. On the other hand, if he truly was a dangerous foreign agent, the police might get a pat on the back and maybe he, himself, might get a mention. There was also the potential for trouble, if he made difficulties for the Sûreté.

The sergeant looked at all of us. We all maintained a straight face.

"Are these two with you?" he asked Montpelier.

"Never seen them before. They might be Baker's associates. They might not be. But I have no papers on them. Have they done anything?"

"Not really."

The sergeant thought about things for a few more moments.

"I will need you to sign a receipt," he said, finally.

I congratulate you for knowing proper procedure."

"Thank you."

"Now, produce the prisoner."

The sergeant picked up the phone and mumbled a few words, no doubt wondering if this was the start of a new and brilliant chapter in his career, or the end of it.

A few moments later Hobey was led out by the warder. Hobey was shambling and disheveled. His collar was torn and his Princeton tie was askew. His hair was sticking out in all directions and he had a black eye and a bloody, swollen lower lip. He had had all day to get himself together, so it was clear he'd spent the time asleep, instead. Or rather, sleeping it off. He looked at me and smiled, or tried to, and then winced. Then he saw Klep and the Inspector and understood what was happening. He knew he had some part to play but also knew it involved merely staying quiet and abject. Not difficult under the circumstances.

"Ah, Monsieur Baker, we meet at last," said the Inspector. He signed the receipt for the prisoner.

"Thank you for your cooperation, Sergeant. I will mention that in my report."

The sergeant smiled in a sickly manner and watched us as the four of us left the station together.

"That was neatly done, Boss," said Klep. He wasn't talking to me.

"Does that surprise you, Klep?"

"No, sir."

We walked to the cars – Montpelier to a shiny four-door Citroen, the rest of us to Kelp's taxi.

"Well, then, I will bid you gentlemen good evening," said Montpelier. "I have other business, unfortunately. I suggest you make yourselves scarce, as they say in the films." He looked at me. "Please tell our friends in America that I send my regards."

The inspector got in the backseat of the Citroen. The chauffeur who was holding the door got in the front and drove off. Hobey and I got in Klep's cab. We headed for the train station hotel.

"I could use a hot bath," said Hobey, wearily.

"You are right about that, boss," said Klep.

"Second the motion," I said.

Chapter Nineteen

"Don't ask," said Hobey. "I don't feel like talking about it. It'll wait till morning. OK?"

"Sure."

Klep and I helped Hobey to his room and left him to his self-loathing and regrets, if any.

"Where to now, boss?"

"You figure I want to go somewhere? It's late, isn't it?"

"Not in France."

"All right, then. Let's pay a visit to Madame Bertrand. She may still be up. Whether she's alone or not is another question. Maybe we should call first."

"I wouldn't, boss. That would give her a chance to give you *l'oiseau.*"

"Meaning?"

"The bird. This way, you'll be there and hard to turn away. No?"

"Yes."

On the way I asked him, "So, Klep, is Inspector Montpelier the real Molière?"

"Oh, no, boss. The real Molière died many centuries ago!"

That was as much as I was going to get out of him, but there really was no mystery about any of it. Hobey and I were under the protection of the friends of our friends, and nothing more would be said about it. Nothing more needed to be said. What favors would be "asked" in return was a different question. But that was not going to be my problem. At least, I didn't think it would be.

There was still a light on in Madame Bertrand's second-floor apartment.

"Still awake, boss. *Bon*! I tell you what — I will wait here until you come back, if it is not too long. Say, thirty minutes? But if you do not come back by then or if I see the light go out of that window, I will come back in the morning. If you need to reach me you can call me at this number." He handed me a card. "It is the apartment of a woman who will be glad to see me. Not far from here."

"Are your woman friends always glad to see you?"

"Of course. Except when their husbands are home. But this one's husband works at night. She gets lonely. Between you and me, I don't think they are officially married anyway. You would think a police sergeant would be more respectful of the customs of the country. But, no."

"I don't suppose the sergeant in question is the same one we just left."

"As a matter of fact, yes."

"No wonder he thought your face was familiar."

"Well, now and then we may have passed in the hallway. Like ships in the morning."

EPITAPH FOR A DREAM

I went past the concierge's doorway, and she came scuttling out with a suspicious expression. But she mellowed when she saw me. Dogs, cats, babies and old ladies all seem to like me. Besides, she probably remembered me as an ambassador from the far-off land of make believe.

"I'm here to see Madame Bertrand," I said.

"*Oui. Bon soir. Et bonne chance.*" And she went back inside her lair.

I went up to the second floor and knocked on the door.

"*Oui?*"

"It's Bruno Feldspar." After all this time I still cringed a little bit at the name. But there were reasons for using it, though I wasn't sure they were very good ones.

"Ah! *Bon!*" She opened the door and I caught a whiff of her perfume, or rather, her scent, which is a more comprehensive and much more intoxicating idea. Wine lovers call this the "bouquet." It is an appropriate word. *Le mot juste.*

"Hello," she said. She looked past me to see if I was with anyone. "I was just thinking about getting ready for bed. Please come in." She was wearing a silvery peignoir that accented her form as though it was designed specifically for her and her alone. And for all I knew, it had been. It was the kind of material the women and goddesses pictured on the classical urns wore. It appeared to be transparent but was only translucent and therefore obviously more seductive. Her dark hair was loose and looked as though she had just run a brush through it, when I knocked. She wore no makeup that I could see. She was old enough to have a grown daughter, but didn't look it. She was at the peak of her physical perfection, regardless of what the calendar said.

Maybe the dim light helped, and maybe my imagination helped, but she didn't need much help from either one. "Would you like a drink?" she said.

"Thank you. Yes. I'm sorry to bother you at this hour."

"At this hour? No, no. This hour is perfect. The day is over, and the evening, too. You know what Cole Porter says about this time of night."

"'Let Us Begin the Beguine?'"

"I was thinking of something else. But that will do, too. Please sit down. Would you like a glass of wine?"

"That sounds good. Do you by any chance have some Tavel? I was introduced to it in Cannes, and I liked it."

"Tavel? Of course. I think it is quite pleasant this time of day. Or any time for that matter. I have a bottle chilling. It is best when it's fairly cold, I think."

"Perfect."

She went into the kitchen and returned with the wine. She poured two glasses from the bar at the side table and then came over and sat on the silver sofa, more or less beside me, although she pulled up her knees and tucked her bare feet under her.

"*Santé*," she said, looking me in the eyes. Her eyes were the same color as Nicole's – maybe even a shade darker. Maybe violet.

"Yes."

"Now, then. I am glad to see you again. Our last visit was too short. But ...."

"Why am I here?"

"Well ... yes, I suppose so. Did you ever find Nicole?"

"Yes, I did. Just briefly. We had a drink in Cannes, and she invited me for dinner at Jean Marc's house, but then she was called away suddenly for some reason and never showed up."

"Ah, yes. She will do that now and then. Wretched child. Were you very put out? Is that the expression? Put out?"

"Yes. And no. I was not put out. I had an interesting talk with Jean Marc, so it was a far from wasted visit."

"I'm sure. He is a very interesting man. You cannot always believe everything he says. He is an artist, after all. But he can be very amusing."

I wondered what to make of that, but didn't pursue it.

"I wanted to stay longer. His villa would make an excellent location for the film we are producing. But I got a telegram from Hobey saying he'd been arrested, so I hurried back."

"Yes, I know. I mean, I know he was arrested. *Quelle surprise, n'est-ce pas?*"

"I managed to get him out of jail just an hour or so ago. Do you know what happened?"

"Of course. I was there." She paused for a moment, as though organizing the story. "Do you know that I knew the man you call Hobey many years ago?"

"Really? No. He didn't say anything about it."

"I was very young. No older than Nicole now. I was an actress. In the cinema. We met in Antibes. At the very villa where you were."

"At Jean Marc's?"

"Yes. But in those days it was owned by an American couple."

"The Blooms."

"Yes. I was there with my mother. Hobey was there with his wife. I could see he was attracted to me. He does not hide his feelings very well."

"No, he doesn't."

"Well, his wife became jealous, and so she started flirting with a Frenchman who was also a guest."

"He wasn't an officer in the Foreign Legion by any chance?"

"I don't know. He might have been. He looked the type. Handsome but a little sinister. You know? Hobey and I met a week or so later in Paris and had a little fling. Nothing too passionate, but a friendly sort of time in bed for a day or so. That was how it was for me, anyway. I think it was something different for him."

"Was he in love with you?"

"I suppose so. He is the kind who falls in love easily."

"I know."

"But his wife ran off with Tommy – that was the Frenchman's name – for a week or so. Whether she found out about us or just did it because she wanted to, I can't say. Hobey was furious. But then it all blew over and people went their separate ways. You know how these things happen, and how they usually end."

"Yes." All too well. Funny how this story sounded so familiar. "I'm surprised he didn't say anything about this the other day."

"Oh, well. Perhaps he thought I'd forgotten. I almost had, you know."

"He didn't go to Cannes – he stayed here because of you."

"I know. I was happy to see him again. It is always good to revive nice memories, no? So the other evening we went to dinner at a popular place here in Lyon. I could tell his old feelings were coming back, but that was all right. I didn't mind. But the worst possible thing happened. There in that very restaurant was Tommy, sitting at the next table."

"Really? A very great coincidence."

"Yes, I suppose so."

"Do you believe in coincidence?"

"Why not? I believe in what I see. And there he was – Tommy, I mean. I can't say who started the fight – it happened so fast. But Tommy is a much bigger man and after a few tables were overturned and people started yelling and screaming, Tommy punched Hobey in the eye and down he went. The police came and all the witnesses said Hobey had started it. I could not deny it. And so they tried to arrest him, but he hit one of the policemen with a champagne bottle and that led to the end of things. One of them hit him with a night stick."

"He's not much of a fighter."

"His temper got the better of him. Besides, he had been drinking. It affects some men that way."

"Yes. They say that when Bogart has a few drinks he thinks he's Bogart."

"Ha, ha! Yes. I understand. I'm surprised you were able to get him out of jail. The police were very angry."

"Friends in high places."

"I see. Well, it helps to be in the movie business." Did I detect some slight irony in her smile? Hard to say. "Would you like some more wine?"

"Yes, thank you."

While she was pouring the wine she had her back to me. The way she stood was meant to be seductive. And it was. It looked very much as though I was about to make a new friend. Well, if I was honest with myself, that was the reason I'd come here. One of them, anyway.

She came back with the wine and sat on the sofa, this time closer to me. The bouquet of the Tavel was nothing by comparison.

"Where are you staying tonight?" she said.

"At the station hotel, I guess."

"How dreary."

"Yes."

"Shall I offer you another idea?"

"Here?"

"Yes. There's plenty of room, and the maid comes at nine. She makes excellent coffee, and she brings fresh brioches and butter."

I remembered just then that someone had said Rosemarie Bertrand was a courtesan. I didn't know what that meant exactly. I wasn't sure whether this offer was a business proposition or simple friendliness. Then of course there was the possibility that she had an eye to getting back into the movie business. If so, what better way to do it? Seduce some chump from Hollywood. But maybe it was nothing more than my boyish charm at work. After all, chemistry does not always require ulterior motives. Does it? But as I looked at her, I frankly didn't care what it was — simple physical attraction or business. If it was business, Marvin Ginsberg's money would never be better spent.

"I like brioche and butter," I said.

"So do I." She reached over and took my hand.

I could hear a car starting in the street below.

"Your driver is leaving," she said.   "Does he know something?"

"Usually."

"Yes, I think so, too. Would you like to see my room?"

She held on to my hand and we went into her bedroom. She was right. There was plenty of room. There was only one bed, but it was twice the size of the standard article.

She turned to me and came into my arms and kissed me, long and perfectly.

"Will you stay with me tonight?" she said, in a fragrant whisper.

"*Here I will dwell, for heaven is in these lips.*"

"How pretty. Where is it from?"

"Marlowe's *Faustus*." I was tempted to say Molière, just to see if she reacted.

"You have said that line to many women, I think."

"Only a few. And never more appropriately than now."

"*Bon.* I like a good lie."

Later –

"What song were you thinking of when I first came in?"

"'Let's Misbehave.'"   She sang in a smoky, throated whisper: "*We're all alone, no chaperone can get our number, the world's in slumber, let's misbehave.*"

"*À votre service, chérie,*" I said.   You pick up these phrases when you travel.

"You should say '*à ton service, chérie.*' Now that we are lovers ... and ... now that you are doing to me ... what you are doing ... there."

"This?"

"Mmm. Yes. That. *Oui.*"

And that's how I learned to use the affectionate second person singular.

Chapter Twenty

"Do you ever think about death?" said Hobey.

"Whenever I go to funerals."

"I think about it," he said, gloomily.

Given his condition, I could believe it. He was probably wishing for it.

"I often think that it's a good thing this whole notion of heaven and hell is nothing more than a fantasy dreamed up by a bunch of ragged shepherds and gloomy monks with piles. To be awake through all eternity? To be conscious, I mean? To sit around on some cloud reliving all the idiotic things you ever did? I don't think so. Not for me. And, even worse, if you're in hell, they're poking you with pitchforks or roasting you on a griddle, while you review your life endlessly – really?"

"Pretty fanciful."

"Yeah. If there's anything at all, it's probably not that dramatic. But *if* there's any afterlife, there will be some punishment either way. I'm sure of that. Maybe it's having to sit through a lousy movie over and over until the end of time. And the only difference is, in heaven the popcorn's free, while in hell the men's room is eternally out of order."

"Which movie do you think it would be?"

"I dunno. Something with Katherine Hepburn. *Little Women*, probably. Well, no thank you. Give me oblivion. Speaking of which, let's get a drink."

We went to a small café near the hotel and sat down outside. There were only a few morning drinkers. Hobey ordered a cognac and I ordered a beer.

"I saw Rosemarie last night," I said.

"How much of her?"

"I don't think I missed anything."

"I suppose she told you about that little fracas in the restaurant."

"Yes."

"No need to go into it further, then."

"Not on my account."

"She's beautiful, isn't she?"

"Yes."

"I remember that she smelled good in the morning. Of course, that was a few years ago."

"She still does."

"Not many people do. I'm no exception, apparently. Women have told me as much. Some women are too frank. Is there a difference between frankness and honesty?"

"There must be. There are two different words."

"Correct. Bravo. Another variation on *le mot juste*." He drank his cognac and ordered another. "I was in love with her once. Rosemarie. And once again a few nights ago. But only briefly. You know Tom Wolfe wrote a book called *You Can't Go Home Again*. It's a good title. I don't know how

169

good a book it is. I do know it's long. But it's the same with women. You can't relive the past. Women forget. They move on. Men are the ones with good memories for love affairs. We have a tendency to remember and brood. 'Alone and palely loitering.' We get stuck in the past. Do you think you'll see her again?"

"Hard to say. It's not likely, under the circumstances."

"No, I suppose not."

"I wouldn't mind, though."

"I can certainly understand."

The "circumstances" were that we were waiting for Klep to pick us up and drive us to Paris. There we'd catch the train to Calais and, from there, the ferry to England. Maybe we'd stay in London a few days. Hobey wanted to see a publisher he said owed him some money, and I was curious whether my friend Amanda was in town. Then we'd take the Pan Am Clipper home. The trip had been a last-minute decision that had a lot to do with Hobey's arrest and the unsubtle suggestion by "Inspector Montpelier" that we clear out of town, while we still had the chance. Besides, I figured I had done what I came to do. I'd found Marvin's dream girl and given her the sad news. Not that she cared. And afterwards she had done what dream girls do. But I could tell myself that Marvin's ghost had no reason to bother me. There was still the question of the Picasso, real or fake. But that would depend on Bunny's evaluation. If it was a fake, there were more than a few possible forgers, most of them hanging around Antibes. But if it was a fake, did I really care who'd painted it? What difference would it make to anyone? It was worthless, and no one even knew it was missing from Marvin's den. I could put it on my office wall next to my

Barbasol calendar. It would remind me every day of a missed opportunity with Nicole and a very fine night with her mother. Either one of them could have posed for the picture. Of course, Marvin had probably spent ten or twenty thousand for it, and had probably paid that to Nicole. But no one was paying me to track down beautiful con artists. And although she made an impression on me, it wasn't that deep. Not deep enough to send me on a fool's errand.

On the other hand, if the painting was a real Picasso, there was a much bigger question – what to do with it? But I put off thinking about that until Bunny made his final evaluation. I more or less hoped it was a fake. That way there'd be no "moral" decision staring me in the face. Moral decisions are usually complicated, and when there is a lot of money involved, they can be difficult. Or easy, depending on how you looked at it.

We could have taken the train to Paris, but I think we both were a little reluctant to say goodbye to Klep, and it really wouldn't take much longer to drive. Klep was glad to do it. He also said that payments were up to date on that route, so there'd be no reason to stop along the way, except if we saw something of interest.

Punctually at ten Klep pulled up in his taxi. There was a large trunk lashed to the roof.

"*Bonjour, mes amis.* I am ready to go. I will put your luggage in what the British call the boot, yes?"

"OK. What's the trunk doing up there?"

"Doing? Nothing. *Il repose.* I am taking it to Paris for a friend. I owe him a favor. So, *voilà!*"

"Does it have two arms and two legs?" said Hobey.

EPITAPH FOR A DREAM

"The trunk or the contents? Ha! You are joking, which is good, after the nights you had. I am what you call pleasantly surprised. But no, when I last saw the contents there was only one arm and one leg. Everything else was missing. This is normal in these situations. It is called distribution. Ha! I am making a joke, too. To be honest, I don't know what's in it. My friend simply asked me to take it, and so I did. The only thing he did say was 'Don't get stopped by the cops.' Ha!"

In a few minutes we were out of the city and on our way north.

"Where shall we stay in Paris?" said Klep.

"No plans," I said.

"I know of a little place on the Rue de la Huchette," he said. "It is the Hotel de Caveau. It is managed by a friend of a friend. A charming residence of artists and writers."

"A dump, then," said Hobey, sourly. "And what's a *Huchette*, anyway? A female huche?"

"Ha! *Très bien*, Monsieur Hobey! Another joke."

"I'm not staying in any Left Bank flea bag. I say we go to the Ritz. I know the bartender there."

"Suits me," I said. Marvin's money was holding up well.

"*Superbe*," said Klep.

"Once we get to the city we can stop and see Sylvia Beach's bookstore. Just to say hello. She'll remember me from the old days."

Then he put his hat over his eyes and fell asleep. Two cognacs did the trick. More than anyone I knew, Hobey got his money's worth from his drinks.

Once again the road ran through the center of every village, town and city. Klep was careful not to arouse the attentions of the local police, but that didn't stop him from waving gaily at every woman he saw on the streets. He made no distinction between young and old, homely and attractive. As much as anyone I ever knew, he was an aficionado of the female species, for its own sake. Woman *qua* woman. Klep's ideas were in stark contrast to Hobey's. Hobey's ideal woman was a misty romantic vision that a real woman would always disappoint and which could only be resurrected and re-established afterwards, by his memory. There he would enshrine her in the gauze of nostalgia. Or the bile of resentment. And then he'd go looking for the next one. Of course, he also had a practical side that had no relation whatever to his imagination. His Hedda Gabler back in LA fit that bill and was nothing more than bed company.

Klep, on the other hand, had no illusions and didn't want any. He dealt only in reality and appreciated all women, regardless of any obvious or subtle deficiencies, deformities or departures from the ideal. If he had any standard it was "One for all and all for one." As for me – well, I could see both sides, and I suppose I preferred some combination of the two. After all, Tavel was neither red nor white, but a nice rosé. And we know what Hemingway said about it. Still, there was the old saying about falling between two stools, and I understand what that meant, too.

Speaking of Hemingway, we arrived in Paris the next day around noon after an uncomfortable night in an auberge owned by a friend of Klep's. Hobey was irritable because the bed in his room had been lumpy and the springs had creaked and groaned throughout the night. Mine was no better. Klep, of course, knew a girl who worked there. She was glad to see him and probably had a better bed, so he greeted us the next morning with a sunny smile.

We arrived around noon and entered the maze of streets that Klep seemed to understand.

"Where did you say you wanted to stop, Monsieur Hobey?"

"At Sylvia Beach's bookstore. It's at 12 Rue de L'Odéon." He turned to me. "This won't take long. I just want to say hello. You'll be pleased to meet her. She was quite the thing in the Twenties. Patron of the writer's art. She gave loans to a lot of struggling scribblers. Not to me, though. Those were 'my salad days when I was green' with money."

"That's good, boss," said Klep. "I will drop you off and then deliver the trunk. By a strange coincidence it is going to the Hotel de Caveau that I spoke about. It's not far from La Rue de L'Odéon."

"What a surprise," I said.

"Yes, isn't it?" said Klep merrily.

"What do you think is in that trunk?" I said when Klep had dropped us at the bookstore and gone off to deliver whatever it was.

"I dunno. With Klep it could be anything – animal, vegetable or mineral. I'm glad we got here without being stopped by the cops. I've had quite enough of French jail cells. Well, let's go say hello to Sylvia."

The bookstore was small and a little shabby and the walls were lined with bookshelves, although one wall was literally covered with framed photographs of authors, famous and otherwise. Mostly otherwise, as far as I could tell. Hobey's eyes lit up when he looked around. He took a deep breath of dusty nostalgia and went over to the wall of pictures. He stared at the wall for what seemed like several minutes.

"Not here anymore. I wonder what happened to it. It used to be here."

At that point a seedy, hungry-looking man emerged from somewhere in the stacks, like a hermit coming out of a cave.

"May I help you?" he said in tones that suggested helping was the last thing on his mind. He wore thick glasses, a shabby cardigan sweater, a flannel shirt and a wool tie. He smelled strongly of tobacco. His fingers were stained yellow and his nails were black. So was his tangled beard. He looked like Rasputin come back to life, partially.

"We've come to say hello to Sylvia."

"Really? How strange. Well, she's not here at the moment. I'm minding the shop."

"Oh. When do you expect her?"

"In a week or so, I suppose. She's visiting friends in the country."

"Oh. That's too bad. How about Adrienne?"

"Well, of course she's with Sylvia." He said this in a waspish tone that suggested a complicated mixture of resentment, suppressed hysteria, superiority and contempt. He was an American who apparently had come to Paris to starve in a garret in the service of his art, and he was plainly successful at the starving part.

Hobey sighed.

"Well, that's disappointing. I guess we'll just look around for a bit. Maybe you could tell her that I stopped. Maybe you could give her a note." Hobey scribbled a short message on one of his cards and handed it to Rasputin.

The man took it, examined it. He obviously did not recognize the name. "I'll be sure to tell her," he said, unconvincingly. Then he scuttled back to wherever he'd come from.

"A writer of unpublished *vers libre*," said Hobey, with a wry smile. "Paris draws them like flies. And they return the favor. Well, since we're here, I just want to check one thing."

I had a feeling what that was.

He searched the dusty stacks for a good fifteen minutes, but did not find what he was looking for.

"Sold out, I guess," he said, putting the best face on it. "Oh, well. 'In a net I gather the breeze.' Have you heard that line?"

"No."

"It's from Petrarch. A kindred spirit. Well, let's go. Klep's parked outside."

He trudged out. His friend from the old days wasn't there, his picture wasn't on the wall, and his book wasn't on the shelves. It was a disappointment, times three. And I knew that, sadly, he was used to it.

Chapter Twenty-One

We got to the Ritz and checked in – a room each for Hobey and me. Marvin paid, bless him. Klep wouldn't stay there. He knew a woman who would be glad to see him.

"She would be hurt if she heard I was in town and didn't stay with her," he said. "But let's have dinner tonight. I know a good place run by friends. It will be our farewell, *n'est-ce pas?*, so we must make it *superbe*. I will come back at seven."

"Let's have a drink," said Hobey after we had checked into our rooms and gotten organized. "I know the bartender."

We went downstairs and into the bar. There were a few very stylish couples seated at the small tables. They were talking quietly. The women were especially attractive, and as usual I began to wonder what they looked like without their clothes. And, as my luscious friend Catherine Moore was fond of saying, her wide eyes all innocence, 'Is that wrong?'

We stood at the bar. The bartender came over.

"Hello, Georges," said Hobey, happily. "It's good to see you. It's been a long time."

EPITAPH FOR A DREAM

Georges smiled professionally. He had no idea who Hobey was, no recollection of him. None. You can always tell that about people. It's not hard. Hobey saw it, too. The blank, not-wishing-to-offend half smile. The last fond memory of Paris was dissolving before Hobey's eyes. But he manfully gave it one more try.

"I'll have my usual, Georges. You remember?"

"I am sorry, sir. Perhaps I am getting old. You know how the memory can go now and then."

"Yes. I do. Well, nice try, Georges," said Hobey, sincerely. "Nice try. I'll have a martini. What'll you have, Riley, Old Sport?"

"The same."

We drank quickly, as though taking medicine. And then we had several more. For a while Hobey didn't say very much. He was brooding a little. It wasn't hard to figure out why. You can't go home again, and apparently you can't go back to Paris, either.

"Who was the Greek philosopher who said you can't step in the same stream twice?" I asked Hobey.

"Heraclitus," he said. "And he was right. Not even in the same stream of consciousness. Ha! A pun, by God! The lowest form of wit. I am devoted to them. Who said 'Whoever would make a pun would pick a pocket'?"

"Doctor Johnson, I suppose," I said.

"A good guess! An inspired guess! But wrong. It was Alexander Pope. Not Pope Alexander. They are two different people. Here's a question for you – which of them was a Catholic? Do you give up? Ha! The answer is – both! It was a trick question. But only one of them was infallible.

The other was a mere poet, like myself. Highly fallible. I leave you to guess which one."

"I thought there was more than one Pope Alexander."

"Could be. It's hard to keep track of them all. I am impressed with your knowledge of Doctor Johnson, though."

"I read a lot," I said.

"I know, Old Sport, I know."

One more martini and Hobey would be asleep in the Ritz Bar. I guessed it wouldn't be the first time. But it was almost seven. Time for dinner.

Klep was sitting in his taxi outside the Ritz main entrance. The trunk was gone.

"Ah, *mes amis*! You have been having a pleasant two hours of *apéritif*. I can see this. *Bon*. Now we go to the place I told you about. It is the *Brasserie Undine*. It is not famous for its cuisine – not yet. But it soon will be. They have only been open for a few years, maybe eight or ten, and it takes time to build the reputation. Is it not? We will go there and order *choucroute* with mugs of foaming beer and talk about the good times we have had together before we must bid one another *bon voyage*. Okay? *Oui!*"

We wound around the narrow streets and crossed over the river and entered into even more narrow streets, many of them dark. It was some sort of industrial section, it seemed.

"I pity the poor Krauts if they even invade Paris," said Hobey. "They'll all get lost trying to find a *pissoir*."

"And Adolf will get his moustache tangled in something at the *Folies Bergère*," said Klep. "He will spend the war with a dancer perched on his nose. But Boches will never come here. It is too dangerous. Especially around this district."

"I hope you're right," I said.

EPITAPH FOR A DREAM

We pulled up outside a small brasserie with a few outside tables and a two sinister-looking couples sitting and smoking. They were dressed for an Apache dance or some sort of gangster costume party. They looked at us suspiciously at first, but then seemed to recognize Klep and nodded noncommittally.

"Let us eat inside," said Klep. "It is cozier."

There were six tables inside and no customers.

"You say this place is up and coming?" said Hobey, dubiously.

"Yes, certainly. It is early in the evening yet. I wanted to get here before the *choucroute* was all gone. *Maman* only makes one batch a day."

The owner was a burly woman with a broad smile of recognition. She hugged Klep and kissed him on both cheeks.

"These are my American friends," he said.

"Welcome, gentlemen."

"She is Alsatian, which is why she understands the secrets of the cabbage."

"I didn't know cabbages had secrets," said Hobey.

"No? I am surprised. But that may be because they are very good at keeping them."

We sat at a corner table while the woman bustled off and returned with mugs of beer.

"We will all have the specialty, *Maman*."

"Of course."

"She is not really my *maman*," he said. "Probably. But she likes it when I call her that. It reminds her of her youth."

We drank our beer and waited. Hobey was a little disappointed with the decor of the restaurant. All the walls

180

were paneled with mirrors, I suppose to make the room look bigger. But that was all. I guess he was expecting posters done by Toulouse Lautrec, or someone. Or maybe Japanese pornographic art. He was even more disappointed when the food arrived.

"What's this?" he said. "It looks like hot dogs on sauerkraut with mustard on the side."

"It is the *choucroute* that I have been telling you about."

"What's the fuss about? I can get this at Nathan's on Coney Island, and get a bun to go with it."

"Ah! I don't think so. Try it and then tell me what you think."

We did. Needless to say it was nothing like a hotdog with sauerkraut. or one thing, the kraut was cooked in wine; you could tell that without any trouble. On top of the bed of kraut were three different kinds of sausage and a circle of boiled potatoes. And the mustard on the side was dark and powerful.

"Good, eh?" said Klep happily.

"Good, yes," I said. Hobey had his mouth full and was chewing with obvious appreciation.

"I stand corrected," he said. "My apologies to the chef. Nathan's never was and never will be like this."

We kept plunging our forks into the kraut and sausage, chewing appreciatively and washing it all down with Alsatian beer. It was good peasant food – hot, filling, delicious.

We were halfway through the dinner when we heard a commotion outside – some sort of scuffling and loud conversation.

"An argument," said Klep, unconcerned. "It is normal in this neighborhood. Not everyone is *très gentil*, like us."

EPITAPH FOR A DREAM

We could hear the sidewalk tables being overturned and a couple of men yelling. Then women starting screaming. The the door burst open and a man dressed all in black with a black beret on his head came rushing in. He was a young man with olive skin. He had a pistol in his hand. He looked wildly to the right and left, and spotted the three of us in the otherwise empty brasserie. He pointed the gun in our direction and fired. The noise was deafening in that little room. The inimitable smell of gun smoke filled the air. The women outside kept screaming and men were shouting. The patroness dropped our refills of beer and jumped back into the kitchen. She moved pretty nimbly for one so fat. I dove to the side of the table and hit the floor. For a moment Hobey was rooted to his chair, stunned and still pretty drunk. But then he hit the floor, too. The gunman fired again. I could see his hand shaking. He was not very good at this, but he was the only one with a gun. Or so I thought. The wooden frame of the mirror above Klep's head was hit and scattered a few splinters. A second or two before and an inch or so lower, and we would have been cut to pieces by shards of glass. The guy's third shot did hit the mirror, and glass flew everywhere. But no one was hit, because by this time all three of us were under the table.

They say in situations like this, time slows down and everyone moves in slow motion. It's not really true. Either your mind goes blank and afterwards you can't remember much of anything, or the surprise and adrenalin rush heightens your awareness, and you see everything as it is happening, and in perfect detail. From my place on the floor I could see Klep's expression change from his usual genial

182

pleasantness into a sudden animal snarl, and he reached in his coat and pulled out his Marine Colt .45 automatic. I'd forgotten about it. He thumbed back the hammer. And this time he was carrying the gun with a round in the chamber. He did not have to work the slide to load it and so was ready for quick action. All he needed to do was cock it. He pointed and fired three shots that sounded almost simultaneous. The gunman in black was knocked back hard against the door jamb, hit by at least one of the shots. A .45 carries an impressive punch. Then he pitched forward on his face. Klep jumped to his feet and ran the few steps to the door to see if there was another gunman anywhere. But no one was outside. The people at the sidewalk tables had all run off, and the street was deserted. After the shocking noise of the gunfire, it was all strangely silent, except for the ringing in my ears.

Klep came back in and looked down at the gunman to make sure of him. He put his foot under the body and rolled it over. There was no need to shoot him again. He was safely dead.

"*Putain*," Klep said and spat on the dead man.

He looked at me and Hobey.

"We had better go," he said. "The noise will bring police. They usually don't like to come to this neighborhood at night, but they feel a responsibility to investigate gun shots. *Eh, bien.*"

Klep reached down and took the man's pistol, examined it with a professional eye and put it in his pocket.

"A souvenir," he said to no one in particular.

"What about the mirror? And the *choucroute*?" Hobey said, absurdly. He was stunned and confused and staring at the dead man.

Klep actually grinned.

"The mirror? Not to worry. Seven years of bad luck for that guy. And the *choucroute*? Well, it's a pity. But when you get home, go to Coney Island and remember the real thing. *Au revoir, maman!*" he shouted.

"Are you all right, Jean Baptiste?" she yelled from the kitchen.

"Yes. He was a novice."

"Thank God."

"And thank the Marines for my pistol. *Semper fi!* Never fear, *maman*. All of this will be taken care of. But we must leave you."

"*A bientôt*, Jean Baptiste," came the voice from the kitchen. "Goodbye, gentlemen. Come back soon."

"Is she serious?" said Hobey

When we were in the taxi and speeding off into the night, Hobey asked the inevitable questions.

"What was that all about? Who was that guy?"

"I don't know," said Klep. He didn't seem overly excited, although he was driving faster than seemed wise. There was no traffic, but we took the corners almost on two wheels. "Maybe someone who wanted the trunk. Or maybe someone from another insurance company. The competition, *n'est-ce pas*? These things happen now and then."

"One of Molière's rivals?" I said.

"Ha! Maybe. What do you think? Racine? Corneille?"

For a moment I was amazed at Klep's literary references, but then it occurred to me that these might very well be the *noms de guerre* of rival gang lords. I was pretty sure we'd never find out.

"What about the body?"

"No problem. The cops will take it away. They will be interested in who he is. Our friends will find out from them. We have good contacts with the police. I am sure he was an amateur, though. Probably his first assignment. Did you see his hand shaking?"

"Yeah."

"It was a good thing. Otherwise, the mirror would be in one piece, and I would not. But he was a punk. This is the correct word, no?"

"Yes."

"Our friends will send someone to clean up the brasserie. They'll be able to reopen tomorrow, and people will hear what happened there and want to come and see. People like to look at other people's bloodstains. It will all be good for *maman's* business. Perhaps she will get a Michelin star out of it. So, all's well that ends well. Have you heard this saying?"

"Yes. It's from Shakespeare."

"Truly? I have heard of him. 'To be or not to be, that is the question.' We answered that punk's question, *n'est-ce pas*? Ha! *Superbe*."

Chapter Twenty-Two

"What do you suppose was in that trunk?" said Hobey, when we were back at the Ritz. Klep had dropped us off with a promise to return in the morning to take us to the train station.

"I imagine we'll never know."

"It reminds me of Alfred Hitchcock. He's a Brit director. Heard of him?"

"Heard of him, yes."

"Well, he talks about a device he calls a MacGuffin. Something that people want, something that drives the action of the movie. It might be an attaché case or an artifact or that kind of thing. But you don't ever really know why they want it. They just do. And the thing is, it doesn't really matter what it is or what's in it. The action and the search are what matters."

"So Klep's trunk could be a MacGuffin."

"Yes. That's what I was thinking. I'm going to remember it. It could come in handy the next time I write a treatment for a picture."

In many ways Hobey was a like a magpie. He would pick up anything that might seem useful or interesting, even though most of the time it turned out not to be.

"Making connections between unconnected things is the source of creativity," he said.

"Thank you, professor. Shall we visit Georges for a nightcap?"

"Why not? Tonight's our last night in *la belle France*," said Hobey. He sighed without any melodrama. "It didn't exactly turn out like I thought. This trip, I mean. I certainly wouldn't write it this way."

"No, you'd do a better job."

In his version the hero would find the girl and take her rapturously to bed, and old friends would all remember him and welcome him back, and the book written long before would still be displayed in the window of Sylvia's bookstore under his picture and a placard saying "Best Seller. Highly Recommended." Even the bartender at the Ritz would remember just how the hero liked his martini, and he would make one and deliver it without being asked, and with a smile that was actually genuine.

"Thanks, Old Sport," he said. "I'd like to believe you're right."

Then I thought that version of the story might only be his first draft. Maybe later when he thought about it, the second draft would have an equal measure of disappointment and disappearances. As he said, he was always gathering breezes in a net.

And then I wondered how I would look back on the trip. We'd been shot at. That wasn't so good. But the guy missed, so all it cost me was a little adrenalin. Other than that, I had no complaints. I'd done what I came to do. Marvin's dream girl turned out to be a crook, most likely, but he was past caring. And the night with Rosemarie was a bonus. She might be involved in this little crime business. It wouldn't surprise me at all. But I didn't care. Not really. And even if I did care, what was I supposed to do about it? I don't think I was rationalizing, although I've always been good at that. I did enjoy staying at the Ritz in Paris and the Carlton in Cannes. There was no telling when or if I'd get to do that again. So, all things considered, it had been a good trip. And I still had a fair amount of the five thousand left. I'd think about what to do about that later.

The next morning Klep arrived right on time and drove us to the Gare du Nord, the station for the train to Calais. There we would catch the ferry to Dover.

"I would take you to Calais in the taxi, *mes amis*, but I find I am called back to the south."

"Trouble about last night?"

"Eh? Oh, no. Nothing like that." And he said no more about it.

"Any idea who the guy was?"

"Not really. The cops are still thinking about it. If his fingerprints are not on file, it will take some time. After a week or so, some woman will wonder why Pierre still hasn't come home, and she'll start to ask questions. Then it will unravel."

We didn't say much on the way to the station. No one likes endings, unless they're love affairs gone stale and tiresome. Then the ending can't come soon enough.

When we were at the station and got our luggage from the boot, Klep grabbed us one by one and gave us each a garlicky kiss on both cheeks.

"*Bon voyage, mes amis,*" he said. "Perhaps we will meet again someday. I hope so."

"Me, too," I said. I wasn't sure I meant it. But I might have.

He got back in the taxi. "One last thing to think about, my friends. I heard something this morning. It is possible that fellow last night was not aiming at me." He wiggled his eyebrows meaningfully. "*À bientôt. Semper fi.*"

And he drove away, waving his left hand out the window.

"What do you suppose he meant by that?" said Hobey.

"What else could he mean? If the guy wasn't after Klep, who was he after? We were the only ones in the restaurant."

"A mistake?"

"Doesn't sound like it."

"But why?"

"Anybody mad at you?"

"Just my wife. But that's nothing new. Maybe a critic. But I don't get it."

"Elementary, my dear Watson. The painting."

When you thought about it for even a minute or so, it really wasn't much of a mystery. Aside from our various friends named Molière, the only people we had met on this trip, the only people who might have something to hide they wanted to protect, were people somehow connected to Nicole and, through her, to the Picasso. Nicole herself, her boyfriend, her mother, Jean Marc – and maybe some others. The painting was the common denominator. If it was a forgery, someone had a motive for keeping us from finding out. Maybe the forger was turning out one Picasso a month and selling them through Nicole – or Rosemarie or Jean Marc – to gullible art collectors willing to take a risk on a possible Picasso at a bargain price. Maybe the forger was Jean Marc himself, or maybe it was Nicole's latest boyfriend. Or maybe someone else entirely.

On the other hand, if the painting was genuine, that meant it had been stolen – stolen most likely from the inattentive and indifferent Jean Marc who would not even notice the thing was gone. In that scenario, most likely Nicole and her boyfriend took the painting and sold it to lovesick Marvin. And did Jean Marc have other Picassos stacked against the walls in his villa? Or a hastily dashed off drawing that might bring serious money? What about works from Jean Marc's other famous artist friends? Was the sale to Marvin just one part of an ongoing business? Or just a one-time opportunity that Nicole saw and took advantage of?

Either way, there was a crime involved – either art fraud or art theft. And, either way, Nicole had to be in on it. Otherwise, why would she grab her boyfriend and run away? I had shown up poking around, asking questions, maybe getting too close to the truth. There was enough money involved to make it worth someone's while to put us, or rather me, out of the way. Or at least try to scare me off the scent. The fact that it was a cheap hitman who wasn't up to the job didn't change the facts. And there was no getting around it – if Klep hadn't been there with his .45, the hitman might have succeeded. It was even possible that the hitman *was* a professional. If they were only trying to scare us away, maybe he didn't want to hit us. Too bad or him that Klep objected to bullets aimed in his general direction. So, as they say, *quelle surprise.*

"What does that have to do with me?" said Hobey.

"Nothing. The way I see it, the guy was after me."

"Really?"

"That's the way it looks. I guess I touched a nerve on somebody down there on the Riviera. I don't know whose. Could be several people. Maybe all of them together. If the gunman had been a better shot, maybe you and Klep would be trying to find a spot for me in Père Lachaise."

"I doubt they'd accept you there. But we certainly would have tried, Old Sport."

"Good to know."

"You know what famous person is buried there?"

"Don't tell me – Molière?"

"Got it in one."

"Really?"

"Yep."

"Well, that's what you call a coincidence."

"Straight out of Dickens."

"You seem a little perkier, now that we think I was the target, not you."

"Somewhat. But not completely. After all, the guy they sent could have hit any of us."

"Well, for your sake I hope the next guy's a better shot."

"So do I."

We could be cavalier about it, but I have to say I was glad to be getting out of France. I didn't think whoever had ordered the shooting would bother going after us – or me – once we were safely gone. This didn't seem like the work of an efficient criminal organization. And I was pretty sure that if professional mobsters were involved, Klep and his friends, including Inspector Montpelier, would have heard something about it. They were well connected.

So this was strictly amateur hour, and the amateurs were probably as glad to see me gone as I was to *be* gone. And maybe they figured taking a few shots at me would be enough to scare me off. From their point of view it would certainly seem that way. After all, I was leaving the country in somewhat of a hurry. They only thing they hadn't figured on was Klep and his .45. So the dead guy might be a troubling loose end, depending on who he was and where they got him. And even amateur crooks don't like loose ends. Unlike professionals, though, amateurs aren't sure what to do about them. But I had the feeling that once I stopped poking my nose where it didn't belong, nothing more would be said or done. As long as they stayed in France, they could figure they were safe.

I did wonder, though – was I so bad an actor that the crooks, whoever they were individually or collectively, saw through my cover story? There was nothing about my story that was inherently implausible. Nothing at all. Hell, anyone could actually *be* a Hollywood producer. All it takes is a telephone and some business cards. It was an easier business to get into than private investigation. A private dick at least needs a license. Being a *successful* producer was something else entirely. But anyone could rent an office, hang out a shingle and sit by a telephone that never rings – until the savings run out. So what tipped them off about me? Why else would they take a shot at me? What would be the point of shooting some random Hollywood producer scouting locations?

Was it Hobey? Had he somehow blown the cover? Was it the night he got hammered, first by martinis and then by the Legionnaire and the cops? Did he say something that aroused Rosemarie's suspicions? Would he remember, if I asked? She didn't indicate anything to me that night I spent with her. Was she swept away by my good looks and boyish charm, or was she just a good actress? Was her enigmatic smile the smile of a femme fatale contemplating an unsuspecting victim? Could she possibly have been ... pretending? Did she order the hit or just accidentally drop the fact that I was really a private dick? And if she didn't order it, who did? As much as I didn't want to believe it, an old song kept coming back to me: "It Had To Be You."

It would seem I was leaving France with more questions than answers. But that was OK with me, because I guess it really didn't matter in the long run. In the long run, of course, nothing does.

"I was wondering. Did you by any chance mention anything to Rosemarie about the real reason we were there?"

"I don't think so. I don't remember saying anything. Why?"

"Just wondering."

Chapter Twenty-Three

"Where shall we stay in London?" said Hobey. "Any preferences?"

"What's the old song? 'Stomping and the Savoy'? Let's try there."

"I don't think the song's about a London hotel. More like some jazz joint in Harlem."

"You prejudiced?"

"Not me. I love all God's chillen. Even the English, although they don't make it easy. The Savoy it is. I hear good things about the Grill."

It took us a full day to get to Calais, cross the Channel and then get to London by train. The London train was crowded and our compartment smelled of fish and chips. A young woman and a ten-year-old boy were stuffing themselves, each holding a greasy-looking newspaper wrapping shaped like a cone.

Hobey asked them, "I've often wondered – does the news print rub off on the chips? And, if so, does it add to or detract from the taste?"

They looked at him blankly and went on eating. The mother apparently did not recognize Hobey's accent. Maybe she wondered if he was a German spy.

"Don't talk to strangers, Alfie," she said.

"Aside from lining the bottom of a canary cage, that is the best use of newspapers," said Hobey, "don't you think?"

Alfie and his mother ignored him and kept eating.

"They must be journalists," said Hobey to me. "Or worse, book critics."

We got to Victoria Station around ten o'clock and took a taxi to The Savoy. Fortunately, I'd had the concierge at the Ritz in Paris make reservations for us. The Savoy was fully booked. The London streets were also full of people, some just emerging from the theaters. Others were young couples seeing the sights. Many of the men were in uniform. The youngsters were having a good time, but I noticed a lot of the older people looked grim-faced and worried. They were the kind who read newspapers and listened to the "wireless." Many were old enough to remember the last war and were worried about what the next one might bring.

The night air was thick with smoke or fog or some combination, so that the lights along the Strand were ghostly and diffused. The little Savoy Theater that was in the same courtyard as the hotel was offering "Henry the Fifth."

"'Once more unto the breach, dear friends,'" quoted Hobey.

"Shouldn't it be 'into' the breach?"

"Maybe. But Shakespeare said 'unto.' He struggled with spelling. But he could write a rousing speech, when he felt like it."

"I'm afraid they'll be needing some of that again."

"I think so, too. But you know Herr Hitler is likely to find the Brits have plenty of it left, bless 'em."

We checked in and went to our rooms.

"I'm going to order a bottle of Scotch and get well," said Hobey. "It's been a long day."

The next morning I phoned Bunny's club, Bellamy's. He had told me to contact him there when and if we came to London. The phone was answered by the porter.

"Mr. Finch-Hayton is not here at the moment," said the porter. "I do expect him this morning. May I give him a message?"

"Yes. This is Mr. Fitzhugh," I said. "Please tell him that I'm at The Savoy."

"Very good, sir."

I had two reasons for wanting to see Bunny. First, of course, he was the key to whether the Picasso was genuine or a forgery. His opinion carried great weight in art circles, and if he authenticated it, Picasso himself couldn't deny it – Picasso who turned out so many pieces of art that he gave some away and probably forgot some as soon as he did them. The other reason was Bunny was my only means of finding Amanda Billingsgate. She was attached somehow to the Foreign Office. She had some kind of shadowy, ill-defined role. She could be back in London or somewhere else in England, or still be in Berlin, in the British embassy there. That was the last posting I knew of and the place she went when she left me in Los Angeles. It hadn't been that long ago, but with tensions so high between the two countries the embassy there might already be closed. Bunny would know where she was, if it was possible to know.

I had breakfast in the hotel, then wandered along the Thames Embankment for a couple of hours. The river was brown and crowded with the noises and smells of river traffic. I couldn't help thinking that all these barges and small freighters would make excellent targets for the Luftwaffe. Slow, ponderous, ungainly. On the other hand, it was hard to believe this peaceful scene of everyday life could or would be "changed and changed utterly." I remembered hearing that phrase somewhere. But I couldn't place it. Hobey would know, I suppose, but it wasn't important.

Toward noon, I met him in the lobby of the hotel. If he had gotten well on the bottle of Scotch, it didn't look like it.

"It must not have been very good Scotch," he said, rather bleary-eyed. "I don't feel myself this morning."

"No doubt they serve an inferior type here at the Savoy. You should write a letter."

"I may, once my hand stops shaking. What are you up to today?"

"Hoping to meet Bunny. You?"

"I'm going to stop by my English publisher's. I am sure he owes me money. I intend to surprise him in his lair. Give him no chance to escape. These publishers are tricky fellows."

We stopped by the front desk for messages. There was one from Bunny asking me to meet him for lunch at Bellamy's at one o'clock.

It was a pleasant day. The sun was out as much as it ever is in London, and we decided to walk. We were going in the same direction. We wandered down the Strand to Trafalgar Square.

"There's a very nice bookshop along Piccadilly," said Hobey. "I think I'll go that way and stop in and have a look."

Well, I knew what he was looking for, so I said goodbye and walked down Pall Mall to the corner of St James's Street, where I turned right. I'd tell my secretary, Della, I'd walked along a street named after her favorite cigarette. She'd get the joke.

Bellamy's was only a block or so up St James's. Precisely at one I went up the steps and into the reception area. I announced myself at the porter's desk.

"Mr. Finch-Hayton is in the library on the third floor. He is expecting you, sir."

The library was deserted except for Bunny. The room looked almost exactly like Bunny's office at UCLA – furnished with leather club chairs made soft and shapeless from decades of use, walls lined with books, of course, a Persian carpet with a few discreet cigar burns, sporting prints where there were no bookshelves, the smell of good tobacco. Bunny was sitting in one of the leather chairs reading *The Telegraph*. He looked up when I came in and seemed to be delighted. Then, again, you could never tell with Bunny.

"Riley! Welcome to London. Good to see you. Take a pew. I thought it would be better to meet up here before lunch. No one ever comes into the library except the older members, and they're all deaf." He stood up and we shook hands. A lot of Englishmen, especially the upper classes, dislike this American habit. But Bunny had acquired it, or at least gotten used to it, in LA.

"Nice room," I said. "It reminds me of your office."

"Not an accident. We have quite a good selection of books on fishing, if you're interested. There's a first edition Izaac Walton. And a very nice edition of Plunkett Greene, the opera singer."

"The singing angler?"

"The same."

"Another time," I said. "How's the authentication business?" "Was the Tintoretto real?"

"The Tintoretto? Ah! You remember that. Well, yes. I think so."

And I knew then that the Tintoretto story had been a cover for something else that brought him to London.

"Not a very good one, I'm afraid. But still worth a small fortune. How are things in Xanadu?"

"Unchanged. Stately pleasure domes as far as the eye can see."

"Did you ever find Marvin Ginsberg's dream girl?"

"As a matter of fact, I did. And a whole lot more."

For the next five minutes or so I gave him the outlines of our adventures, including the shooting.

"No harm done?"

"No. He was a poor shot."

"Yes. Or a good one."

"Yes, that occurred to me, too. Later."

"Have you heard of this fellow Winston Churchill?"

"No."

"You will, I think. One of our politicians. Has the right idea about the Nazis. Knows they can't be trusted. Anyway, as a young man he served in the Boer War and saw some action. He says, 'Nothing is so exhilarating as being shot at and missed.' Rather good, I think. That may not be the exact quote, but it's the gist. Was he right?"

"Well, I can understand that, coming from a soldier. But I was sitting in a restaurant eating a frankfurter and sauerkraut. There was nothing exhilarating about any of it."

"Ah. I suppose not. Lucky the French mafia was there."

"Yes."

"I have a feeling we might find them useful, too – assuming the worst happens in France."

"Meaning what?"

"Meaning the Germans invade. And not only invade, but set up permanent shop."

"What about the Maginot Line?"

"Yes. What about it? That is the question, along with, 'What about the French army?' They pride themselves on their readiness. Let's just hope they're right. But if not, it's wise to prepare for the worst."

"Occupation? Seems unlikely."

"Yes. I agree. But we're in the unlikely business here, in my shop. We're supposed to think of things that might happen and then think what to do about them. If the worst happens in France and the Huns overrun the country, or even if they only manage to slice off a piece, it will be good for us to have local friends who know their way around the underworld. Potential Fifth Columns, you see. We might very well ask you for a contact or two."

"I know the perfect man, if it comes to that."

"Good. We'll need people like that."

I noticed that he used the word "we." If he hadn't been in the game before, when he was in California, he was pretty clearly in it now.

"I'm sort of surprised you don't know them all already."

"It never hurts to be sure. Besides, no one knows all of them. They wouldn't be very good at their business if we did."

"I don't suppose you have any more information on the Picasso."

"I've sent a few letters to my friends in France, but their replies were inconclusive. Picasso is very prolific."

"So I've learned."

"And so are his imitators, and I use that word loosely."

"I've learned that, too."

"The thing is, I don't think I'll be coming back to UCLA for a while. I've asked for, and they've given me, a leave of absence, so that I can stay here and make myself useful."

"I always thought you were a spy, Bunny."

"Did you?"

"Yes. But I suppose that means you won't be able to give me an answer on the Picasso."

"I'm afraid not. I'm sorry."

"I understand. Duty calls."

"Well, yes, as a matter of fact, it does. But I do have an idea for you. There's a colleague of mine in LA – well, he's not really a colleague, because he doesn't work for anyone. An eccentric sort of a bird, but a wealthy one. He's quite a collector. And a legitimate expert in Modernists. I have every confidence that he can give you as good an evaluation as I could."

"Really?"

"Well, almost. Certainly he can give you a solid appraisal. And I am sure his verdict would be accepted by the market, almost unanimously. He's very well known. I have written to him and told him about your project, and he's agreed to take a look at the painting and give you his opinion. His name is Jonathan Woodhouse. He lives in Beverly Hills, as you might expect. My secretary is aware of this, and aware that you will be calling for the painting in my safe. So – I hope that helps. And, once again, I apologize for having to bow out."

"Not at all. As you said, duty calls."

"Yes. She's a harsh mistress, but worth the trouble."

"Speaking of that ...."

"Amanda?"

"Of course."

"I thought you'd ask about her. Well, there's bad news, I'm afraid."

"Uh-oh."

"Yes. She's disappeared. She was working in our embassy in Berlin. But she left work one day and has not been seen again."

"Do you think there was foul play?"

"Almost certainly. The question is, on whose part?"

There had always been a mystery about Amanda Billingsgate. She had been married to an attaché at the British consulate in Los Angeles, and one night after a costume party she shot her husband between the hairline and the eyebrows. The verdict was "accidental." There was some doubt about that, though, because diplomatic pressures were applied and there was every effort to suppress the story. It was the kind of damage control that made you think there was more going on than anyone would admit. There was also the problem of motive – she had one, at the very least. Maybe more. First of all, she didn't like her husband very much. That motive has been more than enough throughout the history of the world. But she was also having an affair with a handsome German diplomat.

When that petered out, she and I had something of a fling. We had a few nights of champagne dinners followed by some really excellent shagging. Whether that was in exchange for my help in extricating her from possible murder charges... well, that was still an open question in my mind. But I have to admit I was sorry to see her go when she was transferred to the British embassy in Berlin.

With her connection to her German lover, there was always the suspicion that she might be tempted to go over to the other side. There were plenty of English people, especially in the upper classes, who thought that Hitler had some good ideas. She might have been on the other side all along.

"Did you ever decide which team she was playing for?" I asked Bunny. I didn't really expect an answer, but I thought he might throw me some oblique indication.

"Nothing definite. We just don't know. But we're looking into the whole question of her disappearance. So far, no leads. This just happened last week."

"What is it you Brits say? – Bloody hell!"

"Yes. I'm sorry. I know you and she became fond of each other."

"A little, yes. It sounds serious. Her vanishing like this, I mean."

"I'm afraid it is. If she was on their team, she's probably gone to ground. If she was on our team, they might have discovered it. Needless to say, they are not the sort of people who pay attention to international law, customs or rules when it comes to things like espionage. If the Gestapo grabbed her, I'm afraid she is, or soon will be, just a memory."

The thought of her lovely face and body at the mercy of Hitler's sadists was ugly beyond words.

"What if she was playing on both teams?"

"Then there would be two sets of people who would be annoyed with her. I'm afraid the Germans would treat her more harshly than we would. For her sake I hope we find her first, even if she's a double. The people I'm with aren't directly involved in the investigation, you understand. So I don't know anything for certain."

Of course.

"But you hear things."

"Oh, well, one can't help hearing things."

"Will you let me know if you hear something definite?"

"If I can. Yes, if I can." He reached over and patted me on the knee. "I'm sorry, old boy. I was fond of her, too."

His use of the past tense was as much as I was going to get from him. And just about as much as I needed.

"And now what would you say to a spot of luncheon?"

"Truth is, I'm not very hungry."

"That's just as well. The food here is appalling."

Chapter Twenty-Four

It was tea-time at the Savoy, and Hobey and I were observing it in the bar with a couple of martinis.

"'What can ail thee, knight at arms, alone and palely loitering?'" said Hobey brightly. He had apparently recovered from his hangover. "Tragic moping is supposed to be my role. You're looking a little peaked."

"Do you remember Amanda Billingsgate?" I said.

"Of course. Brown eyes, blonde hair, lovely shape. Reminded me somehow of butterscotch."

"Yes. Me, too. Well, she's disappeared, somewhere in Germany. I wouldn't be surprised if we don't see her, or even hear of her, ever again. She's got herself mixed up in something. Espionage of some kind. And someone apparently found out about it."

"Bunny told you?"

"Not in so many words. But you know Bunny."

"Yes. He's always been a downy bird."

"Yes, he has. He's involved in something to do with intelligence. He's staying here, because of the war. Everyone knows it's coming."

"Do you think he knows more than he's saying – about Amanda?"

"He knows more than he's saying about everything. As you say – a downy bird, although I don't quite understand that expression."

"Neither do I, but I like it. But didn't you and Amanda have ...?"

"A bit of a fling? Yes. There wasn't enough time for it to develop into anything more. Still ...."

"Yes. I understand. What do you think we should do now? Aside from getting a refill."

"Head for home. Bunny gave me the name of a guy who can help with the Picasso. Bunny's staying here to fight the Huns, and Amanda is ... gone. No reason for us to stay. Did you get your money from the publisher?"

"Yes. I bearded him in his lair. I made him open his books. He resisted, but I persisted and in the end he surrendered. I am quite proud of myself. I extracted every penny of the money due to me. Here is a check for three pounds, seven shillings, three pence, the payment for ten years of English royalties on my last book. Or should I say 'most recent book.' I'd hate to think it was my last."

"Three pounds and change?"

"Yes. Something like fifteen dollars in our money. Not a bonanza, I confess. But it's the principle of the thing. Do you think we can get a decent dinner for that? My treat."

"Maybe for one of us."

"Then I shall treat you, and you shall treat me. Now... how shall we go home? How about an ocean voyage? Perhaps you will meet some fascinating woman and fall in love. Erase all melancholy memories. I picture you in a white dinner jacket meeting the beautiful stranger along the rail of the ship. You offer her your coat to protect her against the chill of the evening breeze. You light her cigarette. The stars shimmer. In the main salon the orchestra is playing Cole Porter. And so on. The screenplay will write itself, though I will help it along. Who should play you? Tyrone Power? Cary Grant? Bela Lugosi?"

"The way things have been going, I would meet a beautiful stranger, and she would fall overboard somewhere in the mid-Atlantic."

"Tut, tut. Self-pity does not become you."

"No. You're right, no one likes a private dick who whimpers. Even so, I suggest we take the Clipper. It'll be faster. I'm starting to miss the palm trees of LA. And I'm sure you're ready to get back to Hedda."

"Ah, Hedda. The Miss Lonleyhearts of the City of Angels. I wonder how many poor souls she's driven to suicide with her inane answers to their heartbreaking questions. She's really a marvel. I've never known anyone so immune to human suffering and despair. She swims every day in a sea of her readers' misery and emerges unaffected and serene. I admire her immensely, even though she looks frightful in the morning and says 'I' when she should say 'me' and vice versa."

"Grammatical mistakes can kill romance."

"Oh, yes. Our friend Bunny once told me he dropped a woman because she mispronounced 'mauve.' That's not a grammatical problem, but the point is similar."

"Yes, he was very extravagant. But in Hollywood he could afford to be."

EPITAPH FOR A DREAM

"And speaking of vice versa, did I tell you the story of our Garden of Allah chum, Dottie Parker, who was asked one time why she was looking so tired and haggard? She said she was 'too fucking busy and vice versa.' Pretty good. Dottie's quite a girl. Not my type, however. Word is she's got a bit of a thing for Hemingway."

I recognized that Hobey's carefree attitude was partly an attempt to jolly me out of my dark mood. It was hard to stay gloomy around him, either because he was always gay and carefree and excited about his next project, even though he suspected it was doomed to failure, or he was so moody and depressed himself that you felt good by comparison. When he was drinking, his moods could go either way, or both.

Well, I said to myself, *Amanda is gone. There is nothing I can do about it.* I certainly had no ridiculous thoughts about going to look for her, no absurd fantasies of rescuing her. She was a big girl who made her own decisions. And the use of the past tense was apparently appropriate. Well, that's how it goes sometimes. As the aforementioned Cole Porter said, "It was great fun, but it was just one of those things." Then I wondered – did I really believe that?

I guess. Pretty much. But it was a damned shame, all the same.

The next day we caught the Pan Am Clipper from London to New York. From there it was a series of puddle jumpers to LA, with the usual miserable and frustrating delays because of weather and mechanical problems. This was no life for a Presbyterian. But we finally did make it to LA, and we returned gratefully to the Garden of Allah Hotel, where the same writers and a few transient actors were standing

208

around the pool, drinking and enjoying the fading sunlight, or ignoring it.

"Home, sweet home," said Hobey.   "Just smell the hibiscus and bougainvillea."

"Hibiscus and bougainvillea don't have any fragrance," I said.

"Not to you, perhaps," he said.   "Did you know that Tahitian women wear a hibiscus blossom behind the ear to advertise their availability?"

"Temporary or permanent?"

"Temporary. Tahiti is known to be a paradise."

"Sort of like the real *Dame aux Camélias*."

"Quite right, Old Sport. Good call. You have profited from your European travels the way we are told people should. You have come back an enlightened man. Bravo. And do you see any exotic women by the pool wearing a flower?"

"No, but there's a fat guy in a sombrero."

"Yes. A writer. You can tell because everything about him is sagging. It's good to be back." He took a dramatically deep breath and sighed. "And look there, just across the way. Miss Lonleyhearts in the flesh. And little else. Perfect! Not Hedda, *qua* Hedda, you understand, but Hedda as personification of the whole human comedy, there on a chaise longue, before our very eyes, chewing gum and answering prayers. This calls for a drink."

So we drank too much that night. The regulars were all glad to see us again. Even Hedda, more or less. One of the regular writers arrived later with three fifths of a mariachi band she'd picked up in a diner on Sepulveda, and they

209

played for tequila. Two writers and an assistant producer had a swimming race and nearly drowned. A couple of would-be starlets came by and took off their tops, hoping to be noticed. They were, but not by anyone interested in their acting. It was good to be home.

Hedda and I had to help Hobey to bed.

"Say, how long were you guys gone?" she said, as we staggered up the stairs to the bungalow she shared now and then with Hobey.

"About four weeks," I said.

"Gee, I'm surprised. Time flies, huh?"

"There speaks the modern-day Penelope," said Hobey. "Would you wait twenty or even ten years for me to return, my darling?"

"Not on your life, buster," she said.

"And who could blame you?" he said. "Such a blossom could not be allowed to wither away unappreciated, if not to say, un-smelled."

She giggled.

"Isn't he cute?" she said to me. I think she was serious.

The next morning was not as bad as I expected. I took an early swim while the rest of the regular hotel guests were still unconscious. That revived me enough to get dressed and go to the office. I had a lot of catching up to do.

Della wasn't there. I couldn't remember if this was one of her half days, or not. She more or less came and went whenever she wanted. Time would tell.

I called Kowalski.

"Where you been, shamus?" he said.

"In Europe assessing the situation for Roosevelt."

"Whadja tell him?"

"That it's a long way away. And the people there talk in strange tongues. Best to stay on this side of the pond."

"I'm with you there. I see all the foreigners I need just driving through Chinatown."

"Anything new on the Ginsbergs?"

"Yeah, we found the hit and run Hudson in a body shop in Yuma. The guy dropped it off and never came back for it. We got a description but nothing else. No prints in the car. Nothing."

"How long ago?"

"Three weeks or so. The guy could be anywhere and back by now."

"How about Ginsberg?"

"You know what Hemingway said in that story."

"Tavel goes best with love?"

"Huh? No – *nada*. *Nada* is *nada* is *nada*, or something like that. Which means *nothing* to you who ain't bilingual."

"I see you're keeping up with your reading group."

"Next week we're doing A. A. Milne."

"Are you really still investigating the Ginsberg cases, or are they too cold to bother with?"

"Well, the wife is definitely listed as an accident, although most of us figure it wasn't. And the husband was probably shot by people covering up the hit. We tried to find another motive, but no dice. It seems the guy was well liked in Hollywood. Hadn't screwed anybody in years. Not in business, I mean. So technically his case is still open, but you know what happens as time goes by."

"Sounds like a song title."

"As a matter of fact, it is. My wife sang it in our little theater last year. It's from a Broadway play called 'Everybody's Welcome.'"

"Can she sing?"

"That depends what you mean by 'sing.'"

"My God, Kowalski, what has become of you? A reading club *and* little theater?"

"It keeps the home fires quiet."

"The other guys know about your secret life?"

"No, and they ain't going to. If they should happen to hear about it, you and I are gonna have a talk."

"Good to know. And ideas about the missing twenty thousand?"

"No, that's been a dead end, too. We figure it's tied somehow to the hit, but there's no way to prove it."

"That seems way too high for a standard hit."

"No kidding. You offer to pay five hundred for a hit and five hundred to disappear and you'd have fifty guys lining up to do it. So where'd all that the money go?"

"I guess that's the question." And in this case, I had an answer. Probably *the* answer. But it was too soon to let Kowalski in on it. In fact, it might *always* be too soon, for a couple of reasons. "So in the time I was gone, all you guys got was a dented Hudson."

"That's about the size of it. And we got a garage guy in Yuma who is the happy owner of a fairly new two-door coupe, only slightly used. The fact that it killed some woman don't bother him."

"Not superstitious."

"I guess not. The guy who dropped it off ain't coming back for it, that's for sure. And we got no reason to keep it.

212

Besides, the last time I checked, Yuma is in Arizona, which ain't exactly our jurisdiction."

"How about the Feds? The guy crossed state lines."

"They ain't interested. Too busy looking for Nazis, Japs and commies. The Arizona state boys helped us out, and they'd probably do it again if we asked nice and polite, but the car's clean and Ma Ginsberg's death is now officially an accident, so what's the point?"

"I'm surprised the guy didn't just leave the car alongside the road somewhere."

"He probably planned to, but he ran out of gas in that stretch of desert on the California side of the river. You don't want to be walking around out there. Not in the summer sun. The guy from the Yuma garage just happened to be driving by and towed him in. Never saw him again. Said he talked kind of funny."

"They talk funny in Chicago."

"New Jersey, too."

"How do you figure he got out of Yuma?"

"The gray dog bus to anonymous."

"Well, thanks. I'll be in touch."

"Like you said, good to know."

Chapter Twenty-Five

Next I called Catherine Moore. She still went by her maiden name because she was pretty sure that someday she'd be divorced, so why change once and then have to change back?

"Who wants to be known as Manny Stair's wife forever," she said, "even after you ain't Manny's wife anymore? Not me. Plus, it's best for my career. You think Betty Grable changes her name every time she gets married or divorced or something?"

She picked up on the second ring, a pretty good indication that she was alone and maybe expecting a call from someone not named Manny.

"Hello, beautiful," I said.

"Sparky! Well, if this isn't a pleasure, I don't know what is. But just to be sure, to which Sparky am I speaking to, huh?"

"Sparky the Detective, home from Europe."

"I knew that. I was only pulling your chain."

"Sounds good."

This was our well-rehearsed routine, always the same banter. But I was never positive that she really recognized my voice at first.

"Guess what I'm wearing," she cooed.

"Well, it's ten in the morning, so I'm guessing ... nothing."

"Wrong. It's a Rolex with diamonds. Manny gave it to me this morning before he left and just after the morning schtup. He said since I was always late I needed a good watch to keep track of how late I was."

"Manny is nothing if not thoughtful."

"I know."

"I'm surprised you didn't already have a watch, all encrusted with diamonds."

"I do, but you have to wind it. And I always forget. I look at it and it's always the same time. This new one winds itself. Don't ask me how. I'm just about to have my shower. I want to see if it's waterproof."

"See if what's water proof?"

"You know," she purred. "I'm pretty sure it is. Want to come over and get sudsy with me?"

"Nothing I'd like more, but I've been away so long that I have a bunch of things to do."

"More important than playing pick up the soap? After being away so long I'd think that would be the first thing on your mind. I suppose you were unfaithful to me with those foreign girls."

"Yes, I was. I lost count. Do you forgive me?"

"Why not? How were they?"

"Nothing compared to you, my darling."

"Smooth talker. Do they shave their legs?"

"Only up so high."

"Well, like the man said, you have to learn to take the rough with the smooth. Ha, ha."

I thought about making a reference to Chaucer's beard jokes, but Catherine wasn't much interested in Middle English literature, and a joke you have to explain isn't a joke. Besides, she'd just tell me I was showing off, which would be true. She could spot a phony a mile off.

"Are you planning to go out to the *Lucky Lady* anytime soon?" I said.

"Oh, I don't know.   I'm always welcome, so there's no particular schedule, you know?   I usually go after Manny's given me a new present."

"Like today?"

"Sure.   It's the best way to make Tony jealous, so he has to come up with quality goods, you know?   He'll see this watch and turn green with envy. 'Course, he's always pretty green already, what with that olive skin, bein' Italian."

"Feel like going there with me today?   This afternoon?"

"Sure, Sparky.   What time?"

"One o'clock?"

"OK.   How about I meet you at the pier?"

"Perfect.   I'll be the one wearing a smile."

"Me, too.   Because I'll be the one arriving in a Rolls."

I'd thought about going to see Tony by myself, but he was always in a better mood when Catherine was around.   Well, who could blame him?   I wanted to thank him for the French friends and also let him know they'd be expecting something in return.   He would know that already; nobody in his business ever did something for nothing.   But it was just good manners to give him a full report on the European connection.   As a little value added, I thought I'd tell him

216

what I'd heard from Bunny about the Brits being interested in the French underground as a possible source for clandestine warfare, if the wheels should come off the French army. That would mean nothing of practical value to Tony, but he would find it interesting. On second thought, if anyone could find a way to turn an international catastrophe into a business opportunity, it would be Tony and his friends. He was already thinking about ways to exploit shortages and the best ways to use the black markets. What was the slogan? *"LSMFT – Lucky Strikes mean fine tobacco."*

Next I called Jonathan Woodhouse. Bunny had given me the number.

The butler answered and I told him who I was and that I was referred by Mr. Finch-Hayton of UCLA.

"Oh, yes, sir. Mr. Woodhouse has been expecting your call. He's not here at the moment. May I have him call you back?"

"No, thank you. I'll be out most of the day. But I'll try again later."

"That will be fine, sir. I'll tell Mr. Woodhouse you called."

Good old Bunny.

I had some time to kill and I was getting hungry, so I got in the car and headed for a diner I knew. It was run by a Greek – all of them are – named Stavros Katavolos. Stavros would greet you at the door and escort you to a booth just as though he was the maître d' at the Savoy Grill. Then he'd hand you a laminated menu that never changed and listed only two available beers – Bud and Schlitz. I liked Stavros. He was proud of his business and dignified. We'd see each other now and then at the Angels games. He always wore a suit and tie to the game. He refused to eat the hot dogs, because, he said, "I am in the food business. I know things."

I also liked the waitresses there. They were all around middle age, and they all had figures that called to mind a Buick's headlights. You couldn't shock them or offend them. They'd heard it all and said most of it all right back. I realize that's a cliché. But that's how they were. When they took your order they called you "Hon," and didn't mean it for a second.

"What'll you have, Hon?" said the one called Rita, once I'd glanced at the menu and set it aside. She wore a hair net over a substantial bun-like arrangement the color of Nedick's orange soda. She wore a much-washed checkered uniform that was limp with age and clung to her the way she wanted it to. She was proud of her assets and had not yet given up. She had pretty brown eyes, and she plucked her eyebrows and replaced them with pencil lines. Why any woman would do this I can't say, but I guess it was the fashion in some quarters.

"How's the meat loaf?" I said, pleasantly.

She smirked. "How do you think?"

"I'll have it anyway. Mashed and brown gravy."

"Mixed veggies?"

"What else do you have?"

"Nothing. The delivery is late."

"OK. I'll have mixed veggies. And I have a question for you."

"Yeah?"

"It's only ten o'clock in the morning. How come the meat loaf's always ready?"

"Because it's left over from yesterday. You want coffee?"

"Is that left over, too?"

"Nope. Fresh this morning."

"OK."

It was good to be home.

"I've got another question for you."

"Do I have to answer first, or do I get to hear it? If I have to answer first, then it's 'maybe.'"

"'Maybe' is better than 'no.' But that's not the question. You get all kinds in here."

"Yeah. So?"

"Just wondering if you ever hear things."

"Like what?"

"Well, I'm working on a case. It involves a hit and run accident. You probably read about it. A producer's wife. Happened at three in the morning just a couple of blocks from here."

"Killed her? Name of Ginsberg?"

"That's right. I wonder if you ever heard anyone talking about it."

"I remember guys talking about the accident when it happened and about her old man getting shot a few days later. Raised some eyebrows."

"Not yours, though."

"No. I hadn't put 'em on yet. But people who were talking were just reading the papers. Kind of like discussing the ball scores. Nothing, really."

"I get it."

"But I'll tell you someone who does know about it. The guy who was with her. He comes in here all the time. Or used to. An actor. The out of work kind."

EPITAPH FOR A DREAM

"I remember seeing his picture in the paper. His name was Richard Lovelace, or something like that, right?"

"Right. Richard Lovelace. That's not his real name. He told me once what it was, but I forget. Nothing unusual. The name, I mean. I haven't seen him lately. Not in the last week or so. I doubt he could tell you anything the cops don't already know. They grilled him pretty hard. He was complaining about it afterwards. But that's all I know."

"It might be worth talking to him. Does he live around here?" I figured he might, since he was a regular.

"In a flop house around the corner. They call it a residence hotel, but it's a flop house. The De Milo Arms."

"Is that supposed to be a joke?"

"No. The guy who owns it is named Joe De Milo. Got any other questions?" She batted her eyelids suggestively and, needless to say, ironically.

"Just the usual one," I said.

"Oh, that again. Well, I'll give you the same old answer: 'Maybe.' But you gotta show me a note from a doctor."

"Oh, well. Another time, perhaps."

"Promises, promises."

I finished breakfast. I have to admit it was pretty good, but then I've always sort of liked leftovers in the morning. Meat loaf stays with you better than Cheerios. You don't mind missing lunch.

I ask Stavros for the directions to The De Milo Arms. It was only a few blocks away, so I decided to walk. People joke about nobody walking in LA, but we were at the fag end of the Depression. Lots of people were walking. The De Milo Arms was a rundown five-story building wedged between a tattoo parlor and a pawn shop – the twin symbols of a lousy neighborhood. Not for the first time I marveled at how fast you could go from the modest prosperity of Santa Monica Boulevard to the slums. There was a faded sign sticking out from above the entrance. "De Milo Arms. Steam Heat."

The lobby of the place smelled like the bottom of an ashtray, and the guy behind the desk, a skinny squirt in a dingy white shirt, fit right in. He looked like a human cigarette butt. He was reading *The Racing Form*.

He looked up. "Yeah?" He didn't seem happy to see me.

"Does a guy named Richard Lovelace live here?"

"Who wants to know?"

"You see anyone else standing here?"

"I see somebody I don't recognize."

I pulled out my wallet and showed him my ID.

He looked at it. He was not impressed.

"A private dick? So what?"

"A private dick with a brother in the vice squad. I told him I'd call him if the jerk behind the desk looked like a cheap pimp, and before you say 'Who're you calling cheap?' I'm going to give you a chance to reconsider your attitude and make nice. So – Richard Lovelace. Know him?"

"I ain't seen him in four days. Maybe five."

"I didn't ask you that. Does he live here?"

"Yeah. He's paid up to the end of the week, so I don't poke my nose where it ain't wanted."

"That covers a lot of territory. Where is he?"

"Room five, second floor. He's the only one on the floor. Is your brother really in the vice squad?"

"What do you think?"

I went up the shabby staircase to the shabby hallway of the second floor. Room five was down toward the end. As I got closer, the De Milo Arms didn't smell like an ashtray anymore. It smelled a whole lot worse.

"Hey! Clark Gable!" I shouted to the desk guy. "Get your ass up here and bring your passkey! Something's getting ripe in room five!"

He came trudging up the stairs and down the hallway with a toilet plunger. And I remembered the lines: *'What a piece of work is man! how noble in reason! how infinite in faculty! in form and moving how express and admirable! in action how like an angel! in apprehension how like a god! the beauty of the world, the paragon of animals!'*

"We been having trouble with the drains," he said.

"This ain't a blocked drain," I said.

Kowalski and his boys showed up fifteen minutes after I called him.

So did the Medical Examiner and the ambulance.

"He's changed since the last time I saw him," said Kowalski. "I hope he doesn't have a mother."

"Your sensitivity does you credit," I said.

"They teach us that in cop school. You touch anything?"

"Nope. Found him hanging just like this."

"They don't make shower rods like this anymore. Good solid piece of work. 'Course, he doesn't look like he weighs much. What brings you here?"

"Just routine. I thought he might have something to say about Ma Ginsberg's so-called accident. Looks like he might have."

"Either that or this is just one hell of a coincidence."

"You believe in coincidence, Kowalski?"

"Nope. They teach us that in cop school, too.

Chapter Twenty-Six

It's not hard to make a murder look like a suicide. But it's very hard to fool the cops into believing it, after they've had a chance to look around. The suicide note was not very convincing, either. It had been typed on the cheap Smith Corona portable that was on the card table in the corner of the room. Maybe Richard Lovelace was a writer as well as an actor. He lived like one. But he didn't write that note. It said that he was devastated (spelled "devasted") over Elaine Ginsberg's tragic death and that he couldn't face life without her. It was signed 'R. Lovelace.'

The cops cut him down and hauled him away in the ambulance. I tried to open the one window, but it was painted shut.

"Is there anything in this world more depressing than a Murphy bed?" said Kowalski, looking around the room.

"A guy hanging from a shower rod?"

"I suppose. Any ideas about this?" said Kowalski.

"Just the same ones you have."

"Yeah. The way I see it, the hitman hired pretty boy to set up the Ginsberg woman. Then the hitman came back a couple of days ago and tidied things up. Exit pretty boy."

"I wonder why the guy waited so long. It's been over a month since the so-called accident."

"It is kinda funny. The only thing I can think is that pretty boy went back to whoever hired him and tried to shake 'em down for a few more bucks. He was broke, from the look of things."

"And Marvin had already put out the word that he was poison. After that he couldn't get hired to wear a sandwich sign."

"I wonder if he shot Marvin," said Kowalski. "For revenge. That'd be great. It sure would make life easier for us flatfeet. Marvin hires killer, killer hires pretty boy to set up Ma Ginsberg, killer runs over Ma Ginsberg, pretty boy shoots Ginsberg, killer hangs pretty boy to shut him up. Very neat. A lot less paperwork."

"Maybe," I said. "But does he look the type?"

"Not anymore."

"My guess is, he was just a loose end. Like Marvin. The killer let him alone as long as he kept quiet. After all, if Richard was an accomplice to murder he'd have every reason to stay quiet."

"True enough."

"But maybe Richard did go back to the guy and ask for more cash. Or maybe the hitman wanted to let a little time go by, so no one would connect the two killings. Maybe he planned to get rid of Richard all along. Either way, this doesn't look much like suicide."

"No way. No pretty boy actor hangs himself over a middle-aged Hollywood hostess. I saw her in the morgue. I admit she wasn't looking her best that day, but even after eight hours at Eve Arden's, she wouldn't have been young love's dream."

"*Elizabeth* Arden's."

"Her, too."

"And nobody signs a suicide note with a phony name some agent came up with. You know, the original Richard Lovelace was a poet in the seventeenth century. Wrote love lyrics. You may remember 'To Althea From Prison'."

"I'll mention it to my reading group."

"Say, what time is it? My watch stopped."

"12:30. You oughta get one of those fancy watches that wind themselves."

"Too rich for my blood. But I gotta go. Important meeting."

"Who is she?"

"What's your wife's name, again? Lois?"

"Yeah. Tell her I'll be home for dinner."

I went back to the diner, collected my car and headed for the Santa Monica pier.

I got there just at one. Catherine was already there, standing by the water taxi, flirting with Perry. She never missed a chance to work her magic on anyone wearing pants, unless it was Katherine Hepburn. Catherine looked exactly like what she was, and then some. She came up to me and held me in a long, fragrant embrace, all softness and silky perfection. She hardly ever wore underwear.

"Hello, Sparky," she whispered. "I'm glad you're home."

"So am I." I kissed her and she kissed me back. When it came to kissing, she knew what she was doing.

"'Here will I dwell, for heaven is in these lips.'"

"Smooth talker. Do you say that to all the girls?"

"Yes. It's my best line. I'll bet you smell this good all over," I said.

"Want to find out? We could go for a ride in the back seat of the Rolls. If you're feeling shy, there's a curtain. But I don't remember you being shy. And Jesus won't watch." Jesus was her devoted chauffeur.

"Think Tony will mind if we're late?"

"I didn't tell him we were coming, so how can we be late?"

"Good point. But I really need to see him. How about afterwards?"

"Sure, Sparky. You know me."

Yes, I did, and I was a happier man for it. Maybe not a better man. But happier.

"I was just showing Perry my new watch. It works, too. I got here right on time."

"Hiya, Chief," said Perry. "Glad you made it back from Gay Paree. They about ready to start shooting over there?"

"Looks like it."

"Think we'll get involved?"

"Could be. You ready to go back in?"

"I've done my time, thanks all the same. Those Krauts come over here, it's another story. But 'til then it ain't none of my business."

"How's Della?"

"As long as the deli don't run out of Braunschweiger and gin, she's as happy as she gets. She'll probably come in tomorrow."

"What's she doing today?"

"I dunno. Probably making some guy glad he's alive. Not personally, you understand. Professionally."

Some months Della's escort service made more than I did as a private dick. But it tended to be a seasonal business. Sales conventions and that kind of thing.

"Well, let's go see the man," I said.

Fifteen minutes later Catherine and I were climbing the companion ladder up to the main deck of the Lucky Lady. Since it was only early afternoon there were only a thousand or so gamblers there. Normally the ship could accommodate three thousand at a time. But it was still a festive scene. The big band was playing and the girl singer was singing "Anything Goes," and the slots were ringing and everyone was having a pretty good time, even the losers. Most of them, anyway.

The goombah security guys all knew Catherine, and in the last year or so they had gotten to know me, too. Tony had put out the word that I was a good guy and a friend and that was all that was needed to generate smiles in guys who didn't smile much, though they did laugh a lot when they were off duty. Gangsters generally have a good sense of humor. Warped, but good. Since they lived strictly by their own rules, the absurdities and restrictions of conventional life were just so many jokes to them. As were their own individual quirks and characteristics. One of the guys was named Sonny the Gherkin, because he had a huge pecker. That kind of thing. They seemed to have an innate understanding that incongruity was the soul of humor. And no one got away with anything. Except the boss. But even he was called The Snail, because of his last name, Scungilli.

227

And because he was always in a hurry. He got the nickname when he was new in the business. *His* bosses gave it to him. If mobsters had one thing in common, it was that they all liked a good laugh.

Tony was in his office behind his massive mahogany desk. As usual, the desk was covered with adding machine tapes and ledgers. Tony was meticulous about his business.

He looked up when we came in and smiled. He was glad to see us. Well, he was glad to see Catherine, and, as I said, he kind of liked me, too. I had done him a favor, and he was the kind who remembered things. That was another thing the mobsters had in common. Someone once said "A senile goombah forgets everything but his grudges." That was only partially right. They don't forget favors, either.

"Hiya, kid! Hiya, doll. Like they say in the movies, this is a pleasant surprise. To what do I owe the pleasure?"

"Does there have to be a reason?" she said, batting her eyelashes.

"No. But there always is."

Catherine skipped over to him and engulfed him in silk and Chanel. I never knew whether she really liked him or just liked the arrangement. It didn't matter.

"Wanna see my new watch?" she said.

Tony groaned.

"It winds itself," she said.

"That's just the watch for you, babe," he said. "She gets wound up all by herself, too," he said, grinning at me. He shook my hand with his usual crushing grip. "I hear you dodged a bullet or two. You and your squirrelly writer friend."

"Word gets around fast."

"That's something to keep in mind."

"Yeah. Some guy took three shots at us. That's one of the reasons I wanted to come out to see you. To say thanks. Your friends became my friends. At least one of them. If he hadn't been along, we might have ended our days in some cheap brasserie, face down in sauerkraut."

"They eat that stuff? Surprises me. Never trust the kraut-eaters. That dipshit Mussolini's gonna find out the hard way. The little guy with the mustache is gonna drag Italy into something she can't get out of. I hate to see it, but it's coming, sure as three aces beats a pair."

"I think you're right. And I was glad to get out of there before it started."

"Did our friends find out who took a shot at you?"

"Not by the time I left. We didn't wait around. I'm guessing you'll hear, sooner or later."

"Probably. Did you find the dipshit producer's girlfriend?"

"Yes. She wasn't too broken up about the news."

"About him being dead?"

"Right. I told her, she shrugged, and then took off with her latest boyfriend."

"Let that be a lesson to you. Never fall in love. That's for dipshits. Right, doll?"

"If you say so," said Catherine. "But does that mean you aren't in love with me?"

"That's what it means."

"That's good. That way things are strictly business. I give you the business and you give me the presents. Ha, ha. But as of today I won't need another watch for a while. Just so you know."

EPITAPH FOR A DREAM

"Speaking of Marvin the Producer," I said, "his wife's boyfriend was found just this morning hanging from a shower rod in The De Milo Arms Hotel."

"Really?"

I might have said the Yankees won yesterday.

"Whoever did it tried to make it look like suicide. But the cops weren't fooled."

"I ain't surprised," said Tony. "It ain't that easy to stage something like that and make it look real. That's what I hear, anyway. So?"

"So I was just wondering if you heard anything about all this."

"Friends don't ask friends those questions. But I'll chalk it up to you being a nice Presbyterian boy from Ohio and not knowing any better."

"I apologize. I just figured it must be an out of town job and nothing to do with our ... friends. Especially since it seemed such an amateurish job."

"Well, we got friends all over. You should know that. You just learned it over in the land of creamy sauces."

"I know. I just thought it might be a lone wolf type job and not related to anybody important."

"I tell you what. If I hear anything and if it don't involve people who matter, I may give you a call. OK?"

"I'd appreciate it."

"But why do you care?"

"That's a good question. I guess because I got involved with Marvin's case and it all seems tied together, somehow."

"Did you get paid?"

"Yes. And then some." I still had a big chunk of the letter of credit available. That was something I needed to think about. It had an expiration date.

"That's all right, then. But you've been piling up some pretty good favors. You might start thinking about saying thanks in some ways other than just saying it."

"Believe me, I have been thinking about that." And that was nothing but the truth, so help me. "I did hear something that you might be interested in."

"Yeah?"

"I stopped in London and talked to a friend who's with the British secret service. Don't ask me which branch. He couldn't tell me."

"Couldn't or wouldn't?"

"Wouldn't."

"That's only smart."

"Anyway, he said there wasn't much doubt that there'd be a war, and soon. And some of the people in the know in England don't think the French army is as good as advertised."

"There's a shock."

"And so they're planning for the possibility that the Germans will not only invade but maybe take over a piece of France. No one believes they'd bite off the whole thing."

"Why not?"

"I guess it just seems unthinkable."

"It ain't unthinkable. I can think it."

"Well, anyway, these Brits are thinking that some of your friends in France might come in handy — as a sort of underground guerrilla force."

"And be an all-around pain in the ass to the Krauts?"

"Something like that. Knocking over a Paris branch of a German bank suddenly becomes patriotic."

"I like it."

"Anyway, the Brits are thinking about it. I figured that was something worth knowing."

"It is. Does our friend Molière know about this?"

"No. I just found out about it on the way back. When I stopped in London." I paused for a moment. "Speaking of Molière, I've been wondering..."

"You do that a lot, kid. What now?"

"Just who the hell is this guy, Molière?"

"It ain't one guy. I'm surprised you ain't figured that out."

"I sort of did. But I just wanted to be sure."

"You know what they say about being sure."

"Measure twice, cut once?"

"No. Making sure killed the cat."

"I thought it was curiosity."

"Same thing."

Chapter Twenty-Seven

I left Catherine on the *Lucky Lady*. She didn't want to miss a chance to make Tony a little jealous about the watch, and he never wanted to miss the chance for a couple of sessions with her – something she laughingly called a five minute tit for tat. As I said, Tony the Snail didn't waste any time about anything.

I went back to my office and called Jonathan Woodhouse. The butler answered. Mr. Woodhouse was in.

He came to the phone, and I introduced myself.

"Yes, indeed," he said. "Bunny told me you would be calling. Some little mystery about a possible Picasso."

"Yes," I said. Personally, I thought it was bigger than that, but I let it go. "Right now the painting's in Bunny's safe at UCLA, but I can get it in the morning. Bunny said you might be kind enough to take a look at it and give your opinion about whether it's genuine."

"I'd be happy to. Why don't you come around to my place about noon tomorrow and we'll have a look, and then maybe you'd like to stay and have a bite of luncheon."

"Yes. That sounds good. Thank you."

EPITAPH FOR A DREAM

He gave me the address – a fancy one – and said goodbye.

I couldn't place his accent. He sounded like one of those people who are born in Kenya or someplace like that and sent to a fancy boarding school in England, where they studied Greek, Latin and buggery. Either that or he was from a place like Milwaukee and came to Hollywood, where he worked with some down-at-the-heels English acting coach and learned to talk like Herbert Marshall.

I wasn't sure I wanted to have "luncheon" with this guy, Woodhouse. As a rule I prefer "lunch," except on days when I have meatloaf for breakfast. Then I skip lunch altogether. And was there a difference between luncheon and lunch? There were two words, after all, and I remembered Klep's short lecture on *le mot juste*. Maybe it was a class thing – "luncheon" for the moneyed, and "lunch" for the rest of us, the "hoi polloi." As an aside, I once went out with a girl who thought "hoi polloi" referred to the upper class, instead of "the many-headed." It was the kind of mistake Bunny would have dropped her for, but I didn't do that until later, because she looked really good in shorts.

Anyway, the way I saw it, Woodhouse was doing me a favor, and I might as well be polite. At least, I thought he was doing me a favor. If he sent me a bill for appraisal afterwards, I'd look at things differently.

Speaking of Herbert Marshall, the actor, I remembered that Bunny was friendly with him. He told me Marshall had been in the Great War and had lost a leg. "Very careless of him," he'd say. It was one of Bunny's favorite jokes. He said he stole it from Oscar Wilde.

I called Bunny's secretary and told her I'd be by to pick up the painting about eleven in the morning. That would be fine, she said, and how was Professor Finch-Hayton doing, and wasn't it a shame that the university would be losing him for a while, and she hoped this nasty war talk was all wrong and that he'd be back at UCLA sooner rather than later.

"Yes," I said.

By then it was cocktail hour – at least it was at the Garden of Allah. About this time of the day, every day, you could hear typewriters falling silent and paper being wadded up and thrown away, so that all the writers, those wretched serfs the producers called "schmucks with Underwoods," would emerge from their sunny rooms and gloomy moods and meet at the pool for drinks. It was, after all, almost three. Those who had offices at the studio left earlier than that so they could be on time at the Garden and not miss out on any of the whining.

Hobey ignored these daily rituals. He started cocktail hour whenever he wanted to, and that usually meant well before three. "As to that," he'd say, "I am a law unto myself."

When I arrived he was sitting by the pool in his favorite chaise longue, next to Hedda. She was wearing red heart-shaped sunglasses, smoking a Chesterfield and reading letters for her Miss Lonelyhearts column. I had to look twice to make sure she was wearing a bathing suit, but she was. What there was of it was vivid orange. It reminded me of Rita's hair – Rita, the waitress.

"Hedda has no color sense," said Hobey. "I tell her that red and orange do not go well together, but what does she say in response?"

"Up yours," said Hedda, on cue.

"Still, orange or not, it covers her maiden modesty, although now and then you can see it peeking out from around the edges. Care for a drink?"

"That's why I'm here," I said.

He reached under the chair for one of the martini pitchers and poured out a tumblerful.

"What's new at the studio?" I said. "Anything come up while we were gone?"

"Lots of things, but nothing for me."

"That ain't true," said Hedda. "What about that castle thing?"

"Ah, well, yes. They want me to write the narration for another of their ten-minute travelogues. This one's about Yeats country in Ireland."

"Really? Too bad you didn't know. We could have stopped there on the way back."

"I know, and there's no money for travel expenses, so it's back to the LA County library for background. But you know, it's a kind of an interesting story. Yeats bought one of those Norman forts – just four floors, straight up. Nothing more than a square stone tower. Nothing at all grand. Certainly not a castle. It's no wonder he got a little strange as he got older. Probably suffered from the damp. You can't make heads nor tails of his later stuff."

"This is the guy who wrote The Song of the Wandering Marvin?"

"'Wandering Aengus.' But yes, that's the guy. Interesting, isn't it? How various threads of our lives seem to intertwine?"

"If you say so. But what's an Aengus? Some kind of cow?"

"A mythical Irish guy. Kind of a Celtic deity, second class."

"Well, it's good that you got another assignment."

"Yes. It's a job, and at least it's more interesting than the last one – that thing about Paraguay."

He took a long pull on his drink and looked pensive. "I've been thinking about this whole Picasso deal and Rosemarie and her lovely daughter I never got to meet."

"So have I – been thinking about it. Come up with anything?"

"Ever heard of Occam's Razor?"

"No."

"It has nothing to do with shaving. It's a theory that says the simplest solution to a problem is usually the right one."

"So?"

I'd been thinking along the same lines, but I figured I wouldn't interrupt. Hobey was very good at figuring out plots for books or movies. He was less good at figuring out reality. But now and then he hit on something.

"So the simplest explanation to all of this is that Nicole sold Marvin a phony Picasso and then took off. Marvin was so smitten, so lovesick that he hired a hit man to get rid of his wife, so that he could go and find Nicole and live happily ever after. Divorce was of course out of the question, because of alimony. Marvin may even have made a profit on the deal, if Elaine was insured. Was she?"

"I don't know. It's worth checking into, although I imagine the cops have thought of that."

"Anyway, the hitman took Marvin's cash, ran over the lady and then decided he didn't want any loose ends and came back and shot Marvin."

EPITAPH FOR A DREAM

"No connection to Nicole, Rosemarie and Jean Marc? No connection to the forgery?"

"No. A coincidence."

"Who painted the Picasso?"

"Jean Marc. Or someone else. Whoever painted it might not even know it was sold as a Picasso. He might have just tried to make a good copy of a real Picasso or to paint something in Picasso's style and done a good job of it."

"What about the signature?"

"Just part of the deception. But there's nothing to say it was intentionally meant to deceive."

"A deception not meant to deceive?"

"Well, if you put it that way, it sounds a little thin. Still ... the artist might have made a copy just to make a copy, for practice. Maybe he didn't even sign it. Maybe Nicole or her boyfriend or somebody added Picasso's name to the bottom. That would be the simplest thing of all to forge."

"Or maybe they removed the real artist's name and substituted Picasso's. And then smudged it a little."

"Possibly. Possibly. Anyway, the artist gave the finished picture to Nicole, because she was the model, and she gave it, or more likely, sold it, to moony Marvin. Told him he was the happy guy in the picture, and he bought it. Literally and figuratively."

"And who killed Richard Lovelace? And why?"

"Who's Richard Lovelace?"

"Elaine Ginsberg's playmate."

"Dead? When?"

"This morning."

"Hmm." He thought about it for a second. Then smiled. "Well, of course! That fits. He must have been in on it somehow. Just how is yet to be determined. And they killed him to shut him up."

"Which always works. So according to your story there's no connection between the painting and the murders of the guy who bought it, the guy's inconvenient wife and her boyfriend, right?"

"Only in the sense that it's a symbol of Marvin's madness, which started the string of three murders. The painting is almost an irrelevant coincidence."

"A MacGuffin?"

"Not quite, but in that ballpark. Marvin would have probably, almost certainly, done what he did, painting or no painting. What do the cops think?"

"The cops don't believe in coincidences. Neither do I. But your explanation is simpler and more reasonable. Tying everything together is hard – hard to see how everything fits."

"Yes, scientists and philosophers have been trying forever to find the one theory that explains everything. An answer to all the questions. I forget what they call it."

"The Single Theory?"

"Yes, I guess so. But no one has been able to come up with anything. It's possible that everything we see is just accidental, just chaos. That none of it makes any sense. Nothing fits together. Like this case, sort of."

"Hey, listen to this," said Hedda. As usual she was pretty much ignoring Hobey and me, focused on reading the letters people sent her asking for advice. "*'I was thinking about things after my boyfriend who was working construction cut off his fingers by accident and bled to death before they could get him to the hospital and I went to my Rabbi and asked him what's the point and he said to me there is no point and that's the point. Then he said he was quitting the rabbi business and opening a deli. I'm confused. What do you think – about things, I mean, and stuff?'* Can you believe these people? What kind of dumbass question is that for Miss Lonleyhearts?"

"I wonder if it will be a kosher deli," said Hobey. "Are you going to answer her?"

"Huh? Are you kidding?"

"*'Are you kidding?'* – There's as good a Single Theory as any," said Hobey. "It reminds me of the line from Steven Crane: 'The man said to the Universe, "Sir, I exist," and the Universe said, "Yes, but that does not create in me a sense of obligation."' Or something like that. The Universe might just as well have said 'Are you kidding?'"

"Coming back to earth," I said, "I think you could very well be right about this case. Maybe the elements don't fit together because they can't. They're unrelated. But I'm going to keep looking for a little while longer."

"The song of the wandering shamus? You '*will find out where she has gone,*' meaning the truth?"

"I guess."

"And I'm going to write a travelogue about WB Yeats and explain his ideas about renovating a four-room castle, which I will make up, since he never said anything about any of that. I'll start by having him install central heating."

He smiled benignly at Hedda. "What do you think, my darling? Will that play in Peoria?"

She smiled her quite beautiful smile. I could see why Hobey liked her. And she had a stunning body.

"Up yours," she said, sweetly.

Chapter Twenty-Eight

In the morning I went out to UCLA to get the picture. Bunny's secretary was waiting for me.

"I have the combination to the safe in my desk, hidden carefully," she said. "But there's a letter for you here from Professor Finch-Hayton. You might want to read it while I get the picture."

"Yes, thank you." What could this mean?

Dear Riley,

Greetings. I just this minute got a response to one of the letters I wrote to a friend in France – someone who knows Picasso well and knows a great deal about his work. He says he talked to him and showed him the photograph that I sent him. Picasso said he seemed to remember doing the painting, because he remembered doing the girl, as he put it. He has a lively sense of humor. Perhaps it sounds better in French. The anonymous man on top in the painting is thinner than Picasso, and younger, but that was just Picasso's sly joke to himself, and about himself. But here's the rub. He's not sure. It was just one of those things, to quote Cole Porter – he dashed it off in a post-coital afterglow, or something like that. Much better for the health than a cigarette. In other words, he remembers the incident, remembers the girl, remembers painting something afterwards and thinks this might be the thing. But he's not sure and frankly doesn't care. Still, it's fair to say that we're at least approaching the truth of the painting. On the basis of this latest information, I'd bet it's genuine. But I didn't have time to study it and subject it to any chemical tests that might prove convincing, one way or another. And I'm afraid I won't be able to as long as this wretched war business is hanging over all of us.

When you see Woodhouse, I would recommend not telling him this story. It will prejudice his judgment. Just let him decide what he thinks, and if you want to tell him afterwards, then fine. By the way, neither my friend nor the Maestro himself knows how the girl, Nicole, got hold of the thing, and neither knows what happened to it. And no one seems to care. Picasso did her, did it, and pretty much forgot everything about both of them. It's good to be a genius.

Cheers,
Bunny

P.S. I'm sorry to say that there's no news of Amanda.

The secretary came back with the painting. It was carefully wrapped and crated, as you would expect.

"Do you think this is really a Picasso?" she said, apparently somehow aware of the mystery.

"It seems very possible."

"Was Doctor Finch-Hayton's letter helpful?"

"Yes. I think so."

I was not surprised about Amanda. And, not for the first time, I wondered if I would ever hear of her again, much less see her. It seemed unlikely. She had "faded in the brightening air," to quote WB Yeats. Or, as they say here in the land of Looney Tunes, "That's All, Folks."

I drove to the address in Beverly Hills. I had the top down on the Packard, as usual – as usual, because it was another perfect day in southern California. If only people could keep themselves from ruining it, I thought. But I wasn't very confident about that. A cigarette tossed carelessly from the car could burn down half the Valley. And over in Europe they were getting ready to do worse. A lot worse. Intentionally.

Then, for no particular reason, I thought of something Blinky Malone used to say: "Never buy sausage from a three-fingered butcher." Funny the things you think about when the day is perfect. Then it occurred to me that it might be a good idea to have a talk with Blinky. He always had his ear to the ground. He was, after all, on the FBI's payroll as an informer. He might know something worth knowing.

You couldn't see Woodhouse's mansion from the street. It was behind a tall stone wall covered with white stucco. The iron entry gates were about twelve feet high and topped with spear points.   An experienced burglar would look for another way in.

There was an intercom at the gate, and I got out of the car and announced myself.   The gates swung open and I drove up the smooth driveway that ran past manicured lawns. There were a few captive deer grazing on the perfect grass and a couple of swans gliding on a large pond.   Like many things in Hollywood, swans looked pretty and had nasty tempers.   The house was as white as the stucco wall and was of no particular architectural style – call it California Big. But it was very pleasant to look at and I'm sure equally pleasant to live in, and much more appropriate than the French chateau or English Tudor houses that were nearby. The driveway ended in a circle at the front door.   I got out, carrying the package.

The butler met me at the door and ushered me into the drawing room, announced me and then left.   The room was huge, with high ceilings and Spanish style exposed beams. There were couches in flowered upholstery and matching chairs, and on the walls were paintings that looked original, mostly by Impressionists.   Everything smelled of money, and it was a good smell.

Woodhouse was a dapper little man of about forty-five or fifty.   He was dressed in California casual: white trousers, a matching white shirt, blue polka dot ascot and a peach-colored sweater thrown over his shoulders.   Why guys did that was beyond me, but a lot of them did.   And he wore two-tone black and white shoes that were the fashion just then. They were handsome shoes.   His pleated trousers were long enough to be correct, and just short enough to show off those shoes.

He was short, slim and had black hair worn slicked down with something shiny. He had a very thin moustache, like Errol Flynn or David Niven. It must have been an English thing. I always thought if you were going to grow one, then grow one. His looked like one of Rita's eyebrows. Rita, the waitress.

Woodhouse got up from his chair and assumed a look that said he was delighted to see me.

"Delighted to see you, Mr. Fitzhugh," he said. "Bunny has told me so much about you."

"I was never convicted," I said. It was my standard smart ass response to that predictable, inane remark.

I usually said it with a disarming smile.

"Eh? Oh, ha, ha! Very droll."

I'd never met anyone or known anyone who used the word "droll," – in English, anyway, so I was clearly in for a new experience of some sort.

"Bunny says you are a private detective."

"Yes."

"How did you get to know him?"

"We worked together on a case a while back. That one also had something to do with artwork and questions of authenticity."

"Ah. I see. I also see you've brought the painting. Shall we have a look? I can't wait. Frankly, I hope it's genuine. I must say, I'm very excited about this."

I hoped he wouldn't get too excited.

We unwrapped the package, and Woodhouse placed it on an easel he had set up for this examination.

"Beautiful," he said. "Just exquisite."

EPITAPH FOR A DREAM

He took out a magnifying glass and peered through it, moving the glass around the whole painting from about nose distance. He was taking his time. I considered that a good thing. "Lovely work," he said, after a few minutes. "Yes, lovely. This artist has promise."

I let that sink in for a second.

"Sounds like you think it's not genuine."

"Oh, it's genuine, all right. A genuine Somebody. It's just not a Picasso."

"Hmm." It seemed superfluous to ask, but I did anyway. "You're sure?"

"Quite sure. Are you an artist yourself, in your spare time, perhaps?"

"No."

"Then I won't go into any technical reasons, such as brushwork and so on. They would only bore you. But I am as sure as I can be that this is not a Picasso."

"And the signature?"

"A very, very good forgery. The slight smear is a giveaway, though. Picasso is quite proud of his name. I do think the picture itself is very well done. Beautiful, really. The expression on the girl's face alone is enough to make some people want to switch teams, if you follow me."

I followed him.

"I wouldn't for a moment suggest that you're being too hasty," I said. "But I'm surprised you can make so quick a judgement. When I showed the picture to Bunny he couldn't decide, and, in fact, wanted to do some chemical tests before offering an opinion."

"Oh, well, that's not surprising. Our Bunny is cautious, because he is often hired to authenticate a picture for a sale.

He can't afford to be wrong. It would ruin him in the business. And so he is very careful and follows a professional procedure. All very understandable. And between us, his real expertise lies in the Italian Renaissance. No one can know everything. If you asked me, for example, to authenticate a Caravaggio, I would take my time, too."

"I'm a little weak on Caravaggio, myself."

"Really? Oh, you're joking. I understand. But with the modernists I am more than sure of myself. I own quite a few, as a matter of fact. And I know many of the artists. Besides, I don't do authentications. I have no reputation to protect. I can make quick decisions, but I assure you, I know what I'm talking about."

"And you're sure about this."

"Yes, dear boy. I'm quite sure. It's a forgery. No doubt about it. Is this a terrible disappointment? I hope not."

Was it? At first it was, but then I thought – was it really? In some ways, if Woodhouse was correct, it was a relief. The fraud would have mattered greatly to Marvin, but he was gone, and so was his wife. There were no children. So no one living had been damaged by the forgery, and if it really was a forgery, no one was losing a piece of art worth a small fortune. What's more, I was no longer faced with temptation – the temptation to keep the painting. Or more precisely, my keeping the painting would mean nothing to anyone. No one had missed it, and it wasn't worth much, if anything. Technically it was theft, of course. But it was the kind of theft that didn't matter and that no one would ever know about. And if that brought to mind discussions with Klep and his sketchy moral position that if no one knew about something, it didn't exist – well, I could live with it. The alternative was to sneak back into Marvin's house and hang the thing over the fireplace. That seemed to me an empty gesture that would mean nothing to anyone, not even me. The only person who might even notice it was back in place was a Mexican maid who would think of it as just one more thing to dust. As for Bunny's information – well, he wasn't positive. His French friend only had a photograph to work with and could not examine the painting the way Woodhouse had just done. Brushwork, and so on. Picasso didn't remember one way or the other, and didn't seem to care. So one expert was certain; the other was pretty sure the other way, but not convinced. I suppose the only sure way to decide was to put the thing for sale at auction and let the market decide. But I couldn't do that. People would ask awkward questions about where I got it. Besides, if Woodhouse was right, it wouldn't sell anyway, except as a curiosity. It wasn't worth the risks and the bother.

"Disappointment?" I said. "No. Not really. It many ways it makes things a lot easier."

"That's not to say it isn't an interesting piece of art in its own right. I would pay something like a hundred dollars for it. But no more."

"What do you think I should do with it?"

"Take it home and put it on the wall and enjoy it. The girl in it is lovely."

"Yes, she is." *And you should see her mother*, I thought.

Well, I did have space for it in the office next to the Barbasol calendar.

"How did you happen to come by it?" he said.

I tried to detect if there was any undercurrent to the question, but there didn't seem to be.

"It's part of a case I'm working on."

"So it belongs to someone?"

"Not really." At least that's the way I saw it now.

"Well, then, if I were you, I'd just give it a good home. Where do you live, if you don't mind me asking?"

Was that an odd question? Hard to tell. And there was something else – the way he said "me asking." I remember having this discussion one time with Hobey and Bunny at a party – how the Americans and the Brits viewed a grammatical question differently. An educated American who was being precise would say "don't mind *my* asking," whereas a Brit would say, as Woodhouse did, "*me* asking." Well, that just reinforced my initial impression that Woodhouse was a Brit, even though he had almost no identifiable accent – just some slightly different usages and pronunciations, here and there. Or, more accurately, it made me wonder, just what was he?

"Where do I live? At the Garden of Allah Hotel. In one of the full time bungalows. But I've got a better spot for the painting in my office."

"That's what I would do, then." He paused and smiled. "I understand that there are some interesting parties at the Garden, now and then."

"Not now and then. That would imply they only happen occasionally. The truth is, they hardly ever stop."

"Maybe I will wander by one evening. Sounds very jolly."

"Jolly is the word for it. And evening starts around three."

"Lovely. And now, would you care for a spot of luncheon? We can sit outside and enjoy the day."

EPITAPH FOR A DREAM

We sat on the patio overlooking the swimming pool. A maid served lunch. It was cold salmon and freshly made mayonnaise, capers and cucumbers and some kind of white wine. Everything was delicious.

"Do I understand that you just returned from Europe?"

"Yes. A couple of days ago."

"Dreadful business going on. Do you think there will be an actual war?"

"I'm afraid so. The people I've talked to all think so."

"It's very distressing. I was born in France. In Paris. My mother was French and my father was the son of a tea planter in Ceylon. English, of course. Very grand in his way, my grandfather. My father came to Paris to study art, and he met my mother, and they fell in love. It was very romantic. My father then became a professor at L'École des Beaux Arts. We lived in Paris until the war, then we came to America when I was almost eighteen. It was the war, you see, that worried my parents. They were afraid I would run away and join."

"So do you consider yourself French? Or English?"

"Neither. Both. I have dual citizenship. But I much prefer it here, although I still have a great many friends in France and in England, where I went to school. Charterhouse. Have you heard of it?"

"No."

"Very posh. But I was only there three years. Not long enough to pick up too fancy an accent. And my French friends tell me I now speak French with an American accent. My poor mother would be so distressed."

"Well, if you don't mind my saying it, you don't seem to have a very noticeable accent of any kind. But there is something. I can't put my finger on it."

"I understand. Some people call it Mid-Atlantic. Halfway between American and English with a dash of French thrown in. In some ways, I'm man without a country, I suppose."

"Or with at least three."

"Don't forget Ceylon. My grandfather is still there, bless him. He's the source of all this wealth." He gestured to include the whole property. That answered an unasked question, and he knew it. "My poor parents, unfortunately, are both gone."

We finished lunch, and I got up to go. It had been very pleasant, I must say. Woodhouse was a very good host — unpretentious, friendly and polite. And if he was also a trifle "aesthetic," well, that was hardly a surprise.

"This was very kind of you," I said, sincerely. "After all, you were doing me a favor by looking at the painting."

"Glad to do it. I'm sorry to disappoint you, if I have. But I couldn't be more sure."

"It's not really a disappointment. As I said, in a lot of ways it simplifies things. So thank you again. And for your hospitality."

"Oh, I enjoy this sort of thing. I like meeting new people. Besides, Bunny vouched for you, and that's more than good enough for me. And who knows, someday I may need a favor, too. You never know when a private detective will become necessary." He smiled as if to say he was a naughty fellow who just might get into any number of scrapes — as if he was someone whose waters ran deeper than the calm surface might indicate.

EPITAPH FOR A DREAM

Could I believe that? I didn't know. Maybe. Most people I knew were more than they seemed to be. Or less. Or, at least, different.

And did I believe him when he said the Picasso was a fake? I didn't know that either. Maybe. Probably. But I did know that believing him certainly made life simpler in a lot of ways.

Chapter Twenty-Nine

I went to my office. Della was there typing and smoking a Pall Mall. She actually smiled when she looked up and saw me. Well, I hadn't seen her in over a month.

"Chief! Welcome home. I'm glad those foreigners didn't do something awful to you. Like teach you to eat snails."

"It was nip and tuck. How're you? How's business?"

"Booming. There's a convention of life insurance agents in town and the California Association of Dentists. The theme of the week is filling cavities. I'm real busy, and happier than a two-peckered puppy. Watcha got there?"

"Remember that painting? This is it."

"That's the one with the girl who's having so much fun."

"Right. Turns out it's a fake. So I'm going to hang it in my office. How are we fixed for picture hooks?"

"I got a nail and a hammer in my desk somewhere. That'll do. But I don't want to look at it too much. Gives me hot flashes."

"When you finish typing up your blackmail letters, do me a favor and call Blinky and ask him to come to the office."

"What's up? Need more documents?"

"No. I just want to talk to him."

Della called, gave Blinky the message and hung up.

"He says to remind you that he's a businessman."

"I know."

"He'll be here in an hour."

"Thank you. I saw Perry yesterday. We took his taxi to the *Lucky Lady*."

"Yeah? How is he? I think of him now and then."

"Aren't you two still married?"

"Don't remind me."

It was good to be home.

I hung the picture on the side wall. I had to admit I liked it.

The thought briefly passed my mind – *What if Woodhouse is wrong? What if that thing hanging there is worth twenty grand, or more?* But then I remembered the old saying: "Where's the best place to hide a leaf?" And besides, I figured Picasso himself would get a kick out of hanging between a Barbasol calendar and a Winslow Homer seascape. The seascape was slightly faded from the sun, but it was that way when I bought it at a garage sale. I figured that's why I got it for fifty cents. Then I thought – *The chances are Woodhouse wasn't wrong in his evaluation. After all Bunny recommended him, and Woodhouse was absolutely certain that it was a fake.* My office was as good a place as any for it to hang. Real or not, no one was going to steal it.

An hour or so later Blinky Malone came slinking in. He nodded to Della and came into my office, furtively. He was a creature of the night, always uncomfortable when the sun was up. He looked behind the door as usual to make sure we were alone. Then he helped himself to the client's chair and took out a toothpick and put it in the corner of his mouth.

He glanced at the picture and raised his eyebrows.

"When did you branch out into porn?" he said.

"It isn't porn. It's art."

"If you say so, but it ain't no mystery what them two are doing, even though it's a little blurry."

"That's why it's art."

"If you say so. How'd them passports work out?" he said. "Must have been OK, since you ain't in jail somewhere."

"The only cop I showed them to spotted them as phonies. Took him two seconds."

His smile faded.

"Well, it was a rush job."

"No harm done. He wasn't a real cop, anyway."

"Oh. A con man, eh? Well, that's better. You can't expect to fool a real professional."

"How are things with the FBI? Still on their payroll?"

Blinky shifted around in his chair. He didn't like his role as a snitch to be mentioned. The wrong people might hear of it.

"Things're quiet," he said.

"Do you ever do any snitching for the cops? Or are you pretty much an exclusive with the Feds?"

"Me and the cops never got along so good. Fact is, me and the Feds only got together, so to speak, because they had something on me, and I made a deal. You know how it is."

"Yeah. I do. That being the case, I suppose it's possible that if you heard something about something that didn't involve the Feds, you wouldn't run to the cops with it. Right?"

"You could say that."

"I just did. And it's also fair to say that you travel in the kind of circles where you hear things."

"You could say that, too. You know I'm a businessman."

"Yes. I do. And because I know that, I'm going to make you an offer. How'd you like to make some real money? Just for scouting around and letting me know what you hear."

"I'd like it. What do you mean by real money?"

"That depends on the information. But high quality stuff would be worth a couple hundred. More than your usual fiver."

"I'd like that, too. So, what are you looking for?"

"A little more than a month ago a woman named Elaine Ginsberg was run over by a car and killed. Her husband was then shot a couple of days later. Then the boyfriend she was with that night was found hanging in a cheap hotel. Whoever did it tried to make it look like suicide, but it wasn't."

"Three murders?"

"Yes."

"They say things run in threes. Like the Andrews Sisters. So?"

"So I want to know if you hear anything about the killings. It might be something as simple as some lowlife flashing some cash. Or it might be a rumor. Anything. The better the information, the better the payday."

"I get it."

"And in case you are tempted to do a little creative thinking, I've got some other people doing the same kind of listening. Guys who are serious. Guys in shiny suits with names ending in vowels. I'll be able to double check anything you give me."

"What do you mean by vowels?"

"Don't worry about it. Just don't try to run anything phony past me. It wouldn't be healthy."

"I get it. You can count on me."

"There you go again. Didn't I just tell you? – no bullshit."

"Yeah."

"Well, then, come back when you have something for me."

"I took a cab over here. I figured you was in a hurry."

"Here's five bucks. Take the bus back and save the difference."

I knew he drove his own car over and used ten cents' worth of gas. But it was always good to let him get away with these little con jobs. It bolstered his self-esteem.

"I'm going over to City Hall," I said to Della, after Blinky had slipped out. "I may be back later."

"Good to know," she said, through a cloud of smoke.

The FBI's unobtrusive office was on the third floor. It was OK for me to drop in unannounced. My buddy Bill Patterson was mostly a researcher with dreams of doing field work. As usual, he was behind his desk surrounded by piles of files.

"Well, look who's back," he said. "Successful trip?"

"More or less."

"What's on your mind? Or did you just stop by to breathe the air of your government hard at work?"

"Just a question or two. You remember a couple of years ago when we got involved in that art forgery case?"

"Sure. Monet, wasn't it?"

"Yes. Well, something similar has come up, and I'm wondering if your art fraud unit is still active."

"I'd have to check to be sure. But I kind of doubt it. We're short-handed in all the offices. Lots of agents have been reassigned because of the war scare. Hell, it's more than a scare, between us girls. Almost all the force not involved in chasing the top ten most wanted are assigned to counterintelligence stuff. There's a lot of bad guys out there and not enough good guys to watch them or catch them."

"I was afraid of that."

"Priorities, old boy, priorities. Would you rather spend your tax dollars catching Nazi spies or nailing harmless scam artists peddling phony Rembrandts?"

"A rhetorical question."

"Yes. I'm afraid you're on your own on this one."

"There's something else that I thought you might like to know about." I told him about the British secret service's interest in the French underworld. I thought he might want to write a report or something about it. It might raise his profile with his bosses and get him out from behind his desk.

"Hmm. That is interesting," he said. "Leave it to the Brits to think ahead. They're the best at this business, I'm sorry to say. But at least they're on our side. Or will be."

"Or maybe it's the other way round."

"We'll be on theirs? Yes. That's the way it looks. But don't tell John Q. Public quite yet. He still thinks the war's none of our business. Speaking of the underworld, how's our friend Tony Scungilli doing?"

"Same as ever. He sends his regards." That wasn't really true, but I figured it would make Bill happy. He and I had done a favor for Tony – strictly within the letter of the law, almost – and Bill had enjoyed the adventure thoroughly. It was his one trip into the field, and he got to carry his gun, loaded. Now he was back among his files and folders.

"Well," I said, "thanks for the information. If you hear of anything in the art fraud department, let me know."

"I will. Say, speaking of the Brits, how's that woman diplomat you were squiring around? Amanda something. I remember she was quite the looker."

"Amanda Billingsgate. She wasn't really a diplomat. She was a spy. And she's disappeared. Somewhere in Europe. Germany, most likely."

"Uh-oh. On an assignment?"

"Maybe. But most likely at Gestapo headquarters."

"In a cell?"

"Maybe. But maybe behind a desk in her own private office."

"Oh. I see. That's very bad."

"No matter how you look at it, yes. It is."

Chapter Thirty

I thought about going back to the office, but there was no need. And I didn't much feel like joining the cocktail hour at the Garden. That last bit about Amanda depressed me, not for any romantic reasons, exactly, but for the thought that she might really be in serious trouble. Given the choice, I'd rather that she was a German double agent than a British agent who had gotten nabbed by those sadistic bastards in the Gestapo.

Well, when I was depressed, there was a sure fire way to get out of it. I stopped at a drug store and made a call.

She picked up after two rings.

"Hello, beautiful," I said.

"Sparky! This is Sparky, isn't it?"

"Sparky, the detective, to be precise. I wouldn't want you to get me confused with any of the others."

"Listen to you! As if there are any others. Guess what. I'm in Malibu."

"I know. I called you, remember."

"Yes. But guess who isn't in Malibu. In fact, he isn't even in California."

260

"Your husband?"

"That's right. He went to Montana to fire a director who's running over budget. So I'm all alone. Want to come over? There's lots of champagne, and it's French, and lots of lobster fresh from Maine. But I don't want to fool with them. They're still alive, and it's the cook's night off. So I'm all alone except for Mr. Moto." Mr. Moto was the Japanese houseboy. That wasn't his real name, but Catherine could never remember it. "So what do you say? Want to come and see me?"

"That's why I called."

"Good. We can make a fire on the beach and roast wienies and watch the sunset. Do wienies go with champagne?"

"Wienies go with anything."

"I think so, too. Do you know that the word 'wienie' comes from Vienna, which is 'Wien' in German? Manny told me that. So that means if you live in Vienna, you're a wiener. Interesting, huh?"

"Yes, I did know that. I read about it."

"You read a lot. That's a good thing. Anyway, afterwards we'll have to come back to the house, because of the sand."

"I know. It gets in places."

"Right. How soon?"

"I'm on my way."

"Yay! I'll have Mr. Moto build the fire on the beach, so we won't have to. He's not doing anything else."

As I said, she was an instant cure for depression, mild or otherwise.

The sun was just about to set when I pulled into Catherine's driveway. The house was partly sheltered by some dunes in front, but as I drove to the front I could see the tasteful outlines of what Manny called his beach house. It was a beach house only in the imagination of a Hollywood mogul. Most people would have called it an average-sized mansion, all teak siding and cedar shakes on the roof. Around back there was a massive stone patio that Manny used to entertain his guests. Tonight Catherine had had Mr. Moto light the Japanese lanterns around the patio and on the walkway down to the beach.

I could see Catherine on the beach standing next to the fire. She was wearing shorts and a skimpy top and she was waving at me like I was some sort of sailor just come home from a long cruise. She once told me not to fall in love with her, because she already had too much on her plate. And I didn't – fall in love with her. But I could have, easily enough, especially seeing her silhouetted by the firelight with the Pacific in the background and the red sun hovering just above the horizon. And I thought, *Beauty may not be truth, but it'll do.*

"Hiya, Sparky," she said, coming into my arms, all soft and fragrant. "I'm glad you came. I brought a picnic basket."

So we sat on the beach and roasted hot dogs and had potato salad on china plates and used silver forks and drank a couple of bottles of champagne. It was Veuve Cliquot 1926. My favorite. I thought about telling Catherine about Tavel, but this was more than good enough.

Off the beach about a half mile or so, a huge yacht was lying at anchor. It had to be almost two hundred feet long. White-hulled, it had cabins almost the entire length of the main deck and another deck above, only slightly smaller. And in front of that was a pilot house that ran the width of the ship. For it was a ship. To call it a yacht didn't do it justice. In the fading light the windows and the bright work gleamed, and it was clear the thing was well cared for. Well, you would expect that. Probably had a crew of ten just to keep it in top condition.

"There's a beauty," I said to Catherine.

"I know. I sometimes get after Manny to get one, but he says he gets seasick. I don't, though, so why should I care? We could keep it over in Catalina at the Yacht Club. It would be fun. You could come and visit. Do you get seasick?

"Nope."

"I want one," she said.

"I don't blame you. Ships are beautiful things. Maybe if the war comes and we get in it, I'll join the navy."

"Oh, don't do that, Sparky. I'd be lonely."

"That'll be the day. Do you have any idea whose boat that is? That ship, I should say."

"As a matter of fact, I do. But I forget. I do know it's called *The Collector*. It's owned by some guy from Beverly Hills. He's some sort of rich guy."

"That figures."

"I know. He's not in the movie business, though. I heard he doesn't do anything moneywise. Collects art. That's why he calls the boat that. Say, do you want to go skinny dipping?"

"So soon after eating? Didn't your mother tell you not to do that?"

"She said not to do a lot of things, and look at me now."

She stood up pulled her tee shirt over her head and wiggled out of her shorts.

"Aren't you worried the boys on that ship are going to see you in the altogether?"

"You know the old saying, if they haven't seen it before, they won't know what it is."

"Yes, I've heard that. But I'll guarantee you, not one of those boys have seen *that* before – not something as perfect as you."

"Smooth talker. Now take off your clothes and let's swim. Then we can go back to the house and take a shower and wash off the sand and salty water and put on something that smells good and then go to bed. Want to?"

And as I dropped my shorts, I thought of Keats again: *"Aye in the very temple of delight, veiled melancholy has her sovereign shrine."* Wrong again, John. In this temple of delight, melancholy is on the outside looking in.

I woke in the gray morning. The French doors were open and the sheer drapes were blowing gently in the morning sea breeze. Catherine was stretched out beside me, her eyes fluttering from some dream, I suppose. There was a soft knock on the door and I got up to see who it was. It was Catherine's maid, Stella, wanting to know if we wanted coffee and should she go to the French baker in town and get some fresh brioches, and I said "Yes, please."

I went back to bed and Catherine rolled over and opened her flawless blue eyes.

"Good morning, Sparky," she said. "Was that Stella?"

"Yes. How long does it take to go to the bakery and get brioches?"

"At least 25 minutes there and back. Just perfect, huh?"

Yes. Just perfect.

Around noon I got up and drove back to town. I wanted to talk to Perry. As an old Navy man and denizen of the waterfront, he generally knew what was going on in and around the various seaports of LA. I was curious about that yacht. The name made me wonder.

Perry was just about to take a load of gamblers out to the *Lucky Lady*.

"Hey, Chief," he said, "wanna see how the other half lives?"

"Why not."

"Hop aboard."

We got underway. There were about a dozen people on board, mostly sailors on liberty. Maybe they'd just gotten paid and were anxious to find ways to lose it.

I stood next to Perry as he steered his thirty-foot water taxi. There was a canopy over most of it so the sports wouldn't get wet from the spray.

"So what's up?" he said.

"I saw an·interesting yacht yesterday. Thing must be close to two-hundred feet long. Named *The Collector*."

"Oh, yeah. I know which one you mean. I've got a buddy who works on her. At least, he did. I ain't talked to him in a while. Goes by the name Bowline. Just a nickname. It took him the longest time to learn to tie a bowline knot. Kept sending the rabbit through the hole the wrong way."

I guessed the rabbit reference was some sort of memory device for sailors.

"Funny thing – he's a pretty smart fella otherwise. Knots just give him trouble. You know, they take that vessel back and forth to Europe when the weather's good. Spend most of the summer in the Med. Greek Islands and that sort of thing. I'm surprised they're back this early."

"Might have something to do with worries about the war coming."

"Wouldn't be surprised. Why're you interested?"

"I'm not really sure. You wouldn't happen to know who owns it?"

"Lemme think. Some guy here in town. Not a Hollywood type. Inherited money. Kind of a normal name as I recall. Woodfield? Something like that."

"Woodhouse?"

"Yeah, that could be it. Why?"

"Still not sure. But do you think you could see if your buddy's still working on the yacht?"

"Sure. If he is, he'll show up at one of the bars around here – that's assuming they stay moored off Malibu. They'll run a liberty boat here. There's nothing to do in Malibu."

Well, he was wrong about that, but I understood his point.

"If he is, maybe the three of us could get together for a beer. I'm curious about that yacht."

"Sure. I'll find out and let you know."

I didn't get off at the *Lucky Lady*. I rode back with Perry. He was taking a load of losers back to Santa Monica. But they, too, were mostly sailors, and if they'd lost their money, they didn't seem to care. It was in a good cause.

"I'll call you," Perry said as I got off at the pier.

I thought about going back to my office but decided against it. It was a beautiful day, of course. It always was. And I figured I might as well take advantage of Manny's business trip to Montana. A day at the beach and then maybe another sunset picnic seemed like a good idea. I stopped at a Rexall and called Catherine.

"Want some company today?"

"Oh, Sparky," she cooed. "Is this Sparky the detective?

"In the flesh."

"I know. I'm just teasing you, sort of like the way you were teasing me last night, only not the same. Come and see me. And ask Della if you can stay overnight."

"I already did."

"Good. Hurry over. I'm just about to take my bath. It's a big tub."

So that was the rest of that day. The cook was back on duty and knew how to deal with the lobsters, and there was lots of champagne left and we boiled the lobsters on the beach over a fire Mr. Moto built, and we ate them with melted butter, fresh baguettes and no vegetables, and I began to think that life wasn't as bad as some of the French philosophers seemed to think. Of course, they were about to have a visit from a couple of million Germans, so I couldn't be too hard on them, even if I could remember who they were. I read a lot, but some things don't stick with me.

The big white yacht was still there, but I couldn't see much activity aboard. Most of the crew was ashore, I guess.

Catherine and I stayed on the beach past sunset. We let the fire burn down and, after taking a swim, stretched out on the blanket. We both tasted pretty salty and learned that, if you're careful, sand doesn't necessarily get in places. Still, a shower afterwards was in order and afterwards we went to bed and slept the sleep of the innocent. Well, Catherine did. I just slept, and that was good enough. I woke up once when it was still dark. I thought I heard a motor boat's engines.

EPITAPH FOR A DREAM

An early fisherman, I supposed. I looked out the open French doors, but there was nothing.

The next morning I drove to my office. It was on the sixth floor of the Cahuenga Building. There were lots of small one- and two-room offices on that floor. The Security Bank and Trust owned the building, but didn't use all of it. They'd built the building about fifteen years before, so it had most of the modern conveniences, like an elevator with a girl in a uniform who operated the thing. Her name was Gladys, as you might expect. She had worked there for the last four years and had given up hoping to be discovered by the movies. She'd stopped plucking her eyebrows and started chewing gum again. Even so, she was not bad looking. Just not good looking.

"Hiya, Gladys," I said.

"You look chipper this morning," she said. "I'll bet I know why."

"I'll bet you do, too."

My office was near the back of the building which meant I had a long walk down two corridors. As I made the turn to the left I saw a half dozen cops milling around and looking busy. It's not easy looking busy while you're eating donuts and drinking coffee, but they were experienced cops and could do it. Thankfully, Kowalski wasn't among them, which meant there weren't any dead bodies anywhere. But I did know some of the cops. O'Malley was a beat cop I saw on the street now and then.

"What's going on, O'Malley?"

"It's the damnedest thing," he said. "Seems like last night some dipshits broke into the offices all along this hallway. Took whatever they could grab and moved on to the next.

268

But it don't make sense. I mean, if you're out of paperclips and typewriter ribbons, you can get 'em at Woolworth's. Most of these offices don't have nothing worth stealing. I mean – an insurance office? An accountant? They don't even keep petty cash. Make any sense to you?"

I had a feeling it did.

"How many got broken into?"

"Ten. Including yours."

What would Klep have said? *"Quelle surprise!"*

I walked down toward my office past the splinters from the jimmied door jams and past puzzled office workers who had no idea what this was about, and in some cases still hadn't figured out what was missing. If anything.

I didn't think I'd have that trouble.

Della wasn't in, but my door was standing open. The office wasn't too much of a mess, although the thieves had scattered some papers around to make it look like the work of desperate and violent men. But sure enough, the Picasso was gone. So was the Winslow Homer. They left me the Barbasol calendar, though.

Well, I thought, the best place to hide a leaf is on a tree branch, and the best way to cover up the theft of a valuable work of art is to have your boys rifle every office on the floor.

Nice try, Woodhouse. But no cigar.

Of course, proving it would be something else again.

Chapter Thirty-One

Well, one thing was clear now. The Picasso was genuine. No one would go to all this trouble for a forgery, not even the forger himself. I remembered when Woodhouse suggested I hang the picture in my home – and asked where I lived – and I said something about hanging it in my office. He didn't bother asking where that was. He didn't need to; it was in the Yellow Pages.

I called Della at home and told her not to bother coming in, but if she knew a good locksmith, and I knew she would, to call them and have them fix the door.

"Anything missing?" she said.

"Just your favorite painting and a roll of Necco wafers."

"They didn't take the seascape?"

"Yeah. I forgot to mention that."

"I guess you can figure what all this means."

"Somebody likes Necco wafers."

"Maybe. But I'll tell you something else – nobody likes a smart ass."

"That's what you think."

"By the way, I talked to Perry last night. He said he's got some information for you about a guy named Bowline. He called the office, but you weren't there."

"I was with someone who likes a smart ass."

"So you say. Anyway, he's got something for you, if you want to stop by the Pier."

"I'm on my way."

I didn't waste any time getting to the Pier.

Perry was loading up another bunch of gamblers.

"Hiya, Chief," he said.

"Hello, Chief. What's the rumpus?"

"I found Bowline. Seems he still works on the yacht. Says he likes the Greek Islands in summer and doesn't mind the Riviera, either. Says there's a beach near Cannes where people go naked."

"Poor people should be able to swim, too."

"Right. Anyway, they just got back, like I heard. I told him you'd like to have a word with him, so I told him I'd meet him today at the Blue Parrot. Noon. Right after I finish this run. I figured if I didn't hear from you I'd at least see what he's been up to. OK with you?"

"Just right. Thanks."

"Want to ride along while I take this last run?"

"Might as well."

When we got to the *Lucky Lady* and unloaded the passengers, Sonny the Gherkin was on the greeting platform and signaled to me.

"Boss says he's got something for you. Nothing big, but he told me if I saw you to tell you."

"Really? Do me a favor and tell him I've got a meeting right now, but I'll be back as soon as it's over."

EPITAPH FOR A DREAM

"OK. What's her name?"

"Lois Kowalski."

"I know her. She could lose a few."

The cops and crooks were well acquainted in this town. Even the wives.

The Blue Parrot was a typical sailor's bar. They were becoming scarcer in Santa Monica as the town gradually cleaned up and became respectable. But there were still a few places near the waterfront where a sailor could get drunk and make a deal with a working girl. The owner was a fat guy. He was his own bartender, because that was the only way he could be sure the bartender wasn't stealing from him. He pocketed every third dollar, but that was just to avoid taxes. The place smelled like beer and sweat and cigarette smoke and cheap perfume from the three or four girls working the day shift. They generally had to be slightly better looking than the night shift, what with the natural light that came through the front plate glass window.

"That's Bowline," said Perry. "The ugly one in the back."

"Which one?"

"The one in the watch cap."

We walked to the table. The floor was crunchy from something.

"Hey, Bowline," said Perry. "This is the guy I was telling you about."

He looked up. His eyes were red-rimmed and he needed a shave, but it was noon, after all. He did his best to smile. He looked better when he didn't. But Perry had told him there could be money in it for him, so he was trying.

"Pleased to meet you," he said. "Have a seat and have a beer."

"Glad to.   Name's Fitzhugh," I said, waving at the barmaid. No sense using the nom de guerre. It might strike this guy as effeminate. "I understand you guys just got back. Have a good trip?"

"Yeah. This time of year things are calm. Another month or so the storms'll start brewing up in the Caribbean, but around now it's smooth. We lost a guy in the Canal Zone. Bar fight, but that happens. What's your interest?"

Well, I thought, there's nothing like the truth, when there's nothing else to use.

"I'm interested in the owner."

"You a cop?"

"Sort of."

"Private?"

"Yes."

"Figures."

"How? In what way?"

"We all figure the guy's into something. No one knows what. Nobody really cares. It's a good billet, so the guys mind their own business."

"How?   I mean, how do the guys know he's into something?"

"Just a hunch. You can usually tell about that kind of stuff."

"Do you know him very well?"

"Who? Woodhouse? No. We hardly ever see him, even when he's aboard, which ain't all that often, except when we're in the Med. But when he is, we don't see him much. He ain't like one of these Hollywood types who buy a yacht and a captain's hat and stand on the bridge and try to look salty. It's a big vessel, and he keeps to himself. He's not what you call a man of the people, if you get me. The stewards see him, of course. And the captain and first mate. But not the working crew."

"How many stewards are there?"

"Two. Filipinos."

"And the rest of the crew?"

"Ten. The captain and first mate plus the rest of us, four deck apes and four snipes."

"Snipes are the guys who work in the engine room," said Perry.

"You still at anchor off Malibu?"

"Yeah, but we'll probably be moving tomorrow. Probably in the afternoon. I don't know where yet. But not far. Maybe Pedro or Long Beach. Word is we're heading down to Mexico in a couple of days, once the boss comes aboard. So we'll need to pull into a slip to load his gear. He travels heavy."

"When you're at anchor, how many people are on board?"

"Just one. Anchor watch. Everyone else is ashore. It's been a long cruise to get here and, like I said, we're going somewhere else pretty soon. No telling how much shore time we'll get coming up."

"The anchor watch is there to make sure the anchor doesn't drag," said Perry. "And to walk around every once in a while. Otherwise there's no reason to have anyone onboard. It's calm out there."

"Do you stand anchor watch ever?"

"Yeah. We all take turns, except the officers and the stewards."

"When's your next time?"

"I had it night before last. Probably won't have to again, because we're getting underway tomorrow or the next day. Like I said, just a short move, down to Long Beach. Maybe San Pedro."

"Was there anything unusual going on last night? Any comings and goings?"

"Couldn't say. I was ashore. Still am."

I paused for a few seconds and studied him.

"How'd you like to make some money?" I said.

"Depends. Doing what?"

"Standing anchor watch."

"I already had it."

"How'd you like to have it again?"

"How much?"

"A hundred bucks now and a hundred bucks afterward. All you have to do is tell the guy who was scheduled for watch tonight that you're feeling lousy and will trade with him. Then when everyone else is gone, you don't do anything and you don't see anything."

"Like the three monkeys – hear no evil and his two cousins?"

"That's it. Simple."

"What's the rumpus?" he said.

"The guy stole something from me, and I have a feeling it's on board that yacht, ready to take a long trip. If he gets away, I'll never see it again."

"Must be valuable."

"It is."

"What is it?"

"Something."

"Oh. And you want to steal it back?"

"'Recover it,' is how I'd put it. But, yes, that's the general idea. And we won't touch anything else."

"And I don't do nothing but look the other way?"

"That's all. And you probably won't even know we're aboard."

"What if it's not there?"

"Then you still get two hundred bucks."

"Yeah, but if it is there and you find it, won't old Woodhouse know the something's missing?"

"He will eventually, but it'll be a while. It'll be crated up tight and we'll leave the crate just the way we found it. We'll be as careful as mice and won't leave a trace, I promise. He'll never know anyone came aboard that night. And when he finally does find out, there'll be nothing he can do about it. Most likely you'll be in Mexico by the time he opens it."

"That's right," said Perry. "And what's he gonna do about it? Yell that somebody stole something he stole? And who's he gonna yell to? The Mexican cops?"

"You gotta a point. You gonna be in this, too, Perry?"

"Wouldn't miss it."

I hadn't asked Perry to join me. But I didn't have to.

"Sounds good to me. How do I collect the second hundred?"

"I tell you what – you look like an honest guy and Perry recommended you, and I trust him. So how about if I give you the two hundred now. It'll save time and hassle."

"OK. Thanks! You can depend on me. I'm good at doing nothing. Ask anyone."

"One more thing. Draw me a quick layout of the yacht – main salon, staterooms, that sort of thing."

"OK."

Ten minutes later we left him at the table. He was a happy man. So was I. I had a plan of the yacht on a napkin, and I had a plan for getting my painting back.

"How do you know the painting's not at the guy's house?" said Perry, as we walked back to the Pier.

"Woodhouse's? I don't. But think about it – he's got a very valuable and very portable piece of art. He's bound to assume that I suspect who took it, right?"

"Yeah."

"So if I had something that valuable, and I had a good idea that the former owner suspected me, I wouldn't want it anywhere near me. What's more, he doesn't know that *I* know he owns the yacht. So it's a perfect place for the painting, even if he weren't planning to leave in a day or so. But he is – which makes the yacht an even better place to stash it. And I'm pretty sure I heard a motorboat fooling around there early this morning."

"Could have been the crew returning."

"Or the crew members who trashed the offices returning with the picture."

"Possible."

"It's also possible that I'm dead wrong. But it's worth checking out. And what's the risk? Hardly any. And what are the odds I'm right?"

"Pretty good, I'd say."

"So would I. Do you think Bowline'll be able to switch with the guy who has watch?"

"There never was a sailor in the history of the world who'd say no to that offer."

"I appreciate your signing on for this," I said.

"Wouldn't miss it, like I said."

"Got any good ideas about how we get out to the yacht? I was thinking of borrowing one of the rowboats people pull up on the beach in Malibu."

"Why bother? I've got an inflatable dinghy. Fits on top of my car. I'll bring it round, and we can paddle it out and back. Very quiet. Slack water's at midnight, so we won't have to fight the tide, either going out or coming back."

"Perfect. Do you know where Catherine lives?"

"Who doesn't? I'll be there around 11:30. You can find something to do till then, I suppose. And wear something black."

Chapter Thirty-Two

We went back to the Pier. Perry had made a deal with one of his buddy's to take over the afternoon runs, so he went home to get ready for the evening's adventure. I jumped on the water taxi, paid my 25 cents and took the ride to the *Lucky Lady*. I didn't know what Tony had for me, but it was something. He wasn't the kind to just issue a casual invitation.

Sonny the Gherkin met me at the companion ladder and escorted me back to the office.

"Hiya, kid," said Tony. "Did you bring Catherine with you?"

"No. I don't know where she is. Probably at the beach house."

"That's good. Every time she comes out here without being invited, it means she's got something to show me that's going to cost me money, one way or another." He shuffled around through the papers on his desk. "I got something here from our friends over in the land of champagne and escargots. Involves you. Fact is, there's a letter here addressed to you, which I read. You don't mind, do you?"

EPITAPH FOR A DREAM

"Of course not."

Mes Amis,

Greetings from your friend Jean Baptiste – the handsome and debonair fellow you know as Klep!

You will perhaps remember that we had a slight contretemps in a place called the Brasserie Undine, which is famous for the choucroute. I have since learned, from people who know, that the fellow who interrupted our dinner was an Italian named Giovanni Martini. Until that evening he was considered a promising artist and was known to be involved with a beautiful Frenchwoman, which is a waste of a beautiful Frenchwoman, if you ask me, but apparently she did not agree. Eh bien! But since that evening he has abandoned art and gone into the fish food business. Superbe!

À bientôt,
Jean Baptiste, also known as Klep

"Make sense to you?" said Tony. "And who's this John the Baptist?"

"Yes, it makes a lot of sense. Klep is the guy our friends over there sent along to watchdog me and Hobey. This guy Martini was involved with Marvin Ginsberg's French girlfriend. He's the one who took those shots at us. Klep finished him."

"That's why he's fish food." It wasn't a question.

"He may have been speaking metaphorically, but there's no doubt Martini's dead. We saw it."

"So what's that tell you?"

"I'm not sure. But I am now sure that Martini and Nicole stole a valuable painting and sold it to Ginsberg for big money. It might have been a one time thing. Maybe Nicole and Martini hatched the plan themselves, maybe even after she got involved with Ginsberg. That may have given them the idea. Or they could be part of a larger group of art thieves and forgers, peddling stolen or phony art to gullible collectors. I just don't know. I don't know if we'll ever know."

"I don't know, either, but one thing I do know, it ain't anything to do with our friends over there, or over here. We ain't in the art business. So even if there's other people involved, chances are it's still a small operation. A few people at most. Probably amateurs, from the sound of it."

"Makes sense. If I had to guess, I'd say it was just a onetime opportunity that Martini and Nicole took by themselves. She's disappeared. And I guess he tried to kill us because we were on their trail, and they panicked."

And maybe they were tipped off by the girl's mother. I didn't mention that little detail to Tony. It didn't really matter.

"You can't trust Italians," said Tony, grinning. "They can be impulsive."

"It does seem like an extreme reaction, if they're just a couple of amateurs."

"That's where you're wrong, kid. Amateurs are the most dangerous kind. They have no sense of what's right and wrong, business-wise. And they scare easy."

"I don't suppose you've heard anything about the Ginsberg murders." I guess I was still trying to find a connection between the murders and the painting.

"Nothing too definite."

"Rumors?"

"Just that whoever did it was a private contractor. None of our friends had a beef with him. No union problems or anything like that. It was strictly a private hit on the wife, and the other two were clean-ups. That's the word, anyway."

"Clean-ups so the trail would disappear."

"Yep. You have to figure the pretty boy got it because he was in on it. Probably got paid for setting her up – getting her liquored up and then out in the street at the right time. Then the hitman didn't want to leave a loose end."

"I wonder why he let a month go by before cleaning up the actor."

"Shoddy work? Could be. You don't have to be smart to be a hitman, you know. Could be the pretty boy took off after the hit and didn't come back to town until a day or so before the hitman helped him commit suicide. Or maybe the pretty boy wanted more money. Ran through the first payoff and wanted more. That's more like it. I don't think we'll ever know that. Of course, I don't really care."

"Think we'll ever find out who Ginsberg's hitman was?" I said.

"Hard to say. He ain't gonna write his memoirs. If he's got any brains at all, he'll lay low and stay there a while. I do know that I'm done thinking about it."

All of which meant that Hobey's theory was essentially right. There was no real connection between the Ginsberg murders and the stolen Picasso, other than coincidence. Ginsberg wanted to be free of his wife. Who knows when the idea of killing her came to him? Most likely that idea predated meeting Nicole, but Nicole fanned the spark of an idea into a flame, and then the picture pumped the bellows. Who knows how many hours Marvin spent staring at the picture and remembering and, more to the point, dreaming. Maybe it was the final push. But that was the only connection. That was all there was. Right?

And what about Woodhouse? Could he be behind some ring of international art thieves, a group that Nicole and Martini were part of? He had the European connections. Or was he just a rich art collector? After all, Bunny had recommended him, so it seemed unlikely that Woodhouse was leading some sort of sinister double life as an international criminal. I came along and he saw the chance to pick up a Picasso for nothing just by lying to me and then pulling some cheap robbery stunt. It had been too much to resist. Once that painting got aboard his yacht and got underway for who knows where, he'd feel he was safe as houses. And he would be. Was I going to tell anyone about it? Hell, no. I had taken the thing from a crime scene – a painting worth at least twenty grand. Some might even call that theft. And if I was dumb enough to want to blow the whistle, who would I tell, anyway? The FBI? They didn't care. The LA cops? Please.

"Well, I can't thank you enough for your help."

"That's OK, kid. Like I said before, one of these days you're going to say thanks some way other than just saying thanks."

"I know. Believe me, I would if I could."

"Don't worry. The time'll come. You should know by now that we deal in favors in this business."

I went back to the Pier and got my car and drove to the office. Building management had repaired the door jamb and the locksmith was there installing new hardware. It was good timing, he said, because he could give me the new keys in person.

"From now on I may leave it unlocked. It'll save money."

"Oh, I wouldn't do that, sir," he said. His professional code was offended. "There are lots of bad people in this town."

I called Catherine to make sure she was still there by herself and told her I'd be coming for dinner, if she'd have me, and that Perry and I also had a little errand to do around midnight and wanted to use her beach.

"Sure, Sparky," she said. "Are you going to rob that big yacht?"

"Yes."

"Oooh. That sounds exciting. I'll have to order some more champagne, though."

"Good. And I'll bring a couple of bottles of Tavel. You know what Hemingway said about Tavel?"

"No. But I bet you do. And you can whisper it to me on the beach."

Then I called Kowalski.

"How's my wife?" he said. "You know – Lois."

"She said to tell you hello. And to bring home a loaf of bread."

"It's always something. What's up?"

"I just heard something about the Ginsberg murders – all three of them."

"Yeah? Anything interesting, like the victims are all still dead?"

"A little better. The guy who did it was a lone professional. Not a local, most likely. Nothing related to the movie business. No union beef. No girlfriend who didn't get a part. Just plain old murder for hire."

"Guy gets tired of his wife, hires some lowlife and it all unravels? That it?"

"Pretty much."

"Who's your source?"

"Can't say, but you can guess."

"Yeah, I can. Well that's nothing more than what we figured."

"I know, but I thought you'd like to have it confirmed."

"OK. I appreciate it."

"Any idea who the guy is?"

"Only that his bus ticket out of Yuma took him to Phoenix. Then he disappeared into thin air. We got a description from the Yuma ticket agent, and he thinks he remembers that the guy was a white male between five eight and six two. And he wore a hat. That narrows it down quite a bit. I'm thinking we should put out an APB. But I don't know what we'll do if he takes his hat off."

"I often wonder – who the hell would want to be a cop?"

"Not me. I was planning to join The Salvation Army and walked in the wrong door. Anyway, thanks for checking in. And tell her I'll be late for dinner."

I grabbed some things I'd need for tonight's sea adventure and headed for a wine store I liked. It was conveniently located in Malibu.

Catherine and I grilled some steaks over the fire on the beach, and I told her what Hemingway said about Tavel and after she tasted it she said she agreed with him. As we watched the sun go down, I kept an eye on the yacht. I could see someone moving around on deck. I used binoculars, and sure enough it was Bowline. There didn't seem to be anyone else on board. I suppose the whole crew, officers included, slept ashore, either alone or not. Either that or they had all left earlier in the day.

When the sun went down Catherine and I had a swim. The sea was as calm as a lake.

"I heard that sharks like to come out at night," she said. "Maybe we shouldn't go out too far."

"I'm not worried. No shark in his right mind would think of eating me when you're right here beside me, wearing nothing."

"Smooth talker."

It wasn't hard to fill the hours until 11:30. Promptly to the minute, Perry arrived.

"Will you be coming back here for the night?" she asked me. She was sleepy and only managed a friendly hug to Perry. He liked it, though, because she was not wearing much.

"Probably not."

"OK. But in case you change your mind, I'll leave the back door open. Thank you for the Tavel. I liked it. We'll have to do it again sometime." She kissed me and toddled off to her bedroom.

"I never heard it called a tavel before," said Perry.

"It's a French expression."

"Figures."

We got the inflatable down from the top of the car. There was a rope looped along both sides for carrying, and we were down the beach and into the water in no time at all.

"Here. Put this on." It was a black wool watch cap. "It folds down over your face. Called a balaclava. Don't ask me why."

We each grabbed a paddle and headed to the yacht. There was no breeze and the tide was slack, and the yacht was only a half a mile or so off shore. About fifty yards away we stopped to make sure there was no activity, but there was nothing to see. Aside from the anchor lights *The Collector* looked like a ghost ship. It showed white and polished metal in the quarter moonlight. We paddled around to the stern. There was a swim ladder there, and we tied off the dinghy and crept aboard. The only noise came from the bilge pumps now and then spouting water out the side of the hull. We went quietly and carefully along the port side, past doors that led to staterooms and a radio room. Everything was deserted. We were looking for the main salon, which was about in the middle of the yacht. It wasn't hard to find because it had windows along the entire length. We carefully opened the door into the salon. We each had flashlights.

EPITAPH FOR A DREAM

We were looking for the crate. I felt sure Woodhouse would have put the picture back in the crate I had brought to his house. It was designed for protecting a valuable piece of art, and I had left it in the office and was going to throw it away later. We looked around the stateroom. There were two large closets, "lockers" Perry called them, but nothing in either of them except the normal stuff – life jackets, boat shoes, sweaters. The forward wall of the room was made of beautifully polished wood paneling with a shelf for objects of art or memory. There was a silver cup sailing trophy from 1920. There were crossed polo mallets, which seemed to me out of place. Above the mallets was a blue and white rectangular banner that said "Yale 1920." There were paintings on the walls everywhere and a few photographs of Woodhouse and his college chums. The paintings looked to be genuine, and they looked expensive. The furniture was very fine leather and the rug on the deck was thick and luxurious. The bookcases were behind glass and contained leather-bound volumes that looked like they had actually been opened. It was a rich man's room in the middle of a very rich man's boat. But there was no Picasso.

"Where now?" whispered Perry.

"Woodhouse's stateroom."

I checked the layout of the boat on the napkin. Woodhouse's bedroom was just behind the main salon. We went out and crept back along the port side and came to what seemed like the right room and opened the door quietly. This was it, all right. The bed was elaborate and ornate, with a carved head and foot. In the corner was a desk with a red leather inlaid top. There was an eight-by-ten photograph in a silver frame on the desk. In the other corner was a comfortable chair and reading lamp. There was one closet-locker in the room. But there was no picture in there. Nothing but clothes.

"Nothing," said Perry.

I began to get nervous. I certainly didn't want to go through every space in a two-hundred-foot yacht. And I couldn't believe that Woodhouse would hide the painting somewhere where someone could stumble across it.

"Look under the bed," said Perry.

"Really?"

"Why not?"

So I did. And there it was.

"Eureka," I said.

I slid the flat crate out onto the rug and took a claw hammer out of the canvas bag I'd brought to carry the painting in. I pulled up the nails on the end of the crate and carefully slid the painting out. It had been wrapped in protective paper.

"Son of a bitch," said Perry, as he flashed his light on it. "That's one hell of a good-looking woman. Who's the guy?"

"Got me. Let's get out of here."

I slid the protective paper and some cardboard stiffener I'd brought back into the crate and replaced the end board. I pounded the nails back in using the cloth to muffle the sound and shoved the crate back under the bed. Then I put the painting in the canvas bag I'd brought.

"One more thing," I said.

I took the photo in the silver frame and slid it into the bag with its back to the back of the painting.

"You know her?" said Perry.

"It's a nice silver frame."

We went out and walked quickly back to the stern ladder, climbed down and stepped aboard the dinghy.

I almost had a heart attack when a voice out of the darkness said:

"You get what you came for?"

It was Bowline.

"Yes."

"That's good." He untied our dinghy rope from the swim ladder and we shoved off and paddled toward shore. The whole operation hadn't taken more than thirty minutes.

"Bowline almost made me lose my dinner," I said.

"Not me. I could see him standing there in the dark."

"Thanks for telling me."

"I didn't figure you for the nervous kind."

We were back on the beach a few minutes later.

"Well, that was easy," said Perry. "Makes you wonder – what kind of a numb nuts would hide a valuable painting under his bed?"

"A numb nuts who never dreamed he'd get caught."

"Now what?"

"Now I'm going to help you put this dinghy back on top of your car, and then I'm going to change my mind about staying with Catherine tonight."

"More tavelling?"

"You said it, brother. More tavelling."

"What if her husband comes back unexpected?"

"I'm feeling so good right now, I just might ask him to join us."

Chapter Thirty-Three

You know how they say in the movies "It's quiet, too quiet." Well, stealing the Picasso – or rather recovering it – was so easy that I worried for a moment that it was just too easy. But it wasn't – too easy, I mean. It was just plain easy.

Perry drove off with the dinghy, and I put the canvas bag with the painting in the trunk of my car and locked it. Then I went quietly into Catherine's bedroom and took off my black sweater and pants and slid into the silk sheets. Catherine rolled over and opened her astonishing blue eyes and snuggled next to me.

"Everything OK?" she said.

"Everything is perfect."

"Good. Kiss me and say something sweet."

"*Here will I dwell, for heaven is in these lips,*" I said.

"Smooth talker," she murmured and fell back asleep.

In the morning I stopped briefly at the office. Della was there, typing furiously at something.

"Hiya, Chief. Any idea who stole our artwork?"

"Yep."

"What are you going to do about it?"

"It's already done. Didn't Perry tell you?"

"Was that who came in last night?"

"Do me a favor, will you please? Find out where this is."

I gave her a note with a kind of address on it.

"Sure. When do you want it?"

"This afternoon, if you can."

"No sweat. I know someone."

"I figured."

"By the way, Blinky called and said to tell you that he doesn't have anything. But he's wondering if trying's worth a fiver."

"When he calls back tell him no."

"I already did."

Then I drove back to the Garden to change clothes. I didn't need another shower.

Although it was still morning Hobey and Hedda were already at the pool. Hobey's shaker of martinis was there with its twin brother.

"Greetings, Old Sport," he said. "Have a drink."

"Thanks. I will. I have some news for you."

"Really?"

"Yes. Your theory about the Ginsberg murders looks like it's correct."

"Occam's razor?"

"Yes. There doesn't seem to be much of a connection between the stolen Picasso and the murders. Just a coincidence."

"I thought so. You can always depend on a writer to see things mere mortals overlook. I congratulate myself."

"Second the motion. How's your travelogue coming? The Irish thing."

"Oh, it's finished. Dashed it off in an afternoon. You can't say much in ten minutes."

"Speaking of that, do you happen to have a copy of that Yeats poem you mentioned? What's it called again? The Song of the Wandering Black Angus?"

I actually knew the correct name, but I was in a good mood. A successful heist plus another night with Catherine were more than enough to put a smile on anyone's face.

"I am appalled at your ignorance," said Hobey. "You make it sound like a barnyard animal that has escaped. But, yes, I do have a volume of Yeats' stuff. Do you need it right now?"

"I'd appreciate it."

"Wait here. Entertain Hedda while I'm gone."

He got up and went to his cabana. Hedda looked at me and smiled. She had a very pretty smile, and I always appreciated her figure, which was on display, as usual, and then some.

"You wanna sticka gum?" she said.

"No thanks. Want me to top off your drink?'

"Why not?"

"How's the journalism business?"

"Great. I got a raise."

"Any of your readers commit suicide?"

"Huh? You joking? How would I know?"

Hobey came back with the book, and I went to my cabana and changed clothes. I made a quick call to Della, and, bless her, she already had the information I wanted.

My next stop was my bank, where I redeemed the balance of the letter of credit. It amounted to almost three thousand dollars, which I considered a very fine payment for services rendered. It was quite a bit more than my usual fee, but I had already decided that there was no sense letting it go to waste. After all, it would only go back into the estate and then into the pockets of the estate lawyers and ultimately the tax people. I understood that some might consider that a rationalization. Well, I could live with it.

It took me a good half hour to drive to Forest Lawn Cemetery, but I was in no hurry. It was another perfect day. It took me another half an hour to drive around and find Marvin Ginsberg's grave. But there it was, finally. It was next to his wife's, and there were the usual messages on both headstones testifying to the affection each had for the other and, in Marvin's case, rejoicing that they were reunited. Well, under the circumstances, the irony was a little over the top, but you still had to smile. Didn't you?

I got out of the car and took Hobey's book and stood there for a moment beside Marvin. Then I read out loud:

> "*Though I grow old with wandering through hollow lands and hilly lands,*
> *I will find out where she has gone and kiss her lips and take her hands*
> *And walk through long green dappled grass and pluck till times and times are done,*
> *The silver apples of the moon, the golden apples of the sun.*"

Well, there weren't any apple trees around that I could see. But there was a nice eucalyptus nearby. That would have to do.

I took out the photograph in the silver frame and put it on Marvin's grave. I turned it away from Elaine's side, out of politeness. The picture was of Nicole, of course.

"There's your dream girl, Marvin. It's the best I could do."

Someone would steal it, naturally. It was a very nice silver frame. But that didn't matter to me. I was not coming back there, so in my memory it would always be there.

Chapter Thirty-Four

I drove back to the Santa Monica Pier. Perry was there at his usual time.

"How was the tavelling?" he shouted.

"Hemingway would approve."

"Who? Well, whatever. What's the rumpus?"

"I need to have a quick chat with the man."

"Hop aboard. By the way, Bowline called, like we asked him to. He said they moved to a slip in Long Beach where Woodhouse came aboard with all his stuff, and they're leaving today."

"Good. Did he say where they're going?"

"No. But he did say they took on enough fuel and stores to be gone for a year, almost."

"Even better."

The usual midday crowd of sailors on liberty were in the boat. They were laughing and joking, and they made me smile just watching them. If the war came, they'd need some happy memories.

I climbed up the *Lucky Lady's* companion ladder. Sonny the Gherkin was on duty as greeter.

"Look who's back," he said.

"The Boss in?"

"He's in his office, as usual. You know the way."

I walked back through the main salon. It was filled with happy people losing their money and a few really happy ones who were winning. The band was playing and the girl singer was warbling into the standup mike, 'What'll I Do When You Are Far Away?', which seemed like a sad note to the happy proceedings, but she sang it so well that I had to stop and listen. *"What'll I do with just a photograph to tell my troubles to?"* Hmm. *"When I'm alone with only dreams of you that won't come true, what'll I do?"*

She finished, and everyone applauded. Man, she could sing. Then I walked back to Tony's office. Paulie, his right hand man, was standing outside the door.

"Hiya, kid. What's on your mind?"

"I'd like to see the Boss for just a minute."

Paulie spoke into the intercom and then buzzed me in.

"Hiya, kid. Is Catherine with you?"

"No."

"That's good. Normally I like to see her, but you know what I mean. What's that you got there?"

"A present. A thank you gift."

I pulled the painting out of my bag and showed it to him.

"Madonna! That's beautiful," he said, pronouncing it in four syllables. "Look at that dame!"

"It's a Picasso," I said.

He looked at me. It was the first time I'd ever seen him surprised.

"For real?"

"Yep. Authenticated as genuine by the foremost experts."

"I heard of him. Picasso, I mean. He's some sort of big shot in the art business."

"Pretty big. Getting bigger, they say."

"You giving this to me?"

"Yes. In return for your many favors."

"This is worth quite a bit of dough."

"Yes. It is."

"How'd you come by it?"

"I stole it."

"Nice!"

He looked at me like a proud uncle.

"Who knows about it?"

"No one. And no one ever will know."

"Sounds perfect. I got just the place for it. Right here in my office."

"I figured." And I couldn't think of a safer place.

"Thanks, kid. I really appreciate this. Like my old man used to say, you done good. Let's have a drink."

We had a couple of glasses of grappa and admired the painting. I thought about telling Tony that the guy I stole it from stole it from somebody who stole it from the owner who didn't remember getting it from the artist who didn't remember painting it. That wasn't precisely true, but it was close enough. But Tony didn't care about details. Most of the time he didn't want to know.

After the second grappa, it was time for me to go. The surprise had worked out just the way I wanted, and it's always good to know when you've reached the proper ending of a scene. As they say in show biz, "Leave 'em laughing." Or, as Tony once said, "When the girl says yes, stop talking."

So I got up and said so long.

298

"Thanks again, kid. And don't be a stranger."

I left. As I was walking through the noisy main salon, the girl singer was crooning a Cole Porter song, "Love For Sale." I stopped to listen. She was really good. Then I went outside to the weather deck to wait for Perry's water taxi. The air smelled fresh and clean after the smoky atmosphere of the main salon.

About a mile away I could see *The Collector* steaming briskly through the lovely blue Pacific, her hull gleaming and her bow wave creamy. Woodhouse was on that yacht, heading south, maybe to Mexico, maybe to the Canal and from there to the Caribbean. I wondered if he would notice that Nicole's photograph was missing. Who knew? Probably not at first, in the hustle and bustle of leaving. I wondered again how she was connected to him. Maybe he was her boss. Maybe he was the head of some international ring of art thieves. Then again, maybe not. Maybe he was just another rich, lovesick sap. Maybe she had conned him the way she'd conned Marvin. I'd never know. But the more I thought about it, the more I realized, I didn't care.

And then I wondered when Woodhouse would reach under his bed and pull out that crate – when he'd pry open the end and carefully slide the protective papers out. And I wondered what he'd say when he found the Barbasol calendar there instead of the Picasso.

I'd never know that, either. But I knew what I said to myself as I watched the yacht heading south.

Superbe!

The End